OLLIE COME FREE

Timothy Patrick

Copyright 2021 by Timothy Patrick
Country Scribbler Publishing, Santa Rosa Valley, CA
All rights reserved.

Vector art courtesy of PCH.Vector/Freepik

Publisher's Cataloging-in-Publication data

Names: Patrick, Timothy, author.
Title: Ollie come free / Timothy Patrick.
Description: Santa Rosa Valley, CA: Country Scribbler Publishing, 2021.
Identifiers: LCCN: 2021902195 | ISBN: 9780989354486 (hardcover) | 9780989354479 (paperback) | 9780989354462 (ebook)
Subjects: LCSH Brain--Injury--Fiction. | Family--Fiction. | Savants (Savant syndrome)--Fiction. | People with disabilities--Fiction. | Artists--Fiction. | California--Fiction. | Suspense fiction. | Mystery fiction. | BISAC YOUNG ADULT FICTION / Disabilities & Special Needs | YOUNG ADULT FICTION / Thrillers & Suspense / General | YOUNG ADULT FICTION / Mysteries & Detective Stories
Classification: LCC PS3616.A8738 O45 2021 | DDC 813.6--dc23

Other Titles by Timothy Patrick

Tea Cups & Tiger Claws

Death of a Movie Star

Dedication

For my son, Taylor

Part One

Gone in a Flash

Chapter 1

"**M**om, I can't find my jockstrap."

Cathy looked across the yard and saw Ollie standing on the patio, his skinny eleven-year-old body dressed only in a pair of baggy baseball pants. And she almost fell for the prank, but then she caught a glimpse of the face that looked just a little too blank. She said nothing and continued setting up tables and chairs. It didn't matter. He got his laugh when a chicken wearing a jockstrap strolled onto the patio.

Ollie laughed so hard he almost fell over. And so did Mariah, his friend who had been helping Cathy set up. The bird slipped free of the garment, and Cathy told Ollie to finish getting dressed. He staggered back into the house.

"Please tell me he doesn't act like that at school," said Cathy.

"All the time," said Mariah.

"And what do the teachers say?"

"They try not to laugh, but it usually doesn't work. Everybody likes Ollie."

"Maybe they should try living with him for a week," said Cathy.

A few minutes later everyone loaded up and drove into town for the baseball game. Ollie and Mariah sat in the back row laughing and talking. Cody, eighteen months older than

Ollie, sat alone in the middle row. Cathy sat up front with her husband, Bob, who drove the minivan and gave Cody the pregame pep talk.

"Now remember what we talked about, Cody. When the ball moves, you have somewhere to go. You're always thinking and moving."

"Yes sir," said Cody.

"And on the cutoffs, set up for the throw before you catch the ball."

"Yes sir, but if Ollie doesn't hit the cutoff, what good does it do? Can you tell him to at least try?"

Cathy saw Bob look at Ollie in the rearview mirror, but he didn't say anything. The boy liked being on the team with his brother but the finer points of baseball didn't interest him, and Bob knew there wasn't much he could do about it.

"Mariah, do you have a ride home from the park?" asked Cathy.

"Yes, Mrs. Buckmeyer."

"And you'll be back at the ranch tomorrow at ten?"

"Yes."

"Thank you. We're going to be busy."

The ranch had started hosting special events such as weddings and birthday parties, and Mariah had become the right-hand wunderkind. Ollie also worked...sporadically...when he came down from the clouds. And Cathy, who didn't need more things to juggle, ran the weekend events because the ranch needed the money. She and Bob had been married for twenty-two years and now they found themselves scrambling like newlyweds to pay the bills. But she didn't complain. She lived on one of the last cattle ranches in Southern California, had a hardworking cowboy for a husband, and had two sons that she adored. That added up to a pretty good life.

After they got to the park, Mariah ran off with some friends, and Cathy and Bob found their seats in the bleachers. And then the game unfolded just like any other. Cathy socialized. Bob watched the game and didn't talk. Ollie goofed off in right field—the least important position on the team, and the place where he did the least amount of damage—and Cody played with his usual intensity.

In the eighth inning the manager brought in a relief pitcher and Ollie, already past his boredom quotient, threw down his glove and marched to the corner of the outfield. He leaned against the foul pole, kicked at the dirt, and waited for the new pitcher to throw his warmup pitches.

And then it happened, but Cathy didn't see the flash of light, and the thing didn't completely register. She screamed, like everyone else, because the crackling explosion had snuck up on her, not because she perceived any specific danger. And no one seemed to be hurt. A nearby man said something about a blown transformer. Cathy scanned the baseball field and saw Cody standing safely near second base. She looked into right field but didn't see Ollie. She touched Bob's arm. When he turned, and she saw the alarm on his face, she knew that something had happened.

He said, "Get Cody and call an ambulance…try the phone in the snack bar."

"What's wrong, Bob? Please tell me!"

He didn't answer. Instead, he stood up, turned to the other parents, and said, "Get your kids and find shelter."

Just then the rain began to pour and a flash of lightning exploded from the sky. Now everyone understood, and the little stand of bleachers erupted into a frenzy that quickly expanded as hysterical parents ran all over the diamond gathering up their bewildered children and herding them to safety—some to their cars, some into the snack bar, some into the wooden equipment sheds that littered the grounds.

Cathy ran toward Cody but continued to search for Ollie. She didn't understand how he had just disappeared. Another bolt of lightning pierced the sky, followed by the angry peal of thunder. She kept running and searching. The rain and the panic made it difficult. She still didn't see him. She also didn't see the smoking cleats that lay neatly on the ground next to the foul pole.

Seconds later, Cathy, with Cody by her side, stood inside the snack bar and stared helplessly out through the serving window. She saw a solitary girl run onto the field that had just been evacuated. It was Mariah, and she led Cathy's eyes to her son, who lay face down in a heap, some thirty feet from where he had been leaning against the foul pole. Mariah knelt next to Ollie and shook him. His body looked limp and lifeless in her hands. Mariah pleaded with him, her desperate cries comingled with the sound of the pounding rain and howling wind that echoed across the field. Cathy felt the panic rise, but then Bob got to the scene, and she steadied herself. Bob nudged Mariah to the side. She rose to her feet and paced back and forth while Bob tended to Ollie.

First, he rolled him onto his back and felt for a pulse. He then tore off the soaked baseball jersey, formed a hardened fist, and pounded it one time onto the bare chest. He checked again for a pulse. He pinched the nose closed and blew into his mouth. The chest heaved. Bob sat back and watched. The chest heaved again. And then again. Ollie tried to move. Bob took off his jacket and sheltered Ollie from the rain.

Cathy began shaking uncontrollably. Cody put his arm around her. Another mother held her hand. There in that snack bar, surrounded by hanging corn dogs, draping licorice ropes, and an unclaimed belly buster, Cathy had just witnessed the death and resuscitation of her son. She, along with all the others who had crowded into the little shack, stood in silence and listened to the distant siren as it pushed against the din of pouring rain, steady, insistent, eventually breaking through and filling the ballpark with an echoing wail and flashing red lights that bounced off a thousand puddles.

Within twenty-four hours Ollie Buckmeyer became a nightly news sensation as the Little Leaguer who survived a bolt of lightning. The story had rock-solid made-for-TV credentials: tragedy, death, and resurrection of an all-American kid who is left for dead and then marches out of the hospital two days later, as normal as normal could be.

Unfortunately, this portrayal mischaracterized the aftermath of that spring baseball game in 1991 because life would prove to be anything but normal for the boy. Three hundred thousand volts can do that to you. As Ollie grew up, his name and the word "normal" would rarely be spoken so freely in the same breath. Other words attached themselves to Ollie, words that sounded like they described two different people, words like slow and fast, cursed and blessed, idiot and genius, awkward and amazing. And artist. That word more than any other.

Chapter 2

When Cathy left her son's bedside and rejoined the crowd in the waiting room, she felt like a pretender. She felt like the doubter who must be found out and thrown overboard to appease the god of the tempest. Word had spread that her son had survived with barely a scratch and these well-wishers—mostly longtime friends, and a few of Ollie's schoolmates—had descended upon the hospital to celebrate with the family. So, Cathy smiled and hugged and shared tears with them. She threw around the M word like confetti at a parade because her little boy had survived and that definitely counted as a first class miracle. But she still felt like an imposter because the mere use of the word "miracle" implies a renewed life that will be lived happily ever after. That's how it works. Throw us in a pit, save us against all odds, and then wrap it all up with a beautiful sunset. We believe in a miracle and a happy ending. We don't believe in a miracle and brain damage.

She participated in the parade mostly for the benefit of her distraught husband, which Cathy didn't really understand because Bob didn't usually act like that. He endured and fought and steeled his resolve. He didn't despair. But there he was, pacing in his ever-present wrangler jeans and plaid cowboy shirt, with red swollen eyes and close-cropped brown hair that had been matted from all the times he had worriedly run his hands across his head. Under normal circumstances this sight would have stopped Cathy dead in her tracks. But she had a son in the ER so she chalked it up to another part of Bob's personality, the black and white part. In that world, if Ollie got hurt while playing baseball, then the blame logically belonged to Bob, because he had forced the boy to play in the first place. Bob, for all his good qualities, had no room for nuances. They only confused a world that was already hopelessly confused. He had only one hope: full recovery.

Cathy also knew that Bob didn't make a habit of hiding from the truth, and that she didn't have the right to hide it from him now. But at this point she had to tackle one problem at a time.

And, of course, Ollie's condition might have improved. Maybe the truth might have bent back upon itself so that the miracle and the happy ending ended up being the same thing. That's what she told herself.

The "truth," as it stood that first day in the hospital, revealed itself to Cathy within minutes of her arrival at her son's bedside. As the doctor cleaned the skin and applied antibiotic ointment, Cathy marveled at her son's appearance. He had a cut on the left side of his head that took six stiches and some superficial fern shaped burns on his back and legs, but, honestly, the whole thing looked better than the usual ER visit for a family with roughhousing brothers. Then she tried to hold Ollie's hand and he pulled away. His reaction had been automatic, subconscious, like the response of someone who doesn't like to be touched. She also noticed that since the time she had come into the room, he hadn't looked at her or the doctor. And he hadn't cracked any jokes. And he answered the questions with clipped sentences or just repeated the question like a parrot. The goofball Ollie she knew didn't act like that. This rigid, unconnected being didn't resemble her boy in the slightest. The mother knew. She didn't know precisely, but she knew.

The next day, just prior to Ollie's discharge, the television cameras and microphones converged upon the hospital waiting room for an impromptu press conference. Cathy didn't see that coming but maybe it kind of made sense. Those were the turbulent days of Iran-Contra and black Monday stock market crashes. She and Bob had felt the pain themselves when, for the first time in the hundred years the ranch had been in his family, they had been unable to pay off the balance on their cattle loan. The bank rolled it over into a new loan but that just meant the new year looked even more difficult than the previous one. So she understood. People need feel good stories and this time around, her family had been designated to provide it.

Bob looked uncomfortable but, still sufficiently buoyed by "the miracle," he stared at the microphones and stiffly answered questions with one- and two-word answers: cattle rancher; happy; very happy; precordial thump; Marine Corps. Realizing that they hadn't exactly stumbled upon a fountain of information, the hungry swarm pointed their microphones at Cathy. One of them said, "What activities does Ollie like best, besides baseball?"

"Ollie likes all the animals on the ranch…and playing with his friends…and teasing his older brother," said Cathy.

Thankfully, just then, Ollie emerged from behind the giant swinging doors, surrounded by a cadre of smiling white lab coats. He sat in a wheelchair and looked absent. After some effort, one of the nurses managed to coax something that almost looked like a smile out of him. The cameras clicked and whirred and the people cheered.

At that moment Cathy saw for the first time a sight that she would see ten thousand times in the future: her son rocking in place. It wasn't a relaxed, musical kind of rock that might signify wellbeing. It was the mechanical glitch of a broken robot. The reporters didn't notice or didn't care to notice.

After the hospital administrator and ER doctor made statements and answered questions, all of which affirmed a completely rosy outlook for her son, someone yelled Ollie's name. Cathy zeroed in on the reporter, a young thing who'd obviously been swept up in the emotion of the story. She looked like she had just graduated from the University of Sunshine with a degree in rainbows. She blurted, "Ollie, you are so cute. Do you have a girlfriend?"

Cathy wanted to jump in and say, "Listen lady: He's eleven years old and has an *E.T.* poster in his bedroom." But, in truth, Ollie had Mariah, a kinda sorta girlfriend. Cathy evaded the question and said, "Oliver has many wonderful things to look forward to, but right now the most important thing is rest and recuperation. And, as you all know, in these matters, mother has the final word, and she says it's time for a comfortable bed and some chicken soup." This elicited some polite laughter and Bob squeezed Cathy's hand in gratitude.

The meeting ended, the crowd dispersed, and one of the orderlies pushed the requisite wheelchair out to the circular drive where Ollie easily climbed into the middle seat of the family's minivan. This sight offered Cathy a sliver of hope because it indicated that at least physically her son had escaped harm. She fastened his seatbelt and accidently touched his arm. He pulled it away and started rocking. She said, "Cody's waiting for you at home." He continued rocking and didn't say a word. Cathy looked up and saw Bob's eyes in the rearview mirror. And then he looked away.

Just as they started to pull out, Cathy saw the ER doctor running toward them. He still had the energetic glow of the press conference on his face and a small paper in his hand. She lowered the window. The doctor handed her a business card and said, "I'm sure there's nothing to be concerned about, but there were some anomalies on the CT scan, and I've referred Oliver's case to our staff neurologist. His name is Dr. Lee and he's expecting your call."

Ollie had been discharged. That's all Cathy had been told. Now suddenly he'd become a "case"? And what on earth was a "CT scan"? Before she had time to ask either of these questions, the doctor left. And she immediately wondered if this new information had been deliberately held back to protect the feel-good story and the hospital's fifteen minutes of fame. Then she took a deep breath, reclaimed her frazzled nerves, and rebuked her warped cynicism.

When the van left the hospital complex and headed onto the open road, Ollie stopped rocking and stared out the window. He stared intensely. And his head didn't move, even minutely, even when something interesting passed by. He just locked his head in place and didn't move a muscle until the van pulled into their driveway twenty minutes later.

Cody met his little brother at the front door with a sly smile and funny insult. Cathy suddenly realized that she'd left him unprepared for this homecoming; he'd gotten plenty of information but it all had come from friends and local news, and it certainly didn't match the disturbing picture that now stood before him. She shot him the standard motherly wide-eyed SOS look, and he got the message, stepping aside to let Cathy escort Ollie to a seat at the kitchen table. Ollie immediately began rocking. The whole family stood and stared.

<center>~~~~~~~~~~~~~~</center>

The odds of getting hit by lightning in any given year are one in six hundred thousand. Bob looked it up. The odds of getting struck on exactly the same day of the year on two different years had to be at least one in ten million. Even though lightning hadn't been part of the first tragedy, for the purposes of figuring probability it came close enough. And this kind of ten-million to one coincidence didn't cut it for Bob. But what alternative did he have? A curse? Punishment for his sins? These possibilities also sounded ridiculous...but maybe not so much.

On a good day fatherhood spooked Bob. Their trust and admiration made him want to run. But he didn't because Cathy had always been there blocking the path. Now, as he stared at his broken son, he wondered if that would be enough.

14

An undulating humming groan radiated from the boy's body as he sat at the table. It started when he lurched forward and ended when his back banged against the back of the chair. Lurch, groan, bang. Lurch, groan, bang. The image reminded Bob of the hijacked bodies and broken brains he had seen at the military hospital in Hong Kong, but he tried to keep his mind from going to such places. As a man of discipline, he understood that the difference between action and paralysis, between healthy fear and debilitating panic, is usually nothing more than a deep breath and a step in the right direction. If anything, this terrible sight represented an unmistakable call to take that step, any step. But there he stood, motionless, thinking about psych wards and little paper cups dotted with lithium pills. And coincidence.

Cathy, always the logical one, started trying to find some favorite little thing of Ollie's that might help him to reconnect with his life. And the boy seemed to respond because he answered some of Cathy's questions. But others he merely repeated or ignored altogether.

"Are you hungry, dear?"

"No."

"I can make you grilled cheese and chocolate milk."

No response.

"There's Max, Ollie. He's coming to say hi to you. Say hi to Max."

"Say hi to Max," said Ollie, without looking at the cat and without interrupting the rocking.

Cathy sent Bob to fetch one of Ollie's toys. Thankful for the chance to at least move his feet, Bob dug into the toy chest and came back with an action figure that looked like a gorilla. It wore a bandolier and carried a gun.

"Yes," said Cathy, "that's his favorite." She sat down next to Ollie, placed the toy on the table, and said, "Ollie, someone needs your help."

"Ollie, someone needs your help," repeated Ollie, but that's as far as it went. No matter how much animation Cathy added, or how many funny voices she invented, Ollie ignored it.

For the next half hour Bob rummaged for toys: superheroes, military heroes, animal heroes; cap guns, ray guns, cowboy guns; talking phones, talking bears, talking gizmos; cars, trains, airplanes. Ollie didn't look at any of them. At the bottom of the toy box Bob found some old coloring books and a half empty box of broken crayons. He shoved them aside to look for something better but found nothing, so he grabbed them.

The instant those tattered and broken castoffs hit the table, Ollie stopped rocking—just for a second—and snatched up the box of crayons. He ignored the coloring books but clutched the crayons close to his body and resumed the rocking and groaning. Bob looked at Cathy. She jumped out of the chair, ran down the hall, and came back with a stack of blank paper, which she placed on the table. Ollie stopped rocking. He carefully took a crayon from the box, placed the rest on the table, and lined up a sheet of paper. And then he started scribbling. He scribbled furiously, deliberately, one page after another in quick succession, like he had a huge backlog that had to be put onto paper without a second's delay.

Bob sat down next to Cathy and they reviewed each drawing as it flew off the assembly line. Each page seemed to portray some sort of landscape with very little variation between one drawing and the next. With the exception of a few simplistic buildings sprinkled through the first half dozen drawings, all the rest depicted line sketches of hills, mountains, trees, and clouds—over and over again. Bob pushed the drawings away and looked at his son, who continued spitting out pages like a haywire copy machine. Despite the initial rush of hope, Bob now wondered if they'd made any breakthrough at all. He honestly didn't see any difference between a damaged brain that forces a body to compulsively rock back and forth and a damaged brain that forces a body to scribble meaningless doodles. He rose from the kitchen table and, without saying a word, left the house through the back door.

∗∗∗∗∗∗∗∗∗∗∗∗∗∗∗

Now, for the second time in as many days, Cathy saw something different in her husband. He didn't usually withdraw like this. He struggled sometimes, but he didn't retreat. And he didn't struggle in an emergency. That was where he usually shined. Something had knocked him off balance, something more than Ollie. But, after half a lifetime together, Cathy knew better than to go rushing in. Bob had his ways and they didn't include a whole lot of conversation. When the time came, he'd drop a few words, like markers on a trail, and she'd pick them up and they'd talk about what she had found.

Just as she put that problem on the back burner, the one at the kitchen table reclaimed her attention: Ollie had stopped drawing. Like a satisfied artist, he had put down the crayon and calmly sat back in the chair. Cathy studied his face. The tension had disappeared. He still avoided eye contact, but the darting, fearful gaze had been overcome by the droopy eyelids of a tired eleven-year-old boy. A half hour later, after devouring a PB&J sandwich, he climbed into bed and fell asleep. Cathy thought about what had just happened. The scene reminded her of Bongo, their Australian shepherd, who routinely became so overcome with his job herding cattle that he ran himself to complete exhaustion. She wondered if the pictures that flew out of Ollie demanded his attention like the straying cattle demanded Bongo's. Thinking that another look at the drawings might help answer that question, she started leafing through them again when the phone rang. With her eyes still on the drawings, she reached for the nearby handset and answered the call at the same time as Bob, who had picked it up from his office out in the barn. He said, "I got it, Cathy."

She started to hang up but heard the words, "This is a collect call from...Ralph Durbin...an inmate at California Correctional Institution." The inner debate between right and wrong ended before it even began; her family had been put through the wringer and a little bit of eavesdropping didn't violate any rule that she particularly cared about just then—especially if it involved Ralph Durbin. She pushed down on the plunger to make it sound like the line had been hung up and then put the phone back up to her ear.

"This call will be recorded and monitored. Do you accept the charges?"

"Yes, operator," said Bob.

"Damn it, Buck. You just cost me a honeybun. I bet my cellmate you had crashed somewhere along the way."

"Yeah…Sorry, Durbin. I had the truck packed and something came up," said Bob.

"Just kidding, bro. I saw the news. But they said everything is good. Right?"

"Yeah…I guess so."

"That doesn't sound convincing."

"The doctors are saying one thing but my eyes are saying something different."

"Yeah, but they got the degree on the wall and you don't," said Ralph.

"That's what I'm counting on." After a pause, Bob said, "Did you catch the date?"

Cathy instantly made the connection and had to stifle her gasp. She knew that date better than her own birthday, and she had even helped pack the truck so that Bob could leave right after the game.

"It's just a coincidence, Buck," said Ralph, and then he cleared his throat. To Cathy, he sounded nervous.

"You don't believe that any more than I do, Durbin. Let's just hope we're going crazy."

"I wouldn't bet against it."

After an awkward pause, Bob said, "What'd you do when I didn't show?"

"Nothing. Cried in my pruno for a few days."

"That's the spirit. Uh...Durbin...I need to ask you something. Do you think the boys would mind if we did it over the phone this year? I don't think I can make it up there for a while."

"They won't mind, Lieutenant. You got a can of beer?"

"Hot and cheap, just like at basecamp," said Bob.

"Then I'm ready when you are."

Cathy heard the hiss of the popping beer can and then her husband said, "Corporal Darin Maloof."

"Semper fi, Loofy. Here's to you and your Broadway show tunes," said Ralph.

With the sound of her husband swigging beer in the background, Cathy said a silent prayer for the soldier's loved ones.

"Private First Class Salvador Reynosa," said Bob.

"Here's to you, Reyno, and your weird Kool-Aid concoctions. Semper fi," said Ralph.

Bob took another drink and Cathy said another prayer.

"Corporal Mark Hochlichtner," said Bob.

"Semper fi, Hokey. Here's to you and your bottle of vinegar."

Bob took the final drink and Cathy said the final prayer. Though uninvited, she felt thankful to be there.

Another long silence filled the phone line before her husband said, "Any news on the appeal?"

"I thought you'd never ask," said Ralph.

"What?"

"They tossed the sentence. Nobody knew about PTSD back then, so now I get a new sentencing hearing."

"That's good news. So...what comes next?"

"The bad news. It's going to take some time…and the lawyer says I'm gonna need some help…He says I need someone to talk about what happened…."

Cathy closed her eyes and took a deep breath.

"I'll do it. Just tell me when and where," said Bob.

"Thanks, Buck. If something comes up, and I can get you out of it, I'll do it." Ralph cleared his throat and continued, "There's something else, Buck. Rachel's going testify against me again. My baby girl is going to point her finger at me and say that I ruined her life."

"I'm sorry, Durbin, I'm sorry."

"Whatever…I'm just a grunt trying not to screw things up."

"That's right, brother. That's what we are. By the way, how many grunts does it take to dig a foxhole?"

"Twenty. One to dig and nineteen to bitch and moan," said Ralph.

"Sounds like you read that straight from the manual. You haven't lost a step. Now listen to me, Durbin. We'll make it through this. And if anything else comes up, you let me know. I don't care what it is, you call me. You got it?"

"Not so fast, Buck. This time the shit hit your fan too, so you gotta let me do my part. It's a two-way street…like they say."

"Alright," said Bob.

"OK…how's Cathy holding up?"

"She's nervous but she's trying to hide it, just like me."

"And…uh…does she know about the…uh…coincidence?"

"I don't think so. She's been so busy keeping everything together I don't think she made the connection, and I hope it stays that way."

"OK. And the gold? asked Ralph.

"Nothing."

"I'm telling you, Buck, you gotta start thinking like a crazy man. You put me up there and I'll dig it up in a month."

"Alright, Durbin."

"OK, Buck…everything else is good?"

"Yep."

"No BS?"

"No BS…except you sold me out for a honeybun. I always thought I was worth at least a cup of noodles," said Bob.

"Later, Buck. Give the cows a kiss for me."

"Later, Durbin."

Cathy waited for the clicking sound of a disconnected call and then hung up the phone. A couple of thoughts banged around in her head. The first, shameful and self-serving, was that Ralph Durbin in a prison cell suited her just fine. The last eight years had been peaceful compared to the eight years before his conviction, and Cathy had no interest in reliving old times. And how typical that Ralph might be able to get out of prison if Bob is willing to go back to a very bad place, dig up some very bad memories, and share them in court. But that's what Ralph had always stood for: looking back and never going forward.

Cathy had been brought up the old fashion way, with Sunday school and the golden rule. She had been taught to love her enemies, but she hated Ralph Durbin with a hate stronger than any repentance she could ever imagine.

The second thought, which really frightened Cathy, had to do with the date. On May twentieth, 1969, Bob lost three members of his platoon after leading them into an ambush. And now, on the exact same day twenty-two years later, Ollie had been struck by lightning. If it had just been the coincidence of the date, Cathy might have been able to reason it away as a tragic fluke. But it was more than that. Bob never recovered from what happened in Vietnam. The happy and carefree young husband never came back. And now Cathy had a son that she didn't recognize and a terrible fear that it might be happening all over again.

Chapter 3

Dr. Stephen Lee, the neurologist who had been referred by the emergency room doctor, repeated himself more slowly as Cathy studiously took notes, "Intracerebral hematoma resulting in damage to the left temporal lobe and dilatation of the temporal horn in the left lateral ventricle of the brain." The words sounded like Greek but Cathy didn't care; when the world spins you hang on to anything you can, even meaningless note-taking. The doctor further explained that this traumatic brain injury, or TBI, had not been caused by electrocution but from the crash of Ollie's head into the ground. The doctor then paused. Cathy stared expectantly. She and Bob sat in the perfectly ordered office, surrounded by plants and diplomas and a bewildering array of plastic display brains. "Mr. and Mrs. Buckmeyer," said the doctor, "I know things don't look encouraging right now, but I'm going to tell you something." Cathy lowered the pen and paper to her lap. He continued, "I have seen many patients recover from a TBI, especially young people. It can take months, or even years, but I have seen it repeatedly. My recommendation is to give it some time. I'd also like to refer you to Dr. Gardner. He's a neuropsychologist in our medical group, and he can tailor therapy for your son that progresses at the same pace as his recovery. I know it's difficult, but I believe in the next six months many of your concerns will be addressed, and we will have a much clearer picture of your son's recovery."

That's it, thought Cathy, *they just need to give it more time! He said it himself, young people recover all the time!*

<hr>

On a fundamental level Bob looked at life differently than his wife. Cathy trusted people. She didn't deny that they do bad things; she just believed that, all things being equal, people have a natural inclination to choose good over evil. Bob didn't trust anyone—especially himself—and if an inclination did exist, he believed it tilted steeply toward selfishness. Cathy expected good things to happen, and it truly surprised her when they didn't. Bob lived in a precarious world that valued contingency, and, since good fortune has little need for a contingency, he had little need for good fortune. Cathy believed in a compassionate God that loves his children. Bob tried to believe in that God, but he struggled.

And Bob had absolutely no doubt that Cathy's worldview beat his every time…with a few exceptions, such as the meeting with the neurologist. Bob sat in that doctor's office and watched as his wife nodded her head and punctuated even the smallest speck of optimism with a little affirmation of her own. She willed the doctor to turn on the hope, and he complied. But what do you say to a person who has too much hope? Nothing. So, Bob listened and watched and thought about all the times her dogged hopefulness had rescued him.

Not quite forty-one, she still had the beautiful, touch-of-crazy auburn hair that he had seen from across the roping arena twenty-four years earlier. She had just nabbed the blue ribbon for barrel racing and Bob wanted to get a better look at the girl and her horse. The horse looked good but the girl with the blue eyes and big smile knocked him out of the saddle. Over time, as they got to know each other, he fell in love with her kindness and infectious enthusiasm. And her hope, the same hope that sometimes now made him feel uneasy.

The next stop on what would become an extensive tour of many different doctors' offices, led them to Dr. Conrad Gardner, the neuropsychologist. He ordered more tests, but, unlike the previous ones that involved instruments that probed the body, these involved written questions and answers, designed to evaluate Ollie's functioning in a number of areas, including intelligence, memory, problem solving, organization, and concentration. He didn't have the capacity to complete the tests without help, and, if he got hold of pencil and paper, he immediately started scribbling, so, by design, the tests required the help of a close family member. Cathy was that person. Depending on the preferences of the professional who administered the test, Cathy read the questions to Ollie and/or coaxed a response from him and/or recorded the answer. By this time Bob had started to take a back seat, but Cathy kept him updated, although he suspected she sometimes withheld bad news. To Bob, no matter how things had been going, it seemed that one test just led to another. And, true to form, when the neuropsychologist had finished, he recommended an occupational therapist...which required yet another test.

Bob had no choice but to be present for this one because the therapist came to the house to interview the whole family. By now almost five weeks had passed since the accident and Ollie's condition had not improved. During the interview he rocked, groaned, and repeated the questions instead of answering them. Unfazed, the therapist efficiently announced that this parroting trait had a name. She called it echolalia. She also said that based upon the interview—and a questionnaire that Cathy had previously completed—she would be able to establish Ollie's "prior level of function."

Prior level of function? thought Bob. *What is there to establish? He functioned like an eleven-year-old and now he functions like a three-year-old.*

After the interview, the therapist conducted a head-to-toe physical assessment that included everything from pencil gripping to jumping jacks. She spoke to Ollie like an over-caffeinated cheerleader and presented each of the numerous activities as a fun game, which helped to keep him involved, more or less. The entire meeting lasted a little less than two hours. A few days later, Bob and Cathy met at the therapist's office, where she presented a report and announced that Ollie showed a high probability for successful occupational therapy related to sensory processing and, to a lesser extent, attentional issues. She also said that one of the previous tests had detected elevated anxiety which could be specifically attributed to the sensory processing disorder, but could also be related to the overall trauma of a brain injury.

In plain English, Bob took it all to mean that Ollie didn't like people touching him, had trouble concentrating, and felt stressed out because his whole world had gone down the toilet.

In addition to the three weekly sessions with the occupational therapist, the neuropsychologist also recommended more physical activity to help relieve stress. Bob took charge of that job but Ollie didn't make it easy because he constantly tried to escape back to his drawings. Cathy suggested they try one of the playgrounds in town, which is where Bob took Ollie on a mild summer day in July, a few months after the accident.

For some reason Bob had expected Ollie to be enticed by the playground equipment and for the tried-and-true kid instincts to take over. That didn't happen. Bob ended up herding Ollie—without touching him—to the different zones of the play area, but Ollie refused to step onto the equipment. Exasperated, Bob violated the no touch rule and physically lifted Ollie onto the merry-go-round where he lowered himself to the deck, held on to the bar, and groaned loudly as the apparatus spun around. The other kids on the playground stopped and stared. Even the little ones, the ones not old enough to recognize their own shadow, recognized that the big boy was different. The parents looked away and pretended not to notice.

A few minutes later, as Bob stared hopelessly at the steps that led up to a swinging bridge and tube-slide, he heard a loud shriek. The sound came from a girl about Ollie's age, dressed in a soccer uniform, who now ran toward them. Her parents stood in the distance, the gear for an afternoon at the park slung across their bodies. It was Mariah. She had been calling daily and sending nonstop get well cards. She shouted Ollie's name and waived her arms wildly as she charged toward them. At first Bob thought that she might be good for Ollie, that she might help him to remember how to have fun, but that feeling evaporated when she wrapped him up in a big hug. Ollie's body immediately stiffened and he released a series of screeching grunts that sounded like a panicked person trying to catch his breath. Mariah didn't let go. Ollie grunted louder. He wriggled his arms free, pushed her away, and screamed incoherently. The shocked girl stared at him. Ollie spastically raised his arms at her. She stepped back. Ollie stepped toward her and awkwardly brought his arms down upon her shoulders with enough force to knock her to the ground. Mariah screamed loudly. The other parents gasped. Ollie also fell to the ground and started sobbing.

The mother yelled her daughter's name and both parents ran to her aid. The mother comforted her daughter and the father stood over Bob as he kneeled down to check on Ollie. The man yelled, "What the hell is the matter with you! Is this what you teach your kid! I ought to knock you on your ass so you know what it's like!"

"Bob rose to his feet and said, "I'm sorry. My son isn't…isn't…feeling well."

"Having a cold isn't feeling well! Attacking a little girl is psycho! And you're probably the psycho who taught him how to do it!"

Bob moved a step closer and, nose to nose, said, "I said I'm sorry, and I meant it."

The man huffed a few more times, took a step back, and started rounding up his family. As they left the scene, he delivered a parting shot, "That boy is dangerous and I hope you realize it before someone really gets hurt."

The angry man left but some of the anger remained—in the stares of the other parents at the playground. Their eyes said, *your son is a freak, and you both need to leave.* Bob lowered his head and concentrated on Ollie, who had started to calm down. Bob patiently coaxed him back to his feet and then guided him back to the truck.

On the drive home Bob constructed an argument against telling Cathy about the incident. No real harm had been done and he didn't believe for a second that Ollie was dangerous. If anything, Bob reasoned, the blame belonged to him. He'd been told all about sensory processing disorder. He knew that Ollie had boundaries that could not be crossed. Not by anyone, not even his own mother, and yet Bob had let someone violate the boundary. And when Ollie had the meltdown—which Bob had also been warned about—he did nothing. He could have easily grabbed his son and carried him to a safe place to recover. But Bob didn't do it because he thought that he knew better. The blame belonged to him.

The argument made sense but, in the end, it didn't work because Cathy would have found out anyway. Better for him to tell an honest version of the incident than for her to get a second-hand version from the grapevine. So, he told her. And then he held her in his arms while she fell to pieces. That day, from beginning to end, had been the worst of their entire married life, worse even than the day of the accident because at least then they had had the comfort of the unknown. Now they knew. Now they had no comfort at all.

〜〜〜〜〜〜〜〜〜〜

Cathy went alone to the final meeting with the neurologist. She had a bad feeling about it and, in reality, didn't want Bob to be there. When they'd first met the doctor, he had showed them into his private office, had taken off his lab coat, and had been friendly and reassuring. He had passed a bouquet of hope to Cathy—if not to Bob. However, as the results of the tests filtered in over the following weeks, and as Ollie stagnated in therapy, the doctor became less reassuring and more clinical—and openly concerned. One of the tests, the Wechsler Intelligence Scale for Children, showed Ollie had an IQ of sixty-nine, which put him in the lowest category. This had happened several weeks earlier, when the doctor had had at least some optimism, so when Cathy protested that the test didn't work with Ollie because of his concentration issues, the doctor readily agreed to try a different test. Now those results had come in and, judging by the white lab coat and businesslike greeting, they didn't look any better. And she was right; Ollie had scored a sixty-five.

Later in the meeting Dr. Lee used the term mental retardation for the first time and mentioned the possibility of institutionalization, if not now, perhaps when she and Bob got older and could no longer care for Ollie. After that Cathy all but checked out.

〜〜〜〜〜〜〜〜〜〜

Bob didn't want to be the kind of man who counts pennies on the way to the hospital. And he would have never let tight finances hurt Ollie's recovery. But when the bills began to pour in, and when he realized that Ollie might need therapy for years to come, he wondered how they were ever going to pay for it all. They had medical insurance but, like many self-employed people, the plan carried a high deductible—a thousand dollars per year—and also required up to two thousand dollars in coinsurance. That was the only plan the ranch could afford.

Income from the ranch had been declining for years. The reasons were easy to understand but not easy to fix. As a starter, the arid Southern California climate had always been difficult for the backgrounding of beef cattle. This phase requires grass pasture but grass doesn't always grow easily in what is essentially a desert climate. One solution, culling the herd down to the size that the ranch could support rendered the operation too small to compete in the modern market. In the past the problem had been solved by negotiating grazing rights on adjacent stretches of unarable land so that even if the grass came in thin, there was always another ungrazed field available. However, the steady climb in Southern California land prices slowly took this option away because landowners quickly learned that while unarable land might not grow strawberries, it grew housing tracts with amazing proficiency—and profitability. At one time there had been ten cattle ranches within thirty miles of Buck Ranch, including the Salto Ranch where the city of Thousand Oaks is now located and the DuMortier Ranch, which Joel McCrea, the Hollywood actor, purchased in the 1930s. All of them had now disappeared, or been turned into hobby farms, or been replaced by housing developments, such as the ones that now surrounded Buck Ranch on all four sides. The other alternatives, bringing in supplemental feed, hauling the cattle to greener pastures, or taking them to market early, took money straight from the bottom line.

The problems didn't stop there because, like they say, when one domino falls, so do the others. In this case, when the ranches closed, so did the processing plants. Now, instead of hauling the cattle twenty miles to market, they had to be hauled a hundred miles which added yet another inefficiency to all the others.

And that word, "efficiency," really represented the main hurdle over which the ranch tripped. Modern, efficient livestock production depended heavily on vertical integration, a fancy term that simply means that a cattle ranch that owns the most supply chain stages—veterinary, transportation, feed, feedlot, processing, distribution—will also be the one that makes the most money. Buck Ranch had no vertical integration. It hadn't evolved. Like a dinosaur, Buck Ranch was noble, beautiful, and growing extinct.

After spending the better part of the last ten years riding this downward spiral, Bob still didn't have a good answer. He had a couple of bad answers, and a ridiculous one. The first bad answer, an obvious one, meant selling out to the developers, which Bob refused to consider. The second, mortgage the land and keep doing what they had been doing, amounted to a slow and depressing march toward insolvency. And, finally, the ridiculous answer, find a pot of gold at the end of the rainbow...or the twelve hundred gold coins that

Jubal Wainwright, line rider, hypochondriac, and part-time stagecoach robber, had buried somewhere on the ranch in 1887. This fairytale had produced five generations of futility and countless dead ends but, try as he might, Bob couldn't stop believing.

Bob had failed before—in the worst possible way—and the territory felt familiar, but he didn't understand why this time it had to be him. His father had fought against the steady loss of grazing land, the same as Bob, but he had been able to keep the ranch going. His grandfather and great-grandfather had battled black leg and anthrax. His great-great-grandfather had guided the ranch through an epidemic of Texas fever that lasted thirty years and the drought of 1871 that wiped out seventy-five percent of the herd. Why couldn't Bob find the answers like they had? Why, after a hundred and fifteen years, did he have to be the one to lose it all?

<hr/>

Razor wire surrounds the fire support base, reflecting the glaring, oppressive afternoon sun. Raw sewage flows in channels on the other side of the wire, rejected by the soggy ground, simmering in the heat. The second lieutenant follows a corporal from the landing zone to the company command post, passing through a hillside pockmarked with foxholes and tattered hooches. The grunts take notice. Their mocking, incredulous stares are not subtle. The lieutenant wears new boots and cammies with perfect press marks. He removes his cover and bends into the command post hooch.

The captain, sitting at a lopsided, makeshift desk, looks tired and unimpressed. He says, "Straight out of Basic and good to go. Is that right, Lieutenant?"

"Yes, sir."

"Maybe even a little eager."

"Yes, sir."

"Well, this isn't TBS, and you don't know shit. You shadow Hunter. You might outrank him but he knows how to save your ass. You don't make a cup of coffee without his nod, got it?"

"For how long, sir?"

"Until I figure out if you're gonna get anybody killed."

When the lieutenant climbs out of the hooch, everything is different. He's no longer at the company support base. He's alone with his platoon in the jungle. He sees Maloof, Reynosa, and Hochlichtner. They look filthy and half dressed. They stare blankly, knowing what he's going to say because he has already said it in a thousand previous nightmares. He can't unsay what has already been said. Maybe back when he really said it, there might've been a way out, but not now. It's too late, and everyone knows it. "Get your gear. We're going after Durbin," says the lieutenant. They don't protest, not even a cuss word.

The lieutenant looks down at his new boots and freshly pressed cammies.

Bob suddenly woke from the dream. He sucked in a slow, deep breath to calm his racing heart. And then another, and another.

Chapter 4

When father came into a room everything stopped. Cody stopped playing. Mom stopped reading. The clock stopped ticking. Then he'd sit down in the giant chair, hide his face behind a newspaper or cow magazine, and everything started ticking right along again.

Father had sad, dark eyes. Mom had smiling, sparkling blue eyes. Father smelled like a day in the barn, like dirt and grease and horse manure. Mom smelled like flowers. Father didn't talk. Mom talked about everything. When father had especially sad eyes, she talked about happy things. Father didn't drink whiskey…but sometimes he did. Mom drank the good stuff, like cream soda and ginger ale. Father didn't yell. Mom yelled sometimes but she didn't scare anyone. Father scared everyone…and, from as early as he could remember, Cody loved his father.

Cody understood his mom. If he made so much as a chirp, she came running, full of hugs and plates of cookies. Cody didn't understand his father. He never came running. Then one day, as no more than a toddler, Cody picked up a baseball that happened to be lying around. Father looked at Cody. He cupped his hands together and talked to Cody. He said, "Throw it here, boy. Put it right in here." Cody threw the ball with a little more zip than your average two-year-old.

Dad laughed. Now Cody understood. He had discovered the magic. It was called a baseball.

That baseball, and the hours spent throwing it, fielding it, and hitting it, eventually led to other, small discoveries about his father. The words came slowly, and so did the bond between father and son, but Cody didn't mind waiting and adding up the bits and pieces over the years, if that's what it took. In the meantime, he learned about the college baseball team his dad had played on; about horses and cows and the stuff he did around the ranch; about the robbery that had happened a hundred years ago practically at their front door. The police never found the gold, but everybody said that it had to be somewhere on the ranch. Father especially liked to talk about the gold. That and baseball.

He didn't talk about the war, except when something accidently slipped out. Then he'd stop talking. Mom didn't know much about it, but sometimes she tried to explain.

Before the day of that baseball game, Cody would've said that he liked his life—if such introspections could be possible from a rambunctious twelve-year-old boy. Maybe he didn't know a good dad from a bad one, but judging by what the other kids had, his stacked up well enough to suit him. Even back at the beginning, when his baby brother came along, Cody got lucky because Ollie liked silly things. He liked the things that mother liked, stuff like itsy-bitsy-spider and peekaboo. And snuggling, holding baby chickens, and getting pushed in the stroller. And, most importantly, Ollie never picked up the baseball. Everything just kind of fell into place; Cody had father, Ollie had mother, and everyone was happy.

But the lightning bolt didn't just strike Ollie; it also zapped Cody's perfect world. It just took him a little while to figure it out. At first, he knew what everyone else knew, that Ollie had dodged a bullet, and they put him on TV. The first real clue, which buzzed by unnoticed, happened when Ollie got home from the hospital. Cody met him at the door and said, "Hey dummy, do you got curly hair now?" But Ollie just stared like a zombie. After that other things also happened. Mother started missing baseball games because she had to take Ollie to occupational therapy, but Cody figured that's where zombies go to get fixed, which meant everything was going to be normal again. Then Father also stopped coming to the games because the whole thing had sent him into a dark mood. But since mom had everything under control, and since the therapist knew how to turn zombies back into nerds, Cody still didn't think too much about it. It took six months to figure out that serious change had blown his way. It happened at open house for the new school year.

Cody had been named starting quarterback for the middle school football team. Middle school in their district included ninth grade and Cody, an eighth grader, had beaten out two ninth graders for the job, but he didn't say a word. He wanted to surprise his father at open house. And he wanted the news to come straight from Coach Zanheiser. For some reason Cody figured that big news delivered from one hard-ass to another packed more of a punch.

On the afternoon of the open house, mom hovered over Ollie more than usual, which barely seemed possible because Ollie never did anything for himself. Mom told him when to eat, get dressed, take a shower, and go to bed. Ollie needed more so mom gave more. It was a mom thing. But on this day Cody knew the mom thing had gone a little crazy when Ollie came out of his room wearing highwaters, purple suspenders, and a neon orange bowtie. He looked like a clown, or one of those freaks who graduates from Harvard at age twelve and then celebrates with some chicken fingers from the kids' menu. She had him dressed in a way that the old Ollie might have liked, but it didn't do anything for the new Ollie because that boy didn't have a clue. The new Ollie was a blob, a blob with a bowtie.

When they got to school Mom decided that they'd visit Ollie's class first. Cody didn't mind because after the accident Ollie had been placed in special ed—one teacher, one class—and that meant there'd be more time for Cody's various classrooms and teachers, including Coach Zanheiser, to top off the afternoon. Mom led the way, and Cody discreetly walked a few steps behind just in case any of his friends caught sight of his weird looking family.

Ollie's class smelled like paste and wet diapers. Cody saw some kids huddled with their parents in different parts of the room. One girl sat in an electric wheel chair. She had skinny legs and her head tilted sideways. A boy on the other side of the room kept shaking his hands, like they had something bad on them. His mom tried to talk to him but he didn't say anything back. The other parents smiled at Cody's parents, and then their eyes drifted over him and Ollie, and Cody hoped that they didn't think he was a retard or something. On the chalkboard a message had been written in perfect cursive handwriting. It said, "Mrs. Huffman welcomes you to open house."

"Hello, Oliver," said the teacher, from across the room, where she stood next to the girl in the wheelchair. Ollie ignored her. She continued, "I'll be right with you, folks. Please feel free to look around the classroom."

Mom smiled and said thank you to the teacher. Cody looked at father to see if mom had reminded him to put on the happy face. No such luck. He looked mean…and mad. Really mad. And Cody immediately knew the reason: Mom hadn't told father what kind of kids go to special ed. Father liked to pretend that Ollie wasn't like those kids. But he was. That's what Cody thought. Now father had gone into def-con four and the fuse had been lit. And, sure enough, a few seconds later, he bolted out the door without saying hi, goodbye, or how do you do.

Mom looked over at the teacher, then at the door, then she started to leave but the teacher stopped her. She said, "Just a moment, Mrs. Buckmeyer. Oliver has a gift for you…and Mr. Buckmeyer." She hurried to a nearby wall and unpinned a large piece of paper. It was just another one of Ollie's drawings. When they got outside and didn't see father, Cody knew that his special day had been ruined.

A slap on the back from father meant ten times more to Cody than a hug and a bunch of mushy words from his mother. And that's all he had wanted, just to see the smallest glimmer of pride, but he didn't get it because of Ollie.

On the drive home, just before sunset, nobody talked, not even mom. Cody sat in the middle row of the minivan next to Ollie, who stared out the window in his usual weird way.

"I'm the starting quarterback," said Cody.

"You're what?" said mom, who didn't know a quarterback from a Quarter Pounder.

"Coach Zanheiser put up the final roster last week and I'm the quarterback. I beat out two ninth graders."

"Oh, Cody, that's wonderful! I'm so proud of you sweetie!" said mom. Father didn't say anything. Mom nudged him and said, "Isn't that good news, Bob?"

"Yes, that's good news. Good job, son."

And that was it.

After they turned on to the dirt road that led to their house, Ollie raised his hand and pointed at something outside. And then his arm froze like a statue.

"Just so you know," said Cody, "Ollie's acting like a freak back here."

Mom looked back and said, "What's wrong, Ollie? Do you see something out there?"

Ollie kept pointing.

"Yes, that's right, sweetie. Those are the hills. Just like the ones you like to draw."

Father stopped the car in the middle of the dirt road. He looked out his window and then at the picture on mom's lap, the one from Ollie's classroom. He did this a couple of times before grabbing the picture and laying it out against the steering wheel.

"What is it, Bob?" asked mom.

Father got out of the car and held the paper up to the sky. Mom followed him. "Look at this picture and then look

42

at the two trees at the top of the hill," said father, as he held up the drawing for mom to see.

"Those are the same trees as on the picture…and here's the cliff," said mom.

"That's right. Those are the hills, the trees, the cliff, and the gorge that runs right down the middle. And there's the mountain in the distant background. And everything is in absolutely perfect proportion." He turned back to the minivan and opened the sliding door. "You drew a picture of this hill, didn't you Ollie?" said father.

"Yes, I drew that picture. I like to draw pictures. Mrs. Huffman says I'm good at landscapes."

Father stood up tall like a baseball player about to launch into a chest bump. He looked at mom, she looked at him, and they busted out laughing. Cody had never seen his father so happy.

That's when Cody knew that father didn't belong to him anymore. He also knew, for the very first time, what it feels like when envy slithers in and wraps itself around an unprotected heart.

Chapter 5

Something had bothered Bob for a while. According to the neurologist, Ollie used rocking and groaning as mechanisms to relieve stress. The doctor called it "self-stimulating" behavior, or "stimming," and said it is commonly seen in people with autism, or, like Ollie, in people with sensory processing disorder. The doctor also said that Ollie's drawing behavior may also be another form of stimming. That's where Bob had a problem. It didn't make sense that Ollie devoted so much focused energy into what the doctor claimed to be nothing more than an involuntary compulsion. When his son took a pencil in hand and bent over the paper, he drew with purpose. Admittedly, his drawings often looked similar to one another, but that didn't mean they were the byproduct of mindless, repetitious, stimming. The composition and subject matter of each one always varied at least in some small way from the others, and, to Bob, that seemed like the exact opposite of mindless repetition. And when Ollie finished drawing, his sessions didn't end with a fizzle, as you'd expect of someone who is being helplessly propelled by a power that is beyond his control. They ended suddenly, under control, with the same energy as he'd had at the beginning. And then he would sit back with the self-satisfied look of a person who had just completed a job. These things had bothered Bob, and now that he'd pinpointed the exact subject matter of one of his son's drawings, he flat out didn't believe the stimming theory.

These doubts provided the impetus for a simple experiment which began by loading Ollie into the van and convincing him to wear a sleep mask over his eyes. He didn't like the mask, and immediately started rocking and groaning, but he didn't take it off either. Then, as Bob briefed Cathy about the experiment he had in mind, they made the fifteen-minute drive to a nearby canyon road.

When they got to the canyon, Ollie took off the mask. His head and shoulders rotated toward the window, and his eyes locked into place. Ollie had been on this road many times before the accident, but now he stared like it was new. Bob started driving up the canyon road and Cathy, also looking out her window, started writing down different things that she saw. Three miles later, after they'd gone up and over to the other side of the hill, Bob pulled over. The first part of the experiment had now ended. Bob coaxed the mask back over Ollie's eyes, and they drove home, where Ollie went straight to the kitchen table and started working.

Twenty-two drawings and sixty-minutes later he finished. He then contentedly ate his PB&J on white—the same lunch he ate every day without fail—while Bob and Cathy went into the living room and laid out the pictures in the order in which they had been drawn. Cathy then began reading the notes she had taken in the order in which she had taken them.

"Carved canyon wall with cement drainage channel," said Cathy.

Bob scanned the artwork and said, "Yes…in the first two drawings."

"Barbed wire at top of canyon."

"Yes, also in the first two drawings."

"Water tank with graffiti."

"Water tank, no graffiti, number three."

"Break in canyon wall and view of winding road below."

"Yes, in number four."

"Yellow car on winding road."

"Nope. Not here."

"High-power lines on top of hill."

"Yes, on number five."

"Passenger jet."

"Nope."

By the time they got to the end, they had confirmed that forty-four of the fifty-seven items from Cathy's list had been depicted in Ollie's drawings. They also knew more about how Ollie's newly configured brain worked. He didn't draw from imagination. He drew from memory, from a huge block of memorized information, stored in one long panoramic recording. They knew this because the items from the notebook had been depicted in their exact sequence, and, more simply, because when they lined up the artwork in the order in which it had been created, it showed the entire five-minute drive, from beginning to end.

But what about the thirteen items he missed? Bob had an idea about that. Cathy had mentioned a couple times that Ollie didn't always draw at the same pace. Sometimes he turned out minimal drawings like these, but sometimes he took his time and added more detail. Also, when he got bored, perhaps when his brain had used up everything it had recorded, he sometimes picked up old projects and added things to them. Maybe Ollie had control over the details of his artwork and toyed around with them to suit his mood. Bob gathered up the drawings, took them back to Ollie, and said, "These are nice, Ollie. Can you add more details to them?"

Ollie dove back into the work, and when he had finished, the drawings included all of the items from Cathy' list, including the passenger jet in the sky, graffiti on the water tower, and the little yellow car on the road below. He had also added dozens of items that Cathy hadn't noticed, all of it from memory.

"But what does it mean, Bob?" asked Cathy.

"I don't know what it means, but I do know one thing: Ollie isn't retarded."

※※※※※※※※※※※※

Dr. Lee stared down at the stack of drawings that Bob had plopped down onto the exam table. Bob hovered next to the silent doctor. Cathy watched from a nearby chair, with Ollie sitting next to her. They had all crammed into the examination room. Bob thumped the paper with his finger and said, "Do you recognize this building here?"

"No, I'm sorry, I really don't," said Dr. Lee.

"That's the southeast corner of the hospital. How about the building next to it?" asked Bob.

"Well then…that would have to be…our building here…yes, that's it. And this one with the courtyard must be the library."

"And this little blue squiggle in the background?" asked Bob.

"That has to be the high school gymnasium…with the blue roof. My goodness."

"These buildings are the first things Ollie saw when he left the hospital, and it's the first things he drew, not even an hour after he got home," said Bob. Then he pulled a page from the bottom of the stack and said, "And this is the last thing he saw that day, the foothills and the two small mountains behind our home, and it's the last things he drew. And these pages in the middle are the rest of the trip, from beginning to end." Bob stopped talking. He had explained it the best he knew how. Now he could only hope that with all his years of education, the doctor might be able to connect at least some of the dots. But he didn't say anything. He just thumbed through the pages, carefully studying each and every one. At one point he glanced at a calendar on the wall, and then he went back to studying the drawings. Finally, without looking up from the artwork, he said, "Ollie, when is your birthday?"

"May first," said Ollie, easily spitting out the answer without interrupting his rocking.

"May first, that was just a few months ago," said Dr. Lee, as he looked at the calendar. "What day of the week was that?"

"Thursday," said Ollie.

Doctor Lee turned to the back of the calendar and said, "And what day of the week will your birthday be on next year?"

"Friday."

Now the doctor turned away from the calendar and faced Ollie. He said, "And what will it be in two years?"

"Sunday."

"And in the year 2007?"

"Tuesday," said Ollie, without a moment's hesitation.

Bob stood up straight, like he'd just been thumped on the head. He wanted to say, *What the Hell!* But he had more sense than that.

Dr. Lee carefully tore off a big piece of white paper from the role attached to the exam table. Then he lowered himself down to Ollie's level, handed him the paper, and said, "Ollie, I'd like to put one of your pictures on my wall. Can you draw my building for me? It's this one right here." He pointed to the building from Ollie's first drawing.

"That's the Cooper Professional Building. It was built in 1968. I like to draw that building," said Ollie.

"How do you know when it was built?" asked the doctor.

"I see it in my head."

"When they wheeled Ollie out of the hospital," said Cathy, in a measured voice, "there was a picture of your building on the wall. It had the date, and he stared at it just like he stares out the car window."

Doctor Lee tucked Ollie up to the desk, Cathy gave him the backup pencils she kept in her purse, and then the three adults slipped away to Doctor Lee's office just down the hall. After taking their seats, and after Dr. Lee cleared his throat a few times, he said, "Mr. and Mrs. Buckmeyer, Ollie is a savant."

"A savant? But he doesn't have autism...does he?" asked Cathy.

"No…some of your son's symptoms are similar, and the location of the TBI is in the same region where we often find brain damage in autistic patients, but I believe that is irrelevant because there are different types of savants and autistic savant is just one of them. Oliver is an acquired savant. He suffered a TBI and then his brain, in ways that we don't completely understand, compensated for the damage and opened up remarkable powers that, ironically, are unavailable to the rest of us. There have been documented cases of this type of acquired savantism for over a hundred years."

"And what was that business with Ollie's birthday?" asked Bob.

"Savants tend to differ greatly one from another. Their histories, disabilities, functionalities, and gifts run a broad spectrum. We see artistic savants, mathematic savants, and even athletic savants. The list goes on, and it is diverse. There is, however, one commonality that we often see in savants: they are calendar calculators. We don't know exactly why. They just do it, like Ollie did. And he confirmed what I suspected."

"But what does it mean? Will it help him be like he used to be? Will we get our old Ollie back?" asked Cathy.

"No, I'm sorry, Mrs. Buckmeyer, it doesn't mean that. Change in personality is sometimes associated with a TBI. But there's another way to look at it. You are getting a new Ollie who can still live a fulfilling life. Just like the old Ollie, he still has hope for the future, and this special gift can play an important role in that future."

Cathy didn't like the doctor's answer. Bob saw it in her eyes. She wanted her son back. She wanted goofy Ollie back, just the way he used to be. For a few awkward moments the three of them stared at each other until Bob said, "So what do we do now?"

"That's the most important question of all because you have a decision to make," said Dr. Lee. "There are two schools of thought: You can treat the condition or you can train the talent. Treating the condition would involve continued therapy to control anti-social, compulsive behavior with a goal of social integration. Training the talent aims for the same goal but does it by emphasizing the gift, or island of genius, as it is sometimes called. So instead of curbing your son's compulsion to draw pictures, you would emphasize and cultivate it. In many cases we have found that when this is done, the patient's gift acts as a conduit to social integration: People see the gift and are fascinated by it; they want to talk to the artist; the artist gains familiarity with varied social settings; he begins to feel accepted and confident; he may never completely understand the rules of human interaction but he is no longer fearful of them. And that makes all the difference in the world. As you can probably tell, my recommendation is for you to train the talent."

<hr />

Cathy understood the concept of "training the talent," but she didn't know exactly how to do it. Other than a year of the requisite piano lessons for the boys—which Cody hated and Ollie loved—they weren't exactly what you would call an artistic family. Between the four of them, Ollie had been the most creative, but his creativity related more toward his offbeat personality and making people laugh, not toward drawing or painting. Now that creative, funny personality had been replaced by a rigid, fearful one, and yet Ollie had become a budding protégé. This glaring irony hit Cathy hard, but she had no choice but to face it head on as she tried to think of ways to help her son grow—the same son who shrank from human touch, avoided eye contact, and had limited communication skills.

Without artistic expertise of her own or the money to pay for someone with it, Cathy had to follow her instincts. This meant lifting most of the time restrictions on Ollie's drawing sessions and giving him the freedom to do what he loved. She also made a point of altering the routes when driving him to and from school or to the therapist so that he had different things to look at. The mere awareness, subconscious or not, that a new vision had been set aside for him, seemed to alleviate some of the fear that drove his behavior. Now he didn't have to robotically stare out the window at old sights because he knew that new ones would always be available. He didn't have to compulsively draw all the images in his head because now he had ones that deserved to be drawn more than any of the others. He still rocked compulsively, but the moaning relaxed just a bit and started sounding more like a hum.

Something else also changed: Ollie began to have fun with his art. He started drawing other things besides landscapes. And instead of strictly replicating the images in his head, he experimented with them by altering the composition or changing the coloring or combining completely unrelated images. Ollie started to explore his creativity.

Cathy first noticed these changes in a particular drawing. He had picked up the image from some television program but it really didn't make sense because he had drawn all the trees upside down. The lower half of the drawing showed a rural street scene with small-town storefronts, old pickup trucks, and people doing the usual people things. And over their heads towered a forest of upside-down pine trees.

He worked on the drawing for several days—longer than usual—sometimes working on the street scene, sometimes flipping it around and working on the forest. At the end of that time, when the drawing seemed to be complete, Cathy asked about it, and Ollie said, "Sometimes things are upside-down." He then picked up a pencil and, in a matter of seconds, changed the whole meaning of the drawing: The trees that looked upside down had actually been a reflection of a forest upon a glassy lake. And when Ollie saw that she finally understood, he laughed like it had been the best joke ever. In that brief moment, with his infectious laugh, unruly blonde hair, and sparkling blue eyes, Cathy saw just a glimpse of the fun-loving son that she used to have.

But all of the changes, as promising as they might have seemed, only related to Ollie as an artist. Cathy saw little or no change in the things that really mattered. Dr. Lee had said that Ollie's gift would pave the way to a better life. Was this the better life, a boy who has fun doing artwork and occasionally flashes images of the beautiful life he used to have? Ollie still required constant care, didn't have a single friend, and rarely showed emotion. Obsessive ritualistic behavior had turned him into a prisoner. It dictated what he ate, the utensils he used, the clothes he wore, the time he woke, the time he slept, and every second in between. And still, nearly a year after the accident, if anyone touched him, he had a meltdown.

Chapter 6

Cody knew that his brother did weird tricks with numbers. Give him a date and he'd tell you the day of the week. Give him a number of any size, and he'd remember it forever. Sometimes this came in handy if you needed to know a phone number or an address on the fly, but mostly it was just a sideshow. Cody didn't pay much attention to it until one morning when he came into the kitchen for breakfast and found Ollie and father sitting at the table almost having an actual conversation—about baseball. Ollie had gotten a hold of father's baseball magazine and had memorized the monthly team batting averages for every team in Major League Baseball as well as all the vital statistics for the entire Dodgers' roster. And father couldn't get over it. Ollie threw out the numbers like a robot, and father made a big deal out of it.

"Hey, Cody, ask him about any stat you can think of. Go ahead. It's crazy," said father.

"Yeah, that's crazy. Maybe later," said Cody. He left the kitchen without his breakfast.

Ollie didn't know squat about baseball, and those numbers didn't mean anything to him. But father sat there grinning like Hank Arron had just come to breakfast. The scene had been laughable, maybe even annoying, but Cody took it harder than that because once again Ollie had taken something that didn't belong to him. The mutual love of baseball had belonged to Cody and his father and not to anyone else in the family.

∿∿∿∿∿∿∿∿∿∿

Cody had his father's looks, minus the perpetual frown and dark rings under the eyes. And, also like his father, he wore his sandy brown hair cut short and neatly groomed. He had brown eyes that continually scanned and evaluated. His facial features added up to utilitarian good looks, efficient and well proportioned. Most importantly, Cody cared deeply about his image and his looks conformed to the image he had chosen: star athlete and always oh so cool. Even at age fourteen, he looked like a living poster for the all-American athlete.

He had also been born with more than his fair share of self-confidence. The good looks and athletic ability turned that confidence into cockiness, but in the past Cody had been smart with the swagger because father didn't like stuff like that. That was also the reason why Cody had mostly stayed out of trouble. But now, in the eighth grade, he stopped caring about what his father thought. Instead of turning away, he turned toward whichever condemned activity looked the most pleasing. And he moved fast, making up for lost time, so that by the end of the school year he had become experienced in the finer points of forbidden pursuits. That's not to say that he got reckless. He couldn't go that far because he'd worked hard building his reputation and didn't care to risk it with a school suspension, which also carried a

58

ban from after school sports for the entire year. So, he played it smooth, forging notes, shifting blame, playing innocent, and charming suspicious school secretaries.

He particularly liked smoking weed and sometimes ditched class to do it. They called it "ditch-&-dope," and in its most awesome form it meant ditching third period and not returning until lunch period ended. This gave them almost two hours to smoke dope, play video games, and raid the refrigerator—and it only cost the absence from one class, for which they provided a forged note. Most of his jock friends didn't smoke weed but Cody still managed to get a little D-&-D every week or two. His grades slipped, but father didn't care enough to notice and mom had her hands full with the retard.

At one of these sessions, in a garage that had been fixed up with a couch and television, Cody and his friend Matt passed a joint back and forth. In between hits, Cody admired the impressive collection of centerfolds that had been stapled to a panel above the workbench. "What's your mom say about those?" asked Cody.

Matt, holding in a toke, gave a strained, choppy answer, "She don't come in here."

"It's a good thing 'cause the place smells like a pot factory," said Cody. The boys, now fully embraced by the prime Maui Wowie, laughed their asses off.

Matt handed the joint to Cody and said, "You wanna know something, man? I could walk through that door with a pipe in my mouth and a big joint stuck in each ear and nobody would say a word."

Cody responded with a surprised grunt.

"I gotta free pass, man," said Matt. "I'll prove it to you." He got up from the couch and pulled out a green ammo box from a cabinet above the workbench. It had yellow stenciled lettering on the side of it. Cody's father also had a few of these surplus boxes. He kept nails and tools in them. Matt put the box on the floor in front of the couch and opened it. Cody bent over from where he sat on the couch and peered inside. He saw a big bag of weed. Matt pulled out the bag and held it up. "This is my old man's stash. What's he gonna say to me?"

Just then a bell rang in the nearby kitchen. Matt took the joint from Cody and stepped through the open doorway to get the frozen pizzas that had been cooking in the toaster oven. Cody used the opportunity to see what other secrets the old man might be hiding. He rummaged through the box and found zig zags, matches, old watches without bands, loose coins, loose keys, and, just as he'd begun to lose interest, something shiny at the very bottom. He pulled it out. It was a gold coin wrapped in a see-through protective cover. His hand immediately plunged back into the box and found four more coins that looked just like the first one. And, like a breeze through the leaves, an easy smile spread across his face.

Cody had grown up in a family that constantly talked about gold coins. At every family gathering, drunk or sober, crippled or healthy, the old farts talked about the same old fairytale. At that very moment Cody could hear his grandfather's voice, "How about you, Cody? Are you the one? I bet you are. You got the gold fever. I can see it." And Cody always thought the same thing: *Yeah, Grandpa, I'll find the gold…right after you find your false teeth. Can I watch TV now?* They all talked about it, but not one of them owned a single gold coin, especially not his father, the biggest dreamer of them all. But now Cody had five of them. He slipped the coins into his pocket and made the stuff in the box look undisturbed.

A few days later Cody got the phone call he expected. The desperation in Matt's voice didn't surprise him either. As Matt choked back tears, with his dad screaming in the background, he begged Cody to return the coins. Cody denied any knowledge of the theft like a guy who'd just committed the perfect crime. And he had. What was the old man going to do, call the police? Not likely, not with the drug story Cody had to tell.

≈≈≈≈≈≈≈≈≈≈≈≈

Professor Phineas Mardikali couldn't say no. Well…he could say no but then he'd feel guilty and lose sleep…not literally…because old geezers don't sleep. They close their eyes and make immodest noises that are sometimes mistaken for sleep. Then they open their eyes, unrefreshed, and continue pushing the rickety cart up the hill, metaphorically speaking. On a spring afternoon in 1992, Phineas had pushed his cart to Bradley Junior High School, where he had been enlisted to judge their annual art contest. He said yes because of the kids, just as a saintly art teacher had once said yes when he had been a kid looking for refuge.

Phineas repeatedly whispered the same words as he walked among the displays: God bless this child. It had been a while since he'd been submerged in a collection of teen and pre-teen art and he had almost forgotten the emotion that often lay so near the surface. And the unequivocal colors and lines. There were unicorns, of course—one frolicking, another making an imposing stand—and a doe-eyed nymph with fireflies for hair, miniature versions of which had probably been dreamily drawn a hundred times in some tattered algebra notebook. Some of the pieces showed a maturity that belied the age of the artists, while others more innocently depicted unambiguous worlds where the sun shined radiantly, good and evil didn't flirt with each other, and hope knew no limits. Some of the works also reflected pain and turmoil, which, given the ages of the artists, didn't surprise the eighty-one-year-old who had been around young people for almost his entire life. He felt thankful that, at the very least, they had found art as a way to express themselves.

He smiled at the ample use of stock-in-trade imagery— prevalent mostly in the younger grades. He saw rainbows, sunrays, blue skies, happy faces, frowning faces, shooting stars, teardrops, hugs, hand-holding, and butterflies. There was also no shortage of youthful idealism in all of the age groups, hinted at in many of the pieces, and energetically portrayed in one particular piece that showed a triumphant spaceman who had grown a crop of corn on the moon. Phineas loved all of them, whether they won a ribbon or not.

One piece, however, interested the professor more than the others. The realistic pencil drawing depicted a freeway with a farm field in the background. A farmer drove his old tractor in the field, going the same direction as the single car on the freeway. The car had been colored a modern yellow. It looked fast, like it had just zoomed past the tractor. The freeway upon which the car traveled, however, had been done in a stark black and white. In contrast to this, the entire farm field in the background, as well as the tractor, had been done in warm, earthy colors that caused the eye to focus on the bucolic tranquility of the background, but only after passing through the coldness and chaos of the fast-paced modern world.

Initially, this panoramic work caught his eye because of its ambition. It measured two feet by five feet and required two easels for the display. It also made him think about the speed of modern life and the direction we are going as a society. But these themes didn't match the age of the artist, a seventh grader, who had to be no more than twelve or thirteen years old. But, then again, the work itself exhibited none of the missteps one might expect from someone so young. It showed expert use of space and balance—no easy feat in a work of this size—and instead of logical coloring that complimented a work of realism, the artist counterintuitively used a targeted coloring technique that showed impressive originality. Professor Mardikali looked forward to meeting the young artist.

⬥⬥⬥⬥⬥⬥⬥⬥⬥⬥⬥⬥

Cody ducked into the bathroom to apply a few drops of Visine to his bloodshot eyes and then traipsed into the auditorium for the all-school assembly. They had gathered for the annual art show awards ceremony—i.e., a parade of nerds and losers; a fashion show of highwaters, pocket protectors, and coke bottle glasses. The members of Cody's posse began migrating to where he stood at the back of the room. They formed a cool-kid cocoon, fashionably protected from the posers and wannabes. Cody saw his mom, also in the back of the auditorium, sitting with the other parents. She didn't have enough of a suspicious nature to detect his altered state so Cody didn't worry too much. Besides, she had her eyes glued on to Ollie, who sat up front with the special ed class.

While waiting for the assembly to begin, Cody's clique put their stamp on the room by teasing and joking a little louder than everyone else, until Mad Dog Maynard, the cranky English teacher, came over and told them to quiet down and take seats.

Mr. Hovey, the principal, stepped up to the podium on the stage and raised his hand, formed in the shape of a zero. This meant zero volume, and required the students to stop talking and to raise their hands, also shaped like a zero. The members of the cool-kid cocoon adopted their best gag-me-with-a-spoon facial expressions and lazily raised their hands, high enough to avoid getting into trouble but low enough to protest being lumped together with mere mortals. Mr. Hovey made one of his speeches and then some ancient professor who probably ate prunes for breakfast and smelled like cheese started announcing the awards for the art show.

Cody's gang responded to the various contest winners in direct proportion to their popularity. A popular but uncool kid got weak applause, and a complete dork got rolled eyes and snide jokes. At the very end, the old fart announced the grand prize winner, but by this time the warmth from Cody's buzz had been burned off and he had begun to tune out. He vaguely heard someone call his brother's name but didn't completely catch on until the girl next to him gasped and gave him a nudge. Ollie had won the grand prize. And then everyone clapped loudly, wildly, like it was a big deal. The girl next to him, one of his favorites, actually had tears in her eyes. She said, "Everyone loves Ollie. He's so great."

"Yeah, he's so great," said Cody.

Ollie climbed the stairs to the stage, but of course he couldn't be normal. Instead of shaking the old man's hand and taking the ribbon, he ignored the geezer, crossed the stage, and took his drawing off of the easels. The room became silent. The old man lowered his outstretched hand and looked confused. Ollie lugged the giant picture down the stairs, up the aisle, and half way through a row of chairs. He stopped in front of Mariah. She used to be Ollie's best friend, before the accident, and before he went apeshit on her in the park. Ollie held out the picture and said, "This is for you, Mariah. I'm sorry for what I did. It was wrong."

Half the girls in the room made that annoying swooning sound that they like so much, and then, a second later, the entire auditorium erupted in applause all over again. It didn't make sense. Ollie didn't have a single friend, didn't talk to anyone, and everyone still loved him. Cody just didn't get it.

<hr>

When the principal explained that the boy was a savant, Professor Mardikali couldn't help himself. He felt disappointed. He'd read stories about these savants and had more or less concluded that, while remarkable, their talents have more to do with an incredible memory and little to do with true creativity. They hear a song once and play it from memory on the piano. They memorize train schedules, batting averages, and entire phone books. And that's where the professor would have left it, fooled by a robotic memory, but no worse for the experience…except for one nagging little detail: He had chosen that drawing especially because of its originality, and, as far as he knew, all the memory in the world couldn't account for that kind of creativity.

After the principal introduced him to the mother, Professor Mardikali took a chance and asked if she might consider enrolling her son in one of his classes at the local community college. She said yes without hesitation.

§§§§§§§§§§§§§§

The day after the awards assembly Ollie got a note from Mariah. She asked him to meet her for lunch in the cafeteria on the following day. And that scared him. It made him feel more confused than the first day in the hospital.

Ollie could remember his old life. When he closed his eyes, he saw happy, colorful pictures of his life when he had friends. He used to talk with them for hours and hours. Back then he knew what everything meant. He knew when the conversation started and when it ended. He knew when to talk, what to say, and when to laugh. He knew how to say funny things that made other people laugh. He knew how to say things with his face and body, without talking at all. Now he didn't know any of those things, and if he ate lunch with Mariah, then she would know it too. She would know that he didn't belong. She wouldn't like him anymore.

But he couldn't say no, so he showed the note to his mother, and she fixed it up with Ollie's teacher.

Everything about the next day felt different. Ollie spent the first two hours of school rocking and groaning and staring at the clock above the chalk board. At ten-forty-seven Mrs. Huffman whispered in his ear. She said he didn't have to go to the cafeteria if he didn't want to. At eleven o'clock the lunch bell rang. Ollie grabbed his lunch and ran out the door but he had forgotten what it felt like to walk to the cafeteria by himself. He didn't like it. When he got to the vending machines outside the cafeteria door, the kids stared and a girl talked to him. Ollie stopped. He needed to say something back to her, but her words had poured into his ears so fast, and each word meant so many different things. If he had time, he could figure them out, but he didn't have time. He walked away. The kids laughed.

He pulled open the door and heard the shrieks and banging plates and loud voices. And the bright lights made a buzzing noise. He didn't like that noise. He didn't like the cafeteria. The kids near the door said things to him, but he didn't say anything to them. He saw Mariah sitting at a big round table with her friends. She had a lot of friends. He walked up to the table and they stared at him. And they smiled. Ollie smiled back because that's what he learned from Mrs. Evertts, the lady at therapy. Ollie sat down next to Mariah, but the bench didn't have enough room and his shoulder touched the girl next to him. He slid away from her but then his other shoulder touched Mariah. He scrunched himself and concentrated on not touching anyone.

"Hey Ollie, you were a big hit yesterday," said one of the boys who used to be his friend. "Everyone's talking about it. They say you stole the show."

Ollie didn't steal things and he didn't understand why the boy said that he did.

"Yeah...and thank you for the picture," said Mariah. "I should've said thank you yesterday but I was so surprised...and embarrassed, I didn't know what to say. I really like it. It must have taken forever for you to draw it," said Mariah.

Ollie didn't understand the words. The buzzing lights made it hard to concentrate. He shouldn't have come. The kids stared at him. He said, "It must have taken forever for you to draw it."

Mariah laughed nervously. The other kids stared down at the table.

"I didn't draw it. You did, silly," said Mariah.

The kids laughed. Ollie laughed, too, because he knew that if he laughed when everyone else laughed, they would think that he understood. He also knew that if he repeated the thing that had made people laugh the first time, they might laugh again when he said it. So, he said, "I didn't draw it. You did. Silly," and then he laughed loudly, but nobody else did. They stared at him.

Mrs. Evertts had taught him a trick to do when he got scared. She said if he did this trick he wouldn't rock and moan and people would like him. He couldn't remember the trick. He rocked and moaned. The kids started to leave, one and two at a time, until only Ollie and Mariah remained at the table. And then she left, too.

Mariah didn't send anymore notes.

68

When Cathy got the phone call to come pick up Ollie, she knew that lunch had gone badly. On the drive home she tried to talk with him, but he screamed at her and violently banged his head against the window. It shattered within the first mile and the sound of blasting wind and loud groaning engulfed the van for the remainder of the drive home.

That afternoon Ollie drew a sad and distorted picture of the tree swing near the side of their house. It had been his and Mariah's special place.

Chapter 7

At Bradley Junior High the ninth graders—considered high schoolers in many other school districts—got certain privileges that the seventh and eighth graders didn't get. The biggest of these being the ninth grade dance, held at the beginning of each school year. This particular dance stood out from the others because it felt like a real high school dance. It started at night time, not after school, had a real disc jockey, good food, slow dancing, decorations, and you could bring a date. Every year this dance kicked off the school year with a blast of excitement. The lower grades gossiped about it and looked forward to their turn. The ninth graders flaunted it.

The year before, as an eighth grader, Cody had gained access to the hallowed event on account of his ninth grade girlfriend. And now at the beginning of his ninth grade year, eighteen months after his brother's accident, Cody decided to return the favor and invite an eighth grader himself. But he didn't tell anyone, especially not anyone in his family.

On the night of the dance Cody hitched a ride with a friend and got to the girl's house right on time. The mother answered and invited Cody inside. From the entryway, where he waited for the girl, Cody saw the father in another room sitting in a recliner, reading the newspaper. He didn't say hello, but he did issue an order from behind the afternoon edition, "You be at the front door of the auditorium at ten o'clock sharp. If you're not there I'm coming in to get you and it won't be pretty. Do you understand?"

Cody gave him a solid sounding, "Yes sir."

Then the girl came out. She looked good, definitely presentable, and Cody estimated that even though he'd invited a non-cool eighth grader, his reputation wouldn't take too bad of a hit. He gave her the corsage, which had cost six dollars, and they loaded into the car to be driven to the dance by the mother. Before they left the driveway, Cody said, "Mrs. Kelley, my mom was wondering if we could swing by my house so she can take a picture of us…since this is my first dance and all?"

"Uh…OK…why didn't she just come inside with you?"

"She didn't drop me off. A friend did," said Cody.

The Kelleys lived on the edge of town and the drive took just a few minutes. Mrs. Kelley waited in the car while Cody and the girl stepped inside the house. From the entryway, where Cody had a clear view down the hallway and into the living room and family room, he hollered for his mom. She answered back from somewhere at the back of the house, saying, "What'd you forget?" And then, as she crossed through the living room, she stopped and stared. She said, "Mariah."

"Hello, Mrs. Buckmeyer."

"Cody, you didn't tell me you were taking Mariah to the dance."

"Yeah, I did. Don't you remember? You must've forgotten. Anyway, did you want to take a picture?"

"Uh…uh…OK…let me get the camera."

"Where's Ollie?" said Cody, innocently. "Maybe he'd like to say hi to Mariah."

Mom stopped in her tracks, whirled around, and said, "No…no…he's in the middle of a project right now and—"

Just then Ollie emerged from the dark hallway. He stared at Mariah for a second and then said, "Hi, Mariah."

"Hi Ollie," said Mariah, awkwardly.

"You're here…you're here…." said Ollie.

"Yep, she's here," said Cody.

And then nobody said a word and Cody let the silence wash over him like a warm shower. Finally, as expected, Mom came to the rescue. She said, "Mariah's mom is giving Cody a ride to the dance and…and…that's why she's here…."

Oh no, that will never do, thought, Cody. He said, "I'm taking Mariah to the dance. She's my date."

"You're taking Mariah to the dance?" asked Ollie.

Yes! Mr. Bonkers is firing on all cylinders tonight! thought, Cody. And then he stared intently into his brother's eyes, searching for the exact moment of impact, when hearing and understanding collide, when the mind staggers and the heart is pierced. Cody wanted to see the pain. He wanted to feel the heaviness of it, and carry it like a cold rock, an undeniable reminder that someone had been hurt almost as badly as he had been. And he got what he wanted. Ollie groaned repeatedly while simultaneously trying to form words, which resulted in a throaty gibberish. Then he spun around and ran to his bedroom. Mission accomplished.

Mariah, Cody, and mother stood there silently. Cody saw the pain in his mother's eyes but it couldn't be helped. Collateral damage. She quietly said, "I don't think the camera has film…and you don't want to be late…."

Later that night, after the dance, and after he had explained to Mariah that their date had been a one-time deal, Cody lay in bed listening to his mom and dad argue. They usually argued about money, but tonight they argued about Cody. Mother said that he needed a father's guidance now more than ever. She pleaded with father to do something. Father argued back, saying that she pampered Cody and spoiled him. At the end of the fight father promised that when he got back from Sacramento, he'd spend more time with his son. But those pathetic words just added to Cody's anger. He didn't want a father who had to be coached. He wanted a father who really cared.

⬩⬩⬩⬩⬩⬩⬩⬩⬩⬩⬩⬩

Cathy eventually learned that Cody had lied to Mariah. He had told her that Ollie wanted her to go to the dance with Cody since Ollie couldn't take her himself. Mariah had been blameless, but it was too late. The damage had been done. Mariah never came back to the ranch. Even later, after Ollie's condition had improved somewhat, she didn't respond to invitations or phone calls. And Cathy couldn't really blame her. She had been attacked at the park and callously used by Ollie's own brother—not to mention the embarrassment in the cafeteria. Not even Mariah had enough determination to overcome so many obstacles.

True to his word, after father got back from the court hearing up in Sacramento, he pushed the daddy-cares button and expected Cody to jump for joy. Cody threw it in his face. He didn't talk baseball with him, didn't ride to the games with him, and didn't so much as nod at him when he faithfully sat in the bleachers. Even after the scouts started coming to watch Cody play, and father got excited, Cody refused to share the joy.

He had learned a valuable truth: Just as you can't force a father to love a son, you can't force a son to love a father. This knowledge opened up an arsenal of weapons for Cody, the same weapons that had been used against him: rejection, ambivalence, preoccupation. And, for his effort, Cody got to see the hurt in his father's eyes. Even the big, bad marine couldn't hide the pain.

He never lost his temper, though, but Cody's mom did. One night, towards the end of his ninth grade school year, she came into his bedroom and Cody saw the anger more than ever before. She stared with a red face and a clenched jaw. Cody said, "What?"

"You listen to me. Sometimes you have to be thankful for what you have and forget about what you don't have. At least your father cares enough to try his very hardest. And if that's not good enough, maybe you need to take a good long look in the mirror!" And then she stormed out.

Chapter 8

The night before Ralph Durbin's sentencing hearing, Cathy saw the light on in the office that occupied a small corner of the barn. Bob often did paperwork at night but not usually this late, so she went out to check on him. She opened the door and saw him sitting at his desk. He smiled at her. Then he stared into her eyes a little longer than normal, holding her gaze away from the bottle that sat at his elbow. Cathy understood. Personal weakness shamed Bob, particularly this one. She sat down in a small leather chair next to the desk. The open bank account ledger sat on the desk next to the whiskey bottle and a small tumbler. She reached for the tumbler, took a small drink, and said, "I read somewhere that if you only open the ledger once a month you have fifty percent fewer headaches."

"But I bet it's a damn big headache," said Bob.

They smiled.

"I'm sitting here wondering what would happen if we sold out and I tried to turn you into a city girl," said Bob.

"Nothing. I'm not the one with the name Buckmeyer on my birth certificate."

"You don't think I could do it?"

"You could do it…but you won't because you think a bunch of Buckmeyers who have been dead for a hundred years are watching your every move."

"Maybe they are. Maybe they're telling me what to do, and I just don't get it." Bob took a drink.

"I'm sure we'll figure something out, and, if worse comes to worse, we could always convert to avocados," said Cathy, with a chirpy voice and an exaggerated smile.

"Sounds wonderful. Is that like converting to Buddhism?"

"Similar…except you get guacamole."

And then they laughed, especially Bob. He laughed good and hard, like it had been held back for too long. And then, when the laughter had ended, he looked into Cathy's eyes and said, "I'm not going to tell them everything. I can't do it."

"You don't have to, Bob. Just talk about Ralph."

"There's no difference, we're the same. I did the same things he did."

"You didn't kill your wife. You're not the same. You could never do something like that."

Cathy heard his forceful, agitated breathing, and saw the tension in his face. He had formed some words but for some reason held them back. Finally, very quietly, he said, "I never got pushed that far because I have you. Ralph wasn't so fortunate. That's the only difference…how far you get pushed…."

"Then tell them just enough to help Ralph. Anything more than that isn't their business," said Cathy.

"Yeah, that's what I'll do, just what they need to know. I won't disturb the fantasy."

"Alright…Can I help you pack?" asked Cathy.

"Sure."

"And are we done with this?" Cathy tapped on the whiskey bottle.

"Yes. I'm done. Sorry, Cathy."

"Just a drink with your friend. Nothing to be sorry about," said Cathy. She took another sip from the glass and handed it to Bob. He polished it off.

Cathy had rightly feared that Ralph's sentencing hearing would create problems. Bob had fought hard to put Vietnam in a place where it did the least amount of damage. And gradually, over many years, he had been successful. He had battled random sights, sounds, and thoughts that used to trigger debilitating memories, and the demons those memories unleashed. He had won a hard-fought truce. But now he would be sworn in as an instrument of the court and ordered to dig up the very same memories that he had so carefully buried. And, because of Ralph, he would obey. And, whether Bob painted a sanitized picture or not, Cathy worried about how far he would be set back.

<hr />

The lieutenant sees Maloof, Reynosa, and Hochlichtner. They look filthy and half dressed. They stare blankly, knowing what he's going to say because he has already said it in a thousand previous nightmares. He can't unsay what has already been said. Maybe back when he really said it, there might've been a way out, but not now. It's too late, and everyone knows it. "Get your gear. We're going after Durbin," says the lieutenant. They don't protest, not even a cuss word.

The lieutenant looks down at his new boots and freshly pressed cammies.

Bob woke from the dream. He sucked in a slow, deep breath to calm his racing heart. And then another, and another.

§§§§§§§§§§§§§§

Bob knew the story. It had Ralph's name all over it, but it didn't belong just to him. The hopelessness of it had been etched into Bob's soul as well. The dread had never left, not even after all these years. Back at the hotel a bottle waited to take away the pain. If only they would call his name and let him be done with it. But they didn't call it, so he waited in the back of the courtroom, not on trial but guilty in every way that mattered. He waited and listened.

Voluntary manslaughter in California carries a penalty that ranges from probation all the way up to eleven years in state prison. Ralph had been sentenced to the maximum, but sometime after the first sentencing, post-traumatic stress disorder, or PTSD, had been added to the *Diagnostic and Statistical Manual of Mental Disorders* and the appellate court ruled that even though the judge had stayed within the parameters of the plea agreement, this medical condition may have directly affected Ralph, and the crime that he committed, and therefore should be considered.

Sometimes a resentencing hearing can backfire on the defendant. The judge can go through the motions and then has full authority to impose an even harsher sentence. But in this case Ralph had already been given the longest possible sentence, so he had nothing to lose. He also got another boost. At the original sentencing his daughter, Rachel, had condemned him to hell. She had been expected to do the same this time but never showed up to the hearing. The prosecutor said that she was sick and he asked for the hearing to be rescheduled. The judge said, "Has Miss Durbin provided a statement that can be read on her behalf?"

"No, your honor, she hasn't," answered the prosecutor.

"She's not here, she didn't provide a statement, and…you haven't heard from her, have you?"

"Uh…your honor…we haven't quite been able to—"

"And she's not returning your phone calls."

"No, your honor."

"Request for a continuance is denied. You may proceed, counselor."

The prosecutor presented a psychiatrist who said that Ralph did not suffer from PTSD at the time of the killing, but the doctor had conducted the examination just three months before the hearing, a full eight years after the crime. The defense expert, on the other hand, pointed to the Separation Health Assessment conducted by a military doctor when Ralph left the Marine Corps. Even though the doctor probably knew nothing about PTSD, she still listed four symptoms that pointed to that condition: chronic sleeplessness, persistent anger, feelings of estrangement, and self-destructive behavior.

Then, late in the afternoon, they finally called Bob's name and he allowed himself to be led through the jungle one last time. He carefully recounted just enough to get the job done, or so he hoped, and described the unrelenting fear that methodically crushed every marine in the jungle, including Ralph, until they either got killed or turned into something less than human.

Just when Bob thought that he had made it through unscathed, the defense attorney asked him to talk about Ralph's most memorable kill. Bob hesitated. The question angered him, and it crossed the line that he had drawn before the hearing. But he had also committed himself to helping Ralph as much as possible. In a barely audible voice Bob said, "Stumpy on the wire."

"I'm sorry. I can't hear you. Can you please speak louder?" said the attorney.

"Stumpy on the wire," repeated Bob, and then he told about the Viet Cong soldier who had been blown into the concertina wire that protected their position. He died on the wire from blood loss, pulpy stumps for legs, and then hanged there for two days, a battlefield scarecrow. Ralph probably didn't actually kill the soldier but he had had the most fun with him, including the painting of a Groucho Marx mustache on the soldier's lip and a cigar shoved into his mouth. And then Ralph posed for a picture with the corpse, smiling like a day at the beach. Right at that point, the attorney produced the picture of Ralph and the corpse, and handed it to the judge. If a picture is worth a thousand words, then the judge gagged on a thousand of the most putrid words in the human language.

Bob didn't tell the worst of the worst, but he came closer than he had wanted. And then Ralph took the stand and did the same thing.

The judge rendered an immediate sentence: seven years and two months, time served. Ralph was free.

※※※※※※※※※※

When Bob returned from Sacramento, Cathy met the truck in the driveway and expected to see one of two facial expressions: weary eyes and an impeded smile or something more relaxed. The first meant Ralph's hearing didn't go well. The second meant some margin of success. Cathy preferred option number one, four more years in prison. Bob didn't know that, though he probably could have guessed. But Cathy didn't see either of those faces. Instead, she saw diverted eyes and a guilty grin. Then Ralph Durbin got out of the truck. He carried a big green duffel bag. And, knowing Bob, this guy wasn't going to be staying for just the weekend.

Bob knew better than to bring Ralph into the house, so he put him up in the old wrangler's bunkhouse a couple of hundred yards up the hill from the house. But this flimsy piece of strategic thoughtfulness did nothing to cool Cathy's anger, and she and Bob tore into each other that night in the most hateful and destructive fight of their entire marriage. Ralph had been back for barely an hour and he had already started tearing apart her family.

※※※※※※※※※※

After Ralph got settled and had been at the ranch for a few weeks, he accepted Bob's invitation to dinner, but it didn't feel right. It felt like an angry tug-of-war between Bob and Cathy over a broken-down old convict, and Ralph didn't want any part of that. And he didn't want to be reminded every time he buttered his bread that his best friend's wife hated his guts. The oldest son, Cody, also had issues, and everyone at the table still seemed to be overwhelmed by Ollie and his problems. It didn't take a shrink to see that this family needed some space. So, Ralph picked up a camping stove and a small refrigerator at the Salvation Army and started taking his meals alone in the bunkhouse—except when Bob fired up the charcoal for the monthly barbecue. Too many prison dreams about forbidden food prevented Ralph from ever having the kind of willpower that could say no to a juicy steak. But, since Bob and Cathy hosted the monthly event especially for the ranch hands, Ralph usually enjoyed the get-togethers without picking up bad vibes or feeling that he had imposed.

At the second barbecue, not more than six weeks after moving in, Cathy approached Ralph where he sat alone at one of the picnic tables that surrounded the barbecue. She had him cornered. Ralph looked for help and saw Bob smiling sadly through the wafting smoke. His face said, "You're screwed, buddy, but good luck anyway." Ralph understood, in fact he had been expecting it, because when you move into a new place you have to fill out an application, so to speak, and Ralph's application looked like shit. Now the landlady wanted to talk about it.

"Can I get you a beer, Ralph?" said Cathy.

"No, I'm good, thanks."

She sat down opposite him and said, "How's the bunkhouse working out for you?"

"It's fine. The Jacuzzi could use a few more bubbles, but I got no complaints."

"Living in a bunkhouse, working on a ranch, bet you never saw that coming. Are you sure I can't get you a beer? If there's one thing I remember, it's you and your beer."

"Cathy, you can ask me anything and I won't hold it against you. I have no right. Ask your questions."

"Why are you here, Ralph?"

"I don't know...I guess because it's kind of hard to get into trouble out here...and I don't have anything else."

"That's not a great answer."

"It's all I got."

"Do you understand that the Bob you knew ten years ago isn't the Bob you know today? He's not your drinking buddy anymore."

"I quit drinking, Cathy."

"Oh yeah? That's the first I've heard."

"'Cause I didn't say anything. I've quit so many times, nobody really wants to hear about it."

Cathy paused for a few seconds before saying, "Bob got drunk the night before your hearing."

"I know. And you think I'm to blame."

"Yeah. It seems like whenever trouble comes our way your name is attached to it. But, to tell you the truth, it doesn't matter, because when Bob falls, he gets back up. He never stops trying. And...I guess...that's what bothers me about you...I've never seen you pick yourself back up."

"In the past, I never did."

"So, what's different now?"

"I never lost anything that I cared about. This time I did." He reached under the collar of his shirt, grabbed the chain that hung around his neck, and pulled it over his head. The chain held a silver locket, shaped like a dog tag.

Cathy took the locket, opened it, and mouthed the word Rachel.

"She's twelve years old in that picture and that's how she looked the last time I saw her, when she told me that I'm not her father anymore."

Cathy handed back the locket and said, "I'm sorry it had to come to that, Ralph, but don't think for a second that this is going to make me trust you. The only thing keeping you here is my husband's stubbornness. If you make one mistake you'll be gone and I'll sleep just that much easier."

"Then why don't I leave now and save you the trouble?"

"No, I don't think so. It'll be better if you screw up first. Let's go with that."

And then she smiled and left, message delivered.

Father looked like a guy trapped in the 1950's—everything respectable and stuffed inside like a pipe bomb. Ralph looked like a hippie that had gotten lost in the desert. He had long, stringy brown hair, a dirty gray beard, and wire brush eyebrows. One look into his lifeless eyes and weathered face and you thought ex-con alcoholic. And you'd be right on target. One look at father, with his discipline and silent sadness, and you'd think trustworthy hero, and you'd be stuck in the bullshit, just as Cody had been for most of his life. Ralph knew what he was. Father still didn't have a clue. No two people ever belonged on opposite sides of life more than these two...except for the thing that held them together, the thing that nobody ever talked about.

Even before Ralph came into the house for the first time in ten years, Cody didn't like him. Cody had heard the phone calls and had seen the way father jumped into action whenever Ralph needed so much as a toothbrush. And now Ralph's presence constantly reminded Cody that he had the kind of father who held back from his own family but never held anything back from a lowlife criminal. That's why Cody hated Ralph.

Chapter 9

By 1996, Cody's senior year in high school, the age of the personal electronic device had fully arrived, but he didn't have money to pay for it—at least not in the style he felt he deserved. And, because of his carefully constructed golden boy image, the feel of a skinny wallet affected him more acutely than it should have. He strolled the school hallways, confident in his domain but always aware of which friends still had last year's mobile phone and which ones had scored a thousand dollar flip phone. When his teammates worked out, he calculated which headsets connected to three hundred dollar Discmans and which ones connected to twenty-nine dollar knockoffs. And when he didn't know, he suspected. He suspected a conspiracy of easy living. He believed others had it better. Their laptops and iPods proved it. A nonchalant charisma allowed Cody to play through this middleclass handicap, but he secretly obsessed.

Of course, the ranch had a never-ending supply of chores, and his parents didn't mind paying for extra work, but that didn't cut it for Cody. That was for losers. That was how idiot cattle ranchers tricked their sons into becoming idiot cattle ranchers. *Here, son, go out and work your ass off all day and maybe I'll slip you a twenty.* Cody knew better.

In the summer before his senior year, he stumbled upon a new website called eBay. People sold things there, and made money. Maybe he could do it too. He clicked on the different categories, trying to get an idea for something to sell, but nothing looked promising. The ranch had cow patties. It didn't have things that people wanted. He kept searching, eventually clicking on a category called "Collectables," which didn't mean anything to him, but a subcategory called "Artwork" popped up, and then another one called "Drawings." Wait a minute. Cody had drawings…or at least he knew where to get them…a never-ending supply—unless Ollie someday gave up the freak show, which didn't seem likely.

Hoping that he had found the solution to his money problem, Cody pilfered ten of his brother's drawings and, with help from his girlfriend's two hundred dollar digital camera, listed them on eBay, each with a starting price of five dollars. The idea had been that after a few days of competitive bidding, he'd end up with an average sale price of ten dollars, which equaled a hundred dollars a week. But it didn't work out like that. Nobody bid and nothing sold. He relisted the drawings with a lower starting price and eventually got one bid on one drawing. It sold for three dollars and sixty-five cents, after fees, and it took two weeks to make the sale.

Cody liked the idea of making money off of his brother, it felt like reasonable payback, but the plan obviously needed to be tweaked.

"Cody Buckmeyer, I need to talk to you."

Cody slipped the headphones from his ears. He knew that tone, and it rarely offered an easy escape, but he tried anyway. Through the closed bedroom door he yelled, "I'm busy."

"Now," shot back his mother.

He stood, dropped the headphones onto the bed, and held a handful of t-shirt up to his nose to see if it reeked like the previous night's party. It did, but his mom didn't usually notice stuff like that, and he didn't care enough to actually change shirts anyway. He slipped out into the hallway and closed the bedroom door behind him. She stood there, staring like a drill sergeant. Cody said, "What?"

"I just got a call from a television reporter. She says you sent a letter."

He remembered something about a letter, and that he had really been into it, but it had been a while ago and the details came up fuzzy. He played cautiously dumb. "Uh...ok...so why would I do that?"

"I don't know. You tell me. She wants to do a story about your brother."

"Who does?"

"The reporter!" yelled mother.

"At the TV station...OK...yeah...that's right, I did send a letter...to help Ollie, that's what it was."

"Cody, how could you do that?"

"Do what? I tried to help. It's no big deal. No one buys his pictures so I figured he could use some publicity."

"She wants to take him up in a helicopter! You told her that he'll draw the Los Angeles skyline from a thirty-minute helicopter ride!"

"Cool! When are they going to do it?"

"They're not! Ollie's never even been near a helicopter, and you had no right making up stories about him."

Cody, once again in control of his manipulative skills, casually called out to his brother, just a few feet away, in his bedroom. "Ollie, let me see your *Kojak* drawing?" Cody heard the sound of rustling papers. He smiled at his mother. She still looked mad. Ollie appeared in his doorway with a large drawing in his outstretched hand. He gave it to Cody and said, "Kojak lives in New York City. I like to draw New York City."

Mother cut him off, "Yes, Ollie, New York City, that's good. I'm talking to your brother now."

"OK," said Ollie. He stood and stared.

Cody showed the drawing to his mother. "This is an overhead view of New York City…like from a helicopter. You and dad were watching an old *Kojak* rerun, Ollie saw the helicopter shot, and drew this picture."

Mother took the picture and studied it. Cody turned to his brother and said, "Do you like helicopters, Ollie?"

"No, I don't like that."

"You can see more things to draw."

"Yeah, I like it."

"What else did you say in the letter?" asked mother.

"Just the usual stuff Ollie does…except on a bigger scale."

"What does that mean?"

"I said he can create an eight-foot-wide drawing of the Los Angeles skyline in less than a week—all from memory."

"You didn't."

Cody smiled big and said, "Whata'ya say, Ollie, do you want to go up in a helicopter and draw a picture of Los Angeles?"

"Yeah. I like Los Angeles."

"If he can do it on the ground from a car, he can do it even better from above, and I think this picture proves it," said Cody.

"You should've talked with us first, Cody. That was wrong." She started to leave but then turned back and said, "And how did you even know about this drawing? You've never taken an interest before."

"I look out for the little twerp. You just never noticed."

She got the warm, fuzzy mother look and said, "That's nice, Cody. I'm glad to hear you say it." She walked back toward the kitchen. Cody called out after her.

"What are you going to do?"

"I'll talk with your father and then maybe to Dr. Mardikali to see what he thinks."

She was hooked. Mother never held back when it came to helping her little boy.

The letter had been nothing more than a garden variety stoner's epiphany where Cody saw the flaw in his moneymaking plan. The pictures on eBay didn't sell because nobody knew the artist. And—after Cody had toked himself to that perfect state, short of oblivion but safely into delusion, where superhuman powers are miraculously discovered—he knew exactly how to fix it. Like a Madison Avenue tycoon, he wrote a letter to the ABC affiliate in Los Angeles and told his version of Ollie's story, but with way too many exclamation points and an uncomfortable number of promises. Despite all of this, and perhaps because of Ollie's previous celebrity, the letter survived the station's various degrees of vetting and managed to elicit a phone call.

~~~~~~~~~~~~~~~~~

A television flickered in a musty and crowded office on the second floor of the faculty building at Crafton Canyon Community College. Ollie's image flashed across the screen. He stood next to a reporter, smiling, pleasantly lost in his world. From behind his desk, Phineas Mardikali, Ollie's faithful old art professor, pointed the remote control and turned up the volume. The reporter said, "I'm here with sixteen-year-old Ollie Buckmeyer. Many of you will remember Ollie as the Little League baseball player who survived a lightning strike. That accident left Ollie with some challenges, but it also left him with a miraculous gift. Ollie is a savant. He has what the experts call an island of genius." Ollie's ink and chalk pastel drawing of Victorian row houses popped onto the screen. The reporter's voice chimed in as the camera panned slowly across this colorful work of art, "Ollie drew this San Francisco street scene after seeing it on a television show for just a few seconds. In those few seconds his brain recorded every detail, from the number of windows in each home, to the exact placement of the wrap around porches, to the turrets, towers, and fish scale siding. There's no doubt that Ollie has a remarkable gift, and if you tune in to the six o'clock news all this week, you will see just how remarkable that gift is. Until then, here's a little hint: We are putting Ollie to the ultimate test. It begins with a helicopter ride and ends with a blank canvas big enough to fill a room. Ken and Nadia, back to you in the studio."

Satisfied that no surprises had been slipped in at the last moment, Phineas put on an overcoat suitable for the cool fall weather, grabbed his cane, and headed straight to the elevator.

When he rounded the final corner on his way to the cafeteria, where Ollie's workspace had been set up in one of the overflow annexes, the professor discovered an energetic and colorful scene. The color came by way of a shiny television news van that had parked on the grass in the quad next to the cafeteria. The energy came from a sizable crowd of students who filled the quad. Not bad for a Monday morning. Those who hadn't been lured by the space-age van with the giant satellite antennae on top had most likely been inspired by the student newspaper, which had put out a special edition about Ollie and the upcoming news special. And the professor had to smile because nobody deserved the attention more than Ollie. The boy had been working with the professor three nights a week for four years, and his faithful perseverance never failed to inspire. Phineas also smiled for the little college that had nurtured Ollie's special talent. The words community college and prestige are rarely spoken together, and the professor took impish pleasure in the possibility of turning that on its ear—if only for a few days. The little fishes in the little pond might just get a little extra sunshine this week, and then life will go back to normal, or so he thought.

With some difficulty, Phineas climbed the few steps that led to the cafeteria, several feet above the hubbub below, and found a spot where he would be easily spotted. Ollie didn't require an inordinate amount of attention but he easily became overwhelmed, and little things, like the sight of a familiar face, helped keep him calm.

A young man with a Bugs Bunny sweatshirt opened the side doors of the news van, retrieved some sort of battery belt which he fastened around his waist, and then hoisted a camera onto his shoulder. Seconds later a black SUV turned off the main campus road onto the walkway that led to the cafeteria. The cameraman filmed the SUV. It pulled up to the entrance of the quad and stopped, about a hundred feet from the cafeteria. Ollie got out of the SUV, walked toward the cafeteria, and met up with the professor, as planned.

Inside the overflow annex, the maintenance department had constructed a ten-foot-long curved wall to which heavy weight drawing paper measuring two and a half feet by eight feet had been attached. To provide an unobstructed view to onlookers, the wall had been built on top of a two-foot-tall platform.

Ollie couldn't hide the smile when he saw the setup. Without fanfare, he climbed the steps to the platform, settled into a tall swivel chair, and began working. And, as usual, professor Mardikali found this unassuming little sequence to be captivating. Good artists often have a refined sense of scale and proportion, but Ollie made it look unusually effortless. He didn't lay down grids or tick marks or a rough sketch. He simply picked up a pen and began recreating—from left to right—the image that had been etched into his memory. He had the ability to instantly calculate the scale and proportion required to transfer an image from his brain onto paper, and the size of the project didn't matter. From miniature to monumental, Ollie just knew.

Several hours after Ollie had begun, the college president popped in to pay his official respects. He noticed that the students in the cafeteria had congregated in a corner of the room that allowed them to watch Ollie from a distance as he worked in the adjoining annex, where the sliding wall had been fully opened. At the various tables the students ate and studied and socialized, and they all seemed to be drawn to the event.

The president wasted no time. He started making phone calls so that by the time the television crew came back to film the first live segment for that night's evening news, they found the annex full of students lounging on two dozen couches that had been borrowed from most every department on campus, including every last couch from the theater arts properties department. The reporter liked the arrangement and included the crowd of lounging students in several of the shots. And Ollie didn't mind the intrusion because he worked in one corner with his back to the rest of the room, he wore music headphones, and he loved being part of a group anyway.

At the end of the first day, after the television people had left and the lights had been turned out, Professor Mardikali felt satisfied—even if he hadn't yet seen the finished product on TV. He got that opportunity later that night when the ten o'clock news re-broadcast the entire segment. Over a hot plate of pastitsio (Thanks to his sister who had packed the freezer with the stuff, along with keftethes, lamb moussaka, and enough baklava to feed Alexander's army), he reveled in Ollie's big moment. He also cringed when the reporter dared to interview a certain over-inflated professor.

A few parts of the piece especially stood out. Ollie had an amazing story, even miraculous, but the professor had come to learn that there is often a painful price to pay because savantism is always accompanied by some degree of brain damage. And the piece didn't shy away from it. They showed some backstory that included candid interviews with a neurologist and a savantism expert. And when they interviewed Ollie, the reporter asked a non-abstract question about what had been seen from the helicopter, which Ollie answered coherently, talking at some length about the Library Tower, the tallest building in California. But then she also asked what it felt like to be a savant and Ollie got painfully lost right out of the gate. Logically, that part should have been left on the cutting room floor, but they included it, and Dr. Mardikali felt that it gave a focused insight into Ollie's life.

The other special moment came at the very end, after the pre-recorded backstory and interviews, after the part showing the imposing challenge that Ollie had accepted, and how much progress he had made after a day's work. This live broadcast segment followed Ollie as he wrapped up work for the day. He put down his pen, took off the headphones, and the students spontaneously applauded. And while Ollie had difficulty understanding personal interaction, he didn't have any difficulty understanding kindness. He smiled at the students, scampered down the steps, and plunged into the crowd like a child plunging into a swimming pool.

<hr/>

Mariah quietly closed the family room sliding door. She turned down the TV volume and pulled a chair up close, like a co-conspirator taking orders. All of her friends had been talking about it, and she wanted to see for herself.

His image flashed across the screen and he looked just like her Ollie. He talked about his artwork. He sounded normal. Mariah felt the faintest little ember of hope begin to kindle. But then they asked a simple question and, like a passing spirit, Ollie disappeared, replaced by someone she didn't know.

<hr/>

Nothing about the second day particularly stood out. Two requests for newspaper interviews came in, and the level of excitement on campus grew—a steady stream of students, visitors, and college employees fed a crowd that now spilled out of the annex and into the cafeteria—but the professor considered this uptick of interest to be the expected natural progression of a weeklong event that has some advertising behind it.

Likewise, for the third and fourth days, Ollie worked happily—oblivious to any kind of performance stress—and a gratifying level of interest continued to build from both on and off campus. All signs pointed to a lovely crescendo for the Friday finale. And when three television news vans greeted the professor, instead of the usual one, he didn't think too much of it. Just more pleasantness. Of course, it meant three interviews instead of one, not counting any newspaper interviews, but Ollie liked talking to people about his art. And it gave him valuable socialization practice, which, at his mother's insistence, needed to be a key part of Ollie's routine.

A feeling of exhilaration permeated the college, and nothing felt out of the ordinary…until the evening of the fourth day when the college president came in again to watch the filming. As he and Phineas stood off to the side, the president talked with more animation than usual and had a sly sparkle in his eye. He looked eager, like a politician on the brink of a landslide victory. Then the head of the maintenance department joined them…at six in the evening…two hours past his hard and fast quitting time. He obediently took notes as the president dictated a list of jobs that had to be completed that very night, including adding a decorative skirt to the platform, adding the name of the college in raised gold lettering to the top of the curved wall, and opening the remaining two annexes to accommodate more seating.

But the event was almost over. It didn't make sense. The president noticed the professor's confusion and said, "Oh, Phineas, I'm sorry, I thought I told you. The story has been picked up by the network. Ten million people are going to meet your little genius…and our college."

Ollie got out of the SUV, as instructed, and walked through the packed quad toward the cafeteria. On this last day the reporter wanted to get another shot of Ollie walking across campus. Only this time it didn't look like a college scene. It looked like a chaotic street party...or a standing room only rock concert. A girl in the crowd yelled, "Good luck, Ollie! We know you can do it!" A young man's voice quickly followed, "Yeah, Ollie, kick butt for the Crafton Cougars!" Ollie stopped, assumed a muscleman pose, and said, "Kick butt for the Crafton Cougars!" The students erupted with laughter and cheered loudly.

Cathy, who witnessed the exchange from inside the SUV, tried to wipe away the silly tears. From the driver's seat the reporter cast a sideways glance at Cathy but didn't say anything. Instead, she pushed a button on the top of the dashboard and spoke by microphone to the cameraman, who had been positioned at the other end of the quad. She said, "Bradly. Tell me you got that shot."

"Of course I got it," said the young man through the car speaker. He then added an exclamation point by briefly poking his head out from behind the camera and flashing a smile across the quad.

The reporter turned to Cathy and said, "What do you think about that, mom?"

"I think it's great."

<hr/>

Mariah drove her old Volvo up the hill to the college. Except for wistful curiosity, she didn't have a good reason for being there. Maybe, like her parents always said, she just didn't know how to let things go.

She parked the car and joined one of the streams of people that flowed toward the cafeteria. Once inside, Mariah's eyes instantly found Ollie. It wasn't hard because he sat all alone on stage, blanketed by bright lights. After some fifty hours his swivel chair had finally worked its way over to the end of the canvas, and he had almost finished the drawing. The auditorium hummed with anticipation.

The platform where he worked had been roped off, and two campus security guards stood nearby, one on each side of the platform. Up against the rope, the first audience section consisted of numerous couches, filled with bubbly college kids who looked happy to have scored front row seating. Also, up against the rope on each side of the couch section, members of the press had set up shop, including reporters, photographers, television cameras, and lighting equipment. After the couches and press sections, hundreds of chairs, all of them occupied, formed semicircle rows that extended back into the cafeteria. The people in the back, behind the chairs, all stood, not even bothering to sit at the cafeteria tables. Lastly, near the far wall, where Mariah now stood, a long line of people waited at the open cafeteria window to buy hotdogs, pizza slices, and soft drinks.

She wove around the perimeter of the room until finding a little space behind some equipment cases. This nook didn't have a seat, or a great view, but it concealed her presence and was close to the exit.

She looked out over the audience. Ollie the artist had brought them there. She didn't know that person, but they knew him because he was famous, more famous than Mariah could even believe. And that meant, on top of the one terrible change, his life had changed even more. Another layer of separation had been wedged between her and the ghost she had been chasing. And that didn't even count any of the changes in Mariah's own life, the years in high school, the accomplishments, the big dreams for the future. Even if she got the miracle that she thought she wanted, would they even know each other like they used to?

Mariah didn't belong to this congregation. They had a reason for being there. She, on the other hand, had come under the flimsy pretense of bumping into an old friend. She had come because a stubborn little girl with big dreams and a strong personality had her foot in the door and wouldn't let it close. But now that veil of willfulness had parted just enough to let in some light. He didn't exist. He had been gone for a long time. Mariah had been wasting her time. And, in her world, very few sins topped that one.

Without even casting a final glance at the stage, Mariah turned and began making her way to the exit. As she weaved through the people, she noticed that they had begun to stir. Their buzz had grown louder. She kept walking. She saw craning necks and leaning bodies. A wave of applause began to build. Overcome by curiosity, she turned around just in time to see Ollie stand up from his chair. They applauded loudly. He kneeled down and signed the bottom corner. They cheered louder. He faced his admirers. He looked happy.

She slipped away unnoticed.

Just like the local news, the network news saved the human interest stuff for the end of the show. And now that time had almost come. They ran a teaser showing footage from when Ollie got struck by lightning, and then broke away for the commercials. Cody sat rigidly in the chair he had pulled up to the family room TV and took a deep breath. He had two fears: that his parents might find out about eBay; and that Ollie might do something stupid and ruin everything. His parents had already been looking at him suspiciously. How was he supposed to know that seventeen-year-olds aren't supposed to be in a good mood for more than five minutes? But that didn't really bother Cody. He knew how to handle mother, and as long as father kept his head buried in cow shit, Cody had nothing to worry about. Ollie, on the other hand, scared Cody. If he did any of his weird space cadet shit on national TV, everything would be ruined.

While the commercials played, Cody looked at his eBay account on the family room computer. What he saw made him want to launch into a victory dance, and it wouldn't have been the first dance of the week. Ever since the first newscast on Monday, his auctions had been popping. He had started with thirty listings, added twenty more when the network came onboard, and now not one of them had a current bid of less than eighty dollars. That equaled a cool four grand, all from just the local publicity. After tonight's coast to coast coverage, Cody had no doubt that he'd soon be seeing numbers ten times that big...unless Ollie screwed up.

The broadcast came back on for the feel-good closing. Cody closed his eyes and uttered a Cody prayer, "OK, Ollie, you little shit, make me feel good."

Peter Jennings, the bigtime anchor, started talking about Ollie. He said, "You wouldn't think that anything good can be said when a child is struck down by lightning, but in tonight's final story, Jessica Williams introduces us to a young man who found a miracle on the other side of tragedy. Jessica…."

The correspondent stood on the baseball field where Ollie had been zapped. Cody couldn't control the anxiety. He wanted to jump out of his seat. Instead, as the story unfolded, he nervously mumbled a play by play commentary: "OK…Ollie plays baseball…seen that; old stuff from the hospital…seen that; Chinese doctor tells sad story…good; old geezer at the college…seen that; pretty picture, another pretty picture, a really pretty picture…good; helicopter…seen that; hero walk at the college…goofy but good; first day…Ollie at work; second day…more work; third day…everybody loves Ollie; fourth day and another hero walk; fifth day, really big crowd…haven't seen that; Ollie almost done; crowd gets excited; finishes the drawing; crowd goes wild; Ollie smiles, keeps smiling, and stares like a dork; good."

Cody liked it. He really liked it. They more or less just ran a compilation of scenes from the previous days that Cody had already seen from the network affiliate. Perfect. Story in a can. You couldn't get any safer than that. But then, without warning, they cut to a live shot of Ollie on stage standing next to the reporter. She held a microphone. Cody said, "Oh shit."

The reporter said, "And here we are live with our young artist who just moments ago finished this monumental ink drawing of the Los Angeles coastal skyline."

The camera slowly panned across the piece before settling on a close-up of Ollie.

"Please let it be over," said Cody.

"What did you like best about this drawing?" asked the reporter.

"No! No questions! Please!" begged Cody.

"I liked the ports, Los Angeles and Long Beach, 'cause they're right next to each other and they have giant cranes and tall ships, and lots of containers. I like to draw those things."

"OK...ok...that wasn't terrible," said Cody.

"I have something for you, Ollie," said the reporter as she held a large photograph up to the camera. "This photograph of LAX was taken from the helicopter when you flew over the airport. Every airplane shown in this photo is depicted in your drawing in exactly the correct position. What do you think about that?"

"I like to draw airplanes."

"Yes, you do. And did you like drawing the tall buildings in the financial district?"

Cody dropped to his knees and said, "Please! Lady! What is your problem!"

"Yes, I like the Library Tower. It's one of my favorite buildings," said Ollie.

"And did you like drawing the Sears Tower?"

Ollie froze and got that scary, confused look in his eye. And then he looked irritated.

Cody banged his forehead against the floor and pleaded with any and all gods who happened to be in the vicinity, "Please! Please! I beg you! Please!"

Ollie said, "No...no...the Sears Tower is in Chicago. I didn't draw that."

Cody looked up at the TV.

The reporter said, "You're right, Ollie. The Sears Tower is in Chicago. Your professor here at the college said I should try to trick you."

Ollie smiled and said, "Professor likes to trick me, but he's not very good."

And then everyone laughed, including the reporter, the crew, and Peter Jennings, when the baton had been handed back for the close of the show.

Cody jumped to his feet and clasped his hands to his head. The little idiot had pulled it off! He had done it! Cody bounced and danced and pumped his fist. He went bonkers like a gameshow winner, and would have gladly kissed some creepy gameshow host right on the lips if given half a chance. And then he watched his auctions blast off to the moon. That first batch netted over thirty thousand dollars, and it didn't stop there. Over time the prices settled back down to earth, but Ollie had become an artist with a name, and for most of the next year Cody made money hand over fist, just as fast as he could steal the drawings.

<hr/>

Very late that night, after all the excitement, after all the wonderful things that had happened, Ollie lay in bed, unable to sleep. He thought about a pretty girl with a radiant face and beautiful smile. She had been there every day in the afternoon, usually in the front row on one of the couches. She read. She talked to the other students. She watched Ollie draw. And whenever Ollie put down the pen and swiveled around in the chair, his eyes found the girl. He couldn't help himself. She looked so lovely, and delicate, like a flower that has to be held very carefully. Sometimes she smiled at him. And Ollie smiled back. But he wished he knew how to do other things besides smile. He wished he could be like the old Ollie.

People liked Ollie's art, and that made him feel happy. They liked to talk to him about his art, and that made him feel like he almost belonged. But on that last night, when he stood on stage, and the people cheered and called his name and wanted to talk to him, he would have traded it all for another smile from the girl on the couch. It hadn't been anything normal, but at least it had been something.

Chapter 10

Ralph sat opposite Bob in the ranch office and watched as he popped open the hot beer. Both of them had bad boozer track records and had given up drinking, but Ralph's bad record trumped Bob's by a longshot so Bob got beer can duty, and Ralph got to talk, which normally came easy. But on this particular anniversary Ralph had trouble finding the words, and Bob noticed. After they had finished honoring their fallen Marine brothers, he said, "Is everything Ok, Durbin?"

"Yeah…uh…everything's good…it's just the usual crap that happens this time of year when I look at my life and wonder what the hell those guys died for."

"Come on, Durbin. Look how far you've come, and you haven't even hit your stride yet." Bob paused and looked down at the beer can on the desk. Then, in a quieter voice, he continued, "I still struggle with it, too. Sometimes the only thing that keeps me sane is the hope that it had to have happened for a reason. Of course, it'd be nice to know that reason, but until then I guess all we can do is our best. And that's what you've been doing, my friend."

It had been a long time since Ralph had heard that kind of encouragement, and he had a hard time responding. He choked out a few words. "Thanks, Buck, I appreciate it."

After a few moments of awkward silence, Ralph pointed up to one of the shelves on the wall, which also happened to be the only uncluttered spot in the office. The shelf contained three potion bottles that had turned green from age, an old medical encyclopedia that had almost deteriorated past the point of recognition, and an ancient pair of field glasses. Ralph said, "Are you telling me that after a hundred and twenty years that's all you got?"

"No, it's worse than that because all that stuff was found the day after Jubal robbed the payroll wagon. In the last hundred and twenty years we've found exactly nothing."

"Wow…uh…I guess that's what you call dedication," said Ralph.

"Thanks, Durbin. You're too kind. Cathy calls it something else altogether."

Ralph chuckled and said, "Speaking of Cathy, I have to say that you're not doing yourself any favors by always trying to include me in things. She may never come around, and I don't blame her, but it sure ain't gonna happen if you try to force it."

"Yeah, I know. It just kind of bothers me."

"You gotta let it go, Buck. If you wanna help, tell me what's up with Cody. I've never done anything to him, and he can't stand the sight of me."

"Yeah…right. Well, if it makes you feel any better, that has more to do with me than with you. In case you haven't noticed, I'm not the best father in the world."

"That's bullshit, Buck. If you want to know about bad fathers, I'll tell you stories that will make you double check your vasectomy."

Bob laughed.

"No, I'm serious. You wanna know the definition of a good father? He tries. Period. And that's you all the way, Buck. You don't need to be listening to that bullshit."

"Thanks, Durbin."

Ralph had previously learned basic horse skills at a ranch for troubled teenagers, but he knew nothing about running cattle, so, for the first year, Bob had started him out as a wrangler. Back then his days mostly consisted of feeding, mucking, repairing fences, and doing routine ranch maintenance. Sometimes, when a herd had to be moved, Bob put Ralph on a babysitter horse and he got to help drive cattle. Over the next few years Ralph's cowboy skills steadily improved and he eventually became a full-fledged member of the team. He worked hard and liked it. Against all probability, Ralph Durbin became a cowboy, even if, with his beard and long hair, he didn't exactly look like one. He lived an uncomplicated life in the bunkhouse, minding his own business, going to sleep with the horses, and waking up with the roosters.

And every month when he got paid, Ralph bought a money order from the post office and sent it to his daughter, whose address he had weaseled out of one of the few family members who still talked to him. For the first couple of years the letters came back unopened but Ralph didn't give up. Like his daily routine, this monthly routine became engrained: write letter asking for forgiveness, buy money order, send to daughter, and get everything back two weeks later. Then one day Rachel accepted his gift. Ralph found out through the mail. The envelope contained an unsigned note and a photograph. The note said:

> *Just so you know where your money is going, this is my son. His name is Francisco and he deserves your money more than you don't deserve to know his name. You are not his grandfather. You lost that right when you murdered his grandmother. You are the owner of a photograph and nothing more.*

Ralph gathered up the returned money orders—close to four thousand dollars—and sent them straightaway back to his daughter. She sent a note, acknowledging receipt, and didn't contact him again, but Ralph could live with that because his life had improved. Now he had two photographs instead of one, now he had a daughter and a grandson. He tacked the picture of Francisco onto the wall of the bunkhouse and looked at it every day. And so did anyone else who happened to come inside, Ralph made sure of it. The baby boy had a bright, happy face, filled with the innocence that every child deserves. He had fun, mischievous eyes, and thick black hair that shined like an oil slick.

<hr>

One day, almost four years after Ralph had come to the ranch, Cathy hopped into her old minivan to go run errands in town. She drove down the dirt road and admired the springtime bloom on the gently rolling hills. Except for the two small mountains on the North side of the property, these beautiful hills dominated Buck Ranch from front to back. But when you live somewhere for thirty years it's easy to take it for granted, and Cathy had been guilty of that. She used to cuss every time a missing ingredient sent her on the forty-minute drive to the grocery store and back. And she'd driven the dirt road a thousand times without admiring any beauty at all.

On a nearby hill, she saw Bob and the other cowboys, shrouded in dust, driving a small herd down to the chutes and the trucks that waited to take them to market. This was payday, supposedly a happy time, but because they had had to cut the finish short on these cattle, no one got any joy out of it. The wastefulness of it gnawed at her husband—Cathy knew that much without a word being said—but they didn't have a choice. They needed the money and the bank refused to extend the loan without further collateral. So, these cattle had been sacrificed so that the rest of the herd could be properly finished. And then they'd do it all over again, no doubt coming up just a little more short than the last time.

Apart from selling out to the developers—a topic that had been regularly discussed and rejected—Cathy didn't see a realistic way forward. She saw the possibility of limping along for a few more years but nothing beyond that. But the good news in all of this was that she no longer had a problem with taking the ranch for granted.

At the end of the dirt road, where ranch property met highway, Cathy saw a small red car parked on the side of the road. The beat-up car looked abandoned and Cathy suspected car trouble of some sort. She continued on in to town, finished her chores, and drove back to the ranch. But

113

when she got there the red car hadn't moved. And a young lady stood outside the car, staring at Cathy as she pulled up to the ranch entrance. Cathy maneuvered the van over to her and lowered the window. The girl, maybe in her early twenties, had tears in her eyes and looked unwell. Cathy said, "Is everything ok?"

"Mrs. Buckmeyer, it's me, Rachel."

"Oh my gosh," said Cathy. She got out, gave Rachel a hug, and said again, "Is everything ok?"

"Yes, I'm ok…sorry if I scared you."

"No not at all. Come on up to the house. The boys would love to see you after all these years."

"I'm sorry…thank you…I really can't."

"That's ok, I get it. If you follow me, I can show you where your father lives. He never stops talking about—" Cathy saw Rachel shaking her head.

"I'm not here to see him."

"Oh…uh…I don't understand, Rachel."

"I'm here to see you, Mrs. Buckmeyer. I need to ask you some questions…face to face…."

"About your father?"

"About Ralph Durbin."

"I see. Well, I'll help if I can," said Cathy.

"Has he changed?" Her voice had a steely, accusatory tone.

"Rachel…I'm the wrong person to ask…I'm sorry…."

"Please, Mrs. Buckmeyer, it's important."

"He hasn't gotten into any trouble. That's the most I can say."

"Does he do his job?"

114

"Yeah, I'd say he does alright."

"And is he drinking?"

"I can't say, I'm not around him very much."

"Do you trust him?"

Cathy evaded the question. "I'm not sure I know what you mean. Trust him with what?"

"Someone's life." The tears, which Cathy had noticed before, started flowing again.

"Bob trusts him."

"I asked about you."

"No, Rachel, I'm sorry. I can't say that I do."

"Thank you for being honest with me. I think I better go now. Thank you."

"Uh…wait a second, Rachel. Maybe I'm not the best person to ask…maybe you should talk with Bob."

Rachel got into her car and lowered the window. She said, "When I was little, I loved coming out here to the ranch. And you were always so kind to me. I never forgot it. Goodbye, Mrs. Buckmeyer."

"Goodbye, Rachel."

She slowly drove away, leaving Cathy behind feeling confused and ashamed. Confused, because Rachel seemed more troubled than you'd expect from someone who is simply thinking about renewing a relationship. She seemed desperate, like perhaps she had something on her mind besides reconciliation. And Cathy felt ashamed because the girl obviously had a terrible burden related to her father, and Cathy had done nothing to relieve that burden. She had been deliberately ungenerous. Ralph Durbin worked hard, had stayed out of trouble, and in almost four years Cathy had never seen him touch a drop of alcohol and neither had Bob. But Cathy didn't have the stomach to admit any of it.

In one area, though, she had been completely honest: She didn't trust Ralph and probably never would. A person just doesn't change like that.

Chapter 11

Ollie's life had changed yet again and, to some extent, so had everyone else's. On the night of his triumph at the college, the family returned home to find that they had been invaded by a band of wannabe promoters…through the answering machine, that affable and indiscriminate sentry. Some of the many phone messages had come from excited family and friends who had seen Ollie on TV, but even more of them came from strangers pitching their services. Agents, producers, writers, gallery owners…and the mayor of Houston, left messages that ranged from drunken to provocative.

As with most issues involving home and harmony, Cathy took the lead in sorting it all out. And once again she relied on Dr. Mardikali, who discarded most of the unsolicited inquiries in favor of his six decades worth of art world experience. From within the bowels of his ancient and overstuffed rolodex, he matched Ollie to a suitable agent, who, in turn, selected a handful of the most promising galleries. Within a few months of the news broadcast, Ollie, only seventeen, had very real prospects of someday being able to support himself. Bob and Cathy had never expected that. And, because of that strange message from the mayor of Houston, they also caught a glimpse of the future: The good mayor made it clear that if Los Angeles had a giant skyline drawing by Ollie Buckmeyer, then, by George, Houston would have one too—and it had better be bigger. Over the years Ollie's agent would field a steady stream of similar phone calls from around the world.

And on the Cody front, things looked almost as good. His antisocial, brooding moods had subsided. Sometimes he almost seemed cheerful. And he had suddenly stopped asking for money. To Bob, this turnaround bordered on miraculous, and he didn't believe in miracles. But, of course, Cathy did. With a wave of the hand, she dismissed her doubting husband and declared that Cody had finally grown up, and the money thing had to be nothing but some friend or sports nut who had fronted her son some cash in advance of the Major League Baseball first-year player draft to be held in just a few months. *Baseball America* and every other reputable source put Cody solidly in the first round of the draft where the bonuses are big—as in high six figures. To Cathy it all made perfect sense. Besides, for the first time in years, Cody seemed to have found some inner peace and that was all that really mattered. Even Bob had to agree with that.

Good news and harmony must make a decent tonic because at this time Bob became more open minded about the ranch's future. He still had a natural resistance to the idea of selling out, but now at least he gave it more consideration than before. For Cathy, the constant scramble for money just didn't make sense anymore. Not when you're sitting on land worth several million dollars. And the idea of mortgaging that land, just to support an operation that barely broke even, had to violate her husband's inherent rancher frugality, even if he didn't admit it.

While selling the ranch may have started to look logical, and even inevitable, explaining it to Ollie looked decidedly unpleasant. He had always loved the ranch, not like a boy who has been groomed to become a rancher, but in the way someone falls in love with nature and becomes a person who can't live without the freedom and peacefulness of wide-open spaces. And then there was the other thing. Ollie still struggled with change of any kind. Even small schedule or menu changes frustrated him. Cathy could only imagine what a U-Haul in the driveway might do.

⬩⬩⬩⬩⬩⬩⬩⬩⬩⬩⬩⬩

Bob drove past the valet parking. The old minivan had suffered enough. She didn't need the indignity of being parked in the premium lot next to a beauty queen. He found another way into the five-star hotel. Before getting out of the van, Cathy touched his arm and said, "Remember, honey, he's not going to do things like we do, but this is his day, and we have to respect that." She had a tinge of worry in her voice and in her eyes. Bob reassured her with a wink and a kiss.

Bob, Cathy, and Ollie had made the early afternoon drive to Beverly Hills where Cody had booked a banquet room for the first day of the MLB draft. After climbing out of the van, Cathy made a final wardrobe and hairdo inspection of the troops, and they started walking. From a distance Bob admired the ornate entrance to the hotel, with its manicured circular drive and towering portico. Two bellboys with a luggage cart had descended upon a big gray Mercedes. The driver of the car, a stylish kind of guy, stood by the car talking to an equally stylish woman. Another bellboy stood at attention at a nearby station.

The raw, rumbling sound of a nearby sports car captured Bob's attention. The powerful roar grew steadily louder and turned into a high pitched whine as the car accelerated, interrupted by the staccato sound of shifting gears. Then the whine became a deafening scream that rattled windows. *This guy is hauling ass,* thought Bob. The car raced into view, going dangerously fast. Then it screeched to a stop just before the hotel entrance. Everybody stared. The racecar, now domesticated, purred obediently as it slowly cruised onto the hotel's driveway. "Idiot," mumbled Bob. It pulled up behind the Mercedes and, with the engine still idling, out popped some hotshot who looked barely old enough to drive.

Cathy recognized him first. She said, "Oh no." Then, just as Bob made the connection, she grabbed his arm and squeezed hard, like a lumberjack, and said, "Bob. Now's not the time."

"Hi guys! How do you like the wheels?" asked Cody, with his arm lazily draped across the gleaming beauty, like a well-traveled playboy.

"Cody!" exclaimed Ollie, with admiration. He ran the remaining ten yards to greet his brother. But then someone else got out of the car, and Ollie suddenly found new things to admire. He stopped and stared. If the car looked dangerous, this girl looked lethal, like a case of spontaneous sexual combustion…unless she had a fire extinguisher tucked somewhere into the pink hot pants.

Cathy said, "Oh no."

Bob said, "Oh, yes."

Cathy said, "Shut up."

Bob said, "Remember, dear, he's going to do things his way and we have to respect that."

Cathy shot Bob a special glare and he wisely stood down. Truthfully, the hot tamale didn't bother him that much. Cody always had girlfriends and had a well-known preference for spice. This one just had more spice than the others. An optimist might have said that his taste had evolved. Others might have called it spice for a price. Bob didn't care to judge.

The sleek blue sports car, a Dodge Viper GTS, troubled Bob much more. It had an aggressive, serpentine appearance. Even at idle the testosterone growl evoked visions of a two hundred mile per hour adrenaline blur. It made you stare. But, with fancy cars (and sexy women), sometimes the smart thing is to look the other way…unless you're a cocky eighteen-year-old. Then you plunk down stupid money, kiss the pink slip, and think you're the biggest badass around. But Cody didn't have that kind of stupid money…unless he'd struck some kind of under the table deal related to his signing bonus. And that, specifically, worried Bob.

Taking money, or signing with an agent, or doing anything else that jeopardizes the player's amateur status before signing the minor league contract is a mistake that can literally cut the signing bonus by tens of thousands of dollars because once the amateur status is lost the player has no bargaining chips. He can't play for a college or junior college. He either signs the minor league contract or he sits at home watching *Leave it to Beaver*. And the team that's trying to sign him knows this. If the kid has taken money or signed with an agent, then they have all the power, and it is reflected in an anemic bonus offer. Bob had warned Cody about this a dozen times, but that had been when he used to listen.

Bob wanted to grill Cody but didn't, mostly for Cathy's sake. In many ways this special day also belonged to her because when Cody had hit the rough patch and shut Bob out of his life, she jumped in and tried to cheer him onto a better path. She became a tireless reconciler, booster, and absolver. And sometimes Cody responded, saying the right things and flashing the right signals. And with each occasional victory Cathy's heart inevitably bobbed to the top like a buoy. She believed in Cody, in his innocent goodness, in the certainty that he must turn to what is right. So, for Cathy's sake, Bob mustered up some pleasantness, which more or less looked like a blank stare, but that was OK. A plastic smile wouldn't have fooled Cody. The two of them had long ago dug their trenches, and now they had to live in them.

Cathy also showed restraint, even if she didn't forego the plastic smile. She exchanged polite greetings, shook the young woman's hand, and said she liked her boots. And the group entered the hotel together. Ollie, unworldly but always observant, followed behind and marveled at the new breed of cat that his brother had found.

This surprise beginning set the pattern for a day full of surprises. The next one followed quickly when they entered the bustling banquet room, which overflowed with food and drink, and Bob found a two-person film crew waiting for them. The MLB sometimes did this for players drafted in the first round. They liked to capture the family's reaction when the player gets the phone call that he's been dreaming about for his entire life; An inspirational, all-American family kind of thing. But nobody had said anything about it. That's what surprised Bob, but it was probably just Cody being his usual uncommunicative self.

After the room had finished filling with people, many of whom Bob knew from Cody's various baseball teams over the years, the film crew began staging the shot which would be shown live on the MLB broadcast, due to start in just a matter of minutes. They put the family in a row of chairs with Cody in the middle and his friends, teammates, and coaches standing behind. And that's where the next little glitch popped up because the head coach of Cody's high school team, the most important of all, didn't show up.

Though not talked about very much, this coach is an integral part of the beginning of a player's career. He talks to the scouts and answers questions that range all the way from ability and knowledge to work ethic and off field behavior. And the higher the draft pick, the more scouts and questions he has to deal with. A first rounder, like Cody, brings an avalanche of inquiries, but the coach gladly accepts the burden because most high school coaches rarely, if ever, have the privilege of producing a first-round draft pick. And they show up to the draft day party, especially when it includes a spot on TV.

And then finally, the last surprise landed with a thud when the film crew unexpectedly packed up and left without ever turning on a camera. They looked sheepish and said something about coming back, but their averted eyes suggested otherwise. Something had happened. Bob suspected the worst but didn't say anything. Cody shrugged it off, calling out to the departing crew to take a few beers for the road.

The nationally televised draft started at three o'clock sharp, and it didn't take long before everyone in the room understood the obvious. The crew had left because they didn't have anything to film; the Milwaukee Brewers, the team holding the number ten selection, the team that had painstakingly researched, that had carefully confirmed signability, and that had publicly declared for Cody Buckmeyer, chose a different player. When the commissioner of baseball announced the other player's name, Cody's friends gasped, and then a blanket of silence smothered the banquet room. Cody's teammates eventually came to his aid with offers of encouragement: "Who needs that cold ass weather anyway, bro?"; "San Diego could use a shortstop."; "Yeah, bro, sunshine and bikinis!" Cathy didn't understand what had happened. Bob quietly explained. Cody ignored everyone and frantically punched a phone number into his mobile phone. Nobody answered his call. He kept trying. One of the two high school assistant coaches also discreetly made a phone call. His went through and, after a few minutes, both of the coaches awkwardly excused themselves.

The Atlanta Braves drafted Cody the next day with the 153rd overall selection. And it turned out that he had not squandered his amateur status after all. The car had been a loaner from a shrewd car dealer who knew that the wild young stud would soon be coming into some money. Cody got a signing bonus of $270,000, average for a player taken in the third round, but a far cry from the million dollars he had been expecting. He paid sixty grand and kept the car.

※※※※※※※※※※※※

Cathy stared at the artwork, racking her brain to figure out how it had ended up on her friend's living room wall.

The friend, who had purchased the drawing online, said, "Is there something wrong?"

"No, no, not at all," lied Cathy. "I'd just forgotten that nowadays the galleries also sell on the internet."

This drawing, one of Cathy's favorites, depicted a hillside that had fallen away, leaving behind a perfect row of orange trees on top of the hill, on the safe side of a stark, chalky fault line. It actually had been a second version of a drawing Ollie had done shortly after the accident, and Cathy treasured the set, completed several years apart, because they showed how much Ollie had grown as an artist. And, despite what Cathy had implied, it had not been sold by a gallery because it had gone missing before any gallery even knew Ollie's name; and Cathy never would have let it go in the first place. She had other questions for her friend but didn't dare ask them because of the humiliating fact that the drawing had obviously been stolen.

Ollie often shuttled drawings back and forth to both the high school and the junior college. And sometimes he got forgetful and left them behind. The theft could have occurred at either place. Or there could be another explanation, one that Cathy didn't want to believe. She and

Bob had quarreled several months previously about Cody's mysterious newfound money. Cathy had scoffed at Bob's suspicions. Now she wondered if, once again, sunshine and roses had blocked her view of the truth.

Accompanied by nagging feelings of fear and disbelief, Cathy went home and found the website, called eBay, and searched for more of Ollie's drawings. She found three. The seller went by the name of "turn2bro." And that's when she knew. "Turn two" is a common baseball term. You hear it a dozen times at every game.

Shaken, but determined to know everything, Cathy began taking inventory of the drawings. Ollie remembered every one ever completed, and she had maintained a log of the ones dispersed to the galleries. Not counting the more primitive artwork from the first year, and allowing for a reasonable amount of unexplained loss, Cathy calculated the numbers and the answer made her cry. At least ninety drawings had been taken. Ninety. Anyone, in a moment of weakness, can steal once or twice. Ninety times takes dedication. It takes a campaign.

Cathy went to bed for two days, feigning sickness when the door opened, listless and numb when it closed. Her mind methodically trolled memories of the early years. She searched for answers. She found unhealthy love. Through a haze of guilt, she saw images of a fearful young mother always standing between a boy and his father. The mother schemes for leniency and subverts healthy consequences. She tries to focus, but the line between love and indulgence is always blurry...until it's too late, and a fresh-faced young man in a blue sports car asks for more.

In the afternoon of the second day Cathy found Bob in his office. She told him that their son was a thief. He listened to the whole story and Cathy, still chastened, told it honestly.

The news saddened Bob, Cathy saw it, but his sadness and hers looked very different. He faced it dispassionately and spoke calculated words, "We won't say anything until the time is right." But those sounded like ambush words, and that scared Cathy. Bob had always said that catching a thief red-handed is a gift from God, and you had better not waste it because it's the only way to make the thief go straight. Bob planned to hit Cody and hit him hard. And, incredibly, Cathy felt the old protective panic rising up all over again. She felt the heavy, pleading heart. She felt the hardening of her face toward her husband.

※※※※※※※※※※※

Fatherhood is like a landmine with a delayed trigger. The dumbass father doesn't get hit. It's the innocent kid who follows behind. That's the one who takes the blast. And then the dumbass father lives with the guilt and the shame.

Nobody, not Cathy, or Ollie, or anyone else, had needed Bob the way Cody had. For some reason the boy had desperately needed his father every day, all day. But Bob didn't give it, or he gave it in measured, unsatisfying portions. The love that is supposed to flow from a father's heart had been dammed to a trickle. And the neglect wasn't a case of someone looking in the rearview mirror and seeing their failure from a month or a year ago. Bob had seen his failure in real time, every day, while he was failing. And every day he promised to do better, but never did. Now his son had grown into half a man, and Bob blamed himself.

Despite all of this, Bob still clung to a thread of hope. He hoped that the world might take over the bungled job and make it right. It had happened to Bob. He had been wild and selfish. And then the world kicked his butt, and he grew up. He didn't want Cody to have a Vietnam, nobody deserved that, but he did want the demolition that only a harsh and indiscriminate world can accomplish. He wanted the lies and arrogance and manipulations to be stripped away, for Cody to be left naked, standing before a mirror. And this was never going to happen with him tucked snugly into his boyhood bed. In less than a month Cody had to report to the Eugene Emeralds—the Braves affiliate up in Oregon—but Bob didn't want him leaving on his own terms. He wanted him booted out the door with a thump on the head and something to think about. But this would take some planning, and Bob had decided to start with the draft day disaster.

There are three common reasons why a player unexpectedly falls in the draft: signability, medical, and character. Cody had decided against playing college ball, had been agreeable to the money being offered, and had been willing to sign. And he had been transparent about his physical condition. That left off field character issues. Bob knew it had to be that, but he didn't know any specifics, so, from the seclusion of his office, he telephoned a college coach who had been a teammate of Bob's back in the day. The two had stayed in contact over the years, most often talking about Cody's blossoming baseball prospects. The coach had closely followed Cody's amateur career. And, because he had constant contact with the scouts, he knew the most recent scouting reports.

∾∾∾∾∾∾∾∾∾∾∾∾

The voice that called through the bedroom door startled Cody.

"Feel like throwing the ball around?"

"Yeah…uh…ok," said Cody. He had nothing on the old man except rejection, and didn't like giving it up, but he hadn't thrown a baseball in almost two months and needed to start getting back in shape. He pulled the sports bag out of the closet and headed to the back yard. On the way out the door his mother called after him. Cody didn't answer. She followed onto the back patio, obviously with something on her mind, but Cody didn't feel like dealing with two needy parents at the same time.

Father waited at the far end of the backyard. He stared weirdly as Cody approached, and Cody suspected some feeble delusion about a father and son reconciliation just before Cody had to leave home for the short baseball season up north.

"How about a little long toss? Keep the arm in shape?"

"Yeah…that's fine," said Cody. He kneeled down, unzipped the sports bag, and pulled out his stuff.

Long toss starts short, to warm up the arm, and gradually expands until the two players are far apart. The beginning, when the players are very close together, is a good place to talk or kid around.

After putting cleats on his feet and the small shortstop's glove on his left hand, Cody flicked a baseball over to his father.

He lobbed it back and said, "How's the car?"

"Good."

"I'd ask how fast it goes but then I'd have to lie about it to your mother," said father, with a weak chuckle. He caught the ball bare handed and tossed it back.

"Yeah…right," said Cody. He expanded the range with a single step backward.

"After you get settled in up north, your mother and I are thinking about driving up to visit. Maybe catch a few games." Then, with a quick catch and throw, he said, "How's that sound?"

Cody took another step back, threw the baseball, and said, "That's fine."

"Maybe stop in 'Frisco and do some sightseeing."

Who the hell cares? thought Cody. He took the return throw, but this time, when he stepped back, he noticed his mother staring out of the kitchen window, eyes locked like a laser. She had a convenient habit of tipping her hand before big things come down. Cody eyed his father suspiciously. This no longer felt like a bury-the-hatchet-goodbye. It felt like an ambush, Mayberry style. Cody sent the ball back with a little bit of zip.

Father easily gloved it and wound up for the return but stopped in mid motion. He dropped his hands to his sides and said, "I just remembered something I need to ask you. We found some of Ollie's drawings up for sale on the internet and we're wondering if you know anything about it?"

And bingo! The old boy sets the trap. But guess what, asshole, I saw this coming way back…like three months back, thought Cody. He said, "Oh…wow…I was hoping to surprise you with that right before I left, but I guess now is ok. Wait here. I have something for you and mom."

Cody jogged into the house. Mother didn't yell at him for wearing cleats. Instead, she fell in behind and trotted down the hallway. When Cody came back out of his bedroom, with a white envelope in hand, she reversed course and followed like a dog all the way out to the backyard. And if she had not followed on her own, Cody would have dragged her along because you don't beat father without a heavy dose of mother. With the three of them facing one another, Cody handed the envelope to his mother and said, "I don't want you to lose the ranch. I know how much you love it, and I wanted to help."

Mother opened the envelope, gasped loudly, and pulled out a huge stack of cash.

"See. That's why I wrote the letter to the news station. There's nineteen thousand dollars there. I was shooting for twenty, but father beat me to the punch. You'll get the rest next week."

Mother fell right in line, like usual. She started to gush, "Oh Cody, we're so sorry—"

"Cathy!" yelled father with a booming voice that echoed off the hillside. Mother froze. Father dropped his glove to the ground and pulled a folded piece of paper from his back pocket. He held it up and said, "This is your bank statement, Cody. Think about it before you dig the shit hole any deeper."

Cody paused. The old man had him. But, after thinking about it for a second, Cody realized that he didn't really care. He didn't care about the man, and he especially didn't care about his self-righteous code of honor bullshit. He said, "Yeah, so I made some money. That's more than you ever do."

"You didn't make money. You stole from your brother."

"Those drawings have been sitting around for five years. The dog could've pissed on them and no one would've said a word."

"Then why lie about it? And not just one lie. You piled one on top of another. That white envelope is the little lie you put together just in case we got too close to the big lie. That's scary! Not only are you a liar, and a thief, but most of all you're a conman." He took a breath. Cody tried to answer back, but father held up a hand and said, "Save it Cody. I'm not interested in your stories. Get your stuff together. You are out of here by morning. I don't want to see your face when I wake up."

"Bob...please..." said mother.

Father picked up his glove and started walking to the house. After a few steps, he turned back and said, "You should know that the Brewers dropped you because of chronic drug use."

"What!" said mother.

"That's what this is really about, isn't it! About you and your pathetic baseball fantasy!"

"If you fix your life and never play another game of baseball, I'll be the happiest father in the world."

"Bullshit!"

132

"Please, Cody, just listen to your father," said mother.

~~~~~~~~~~~~~~~~

Cody waited all night long for sounds of a heated argument, and for the gentle tap on his bedroom door, and for the sight of his mother's red, tearful eyes. He expected a thorough scolding, followed by a full and unconditional pardon. It didn't happen. He left first thing in the morning without saying goodbye.

~~~~~~~~~~~~~~~~

The lieutenant sees Maloof, Reynosa, and Hochlichtner. They look filthy and half dressed. "Get your gear. We're going after Durbin," says the lieutenant. They don't protest, not even a cuss word. What would be the point?

The lieutenant looks down at his new boots and freshly pressed cammies.

Bob woke from the dream. He sucked in a slow, deep breath. And then another, and another.

Chapter 12

Procrastination is fueled by talky talk. It burns hot on ripe words and marinated monologues. Cathy and Bob (mostly Cathy) had funneled five years' worth of words into their procrastination. They had talked it to the moon and back. And then, just when another journey looked imminent, they jumped ship when Cathy figured out a way to keep the ranch.

This reprieve, wrapped in a compromise, began with an errant assumption about the money in Cody's white envelope. Cathy had thought that it might allow them to keep the ranch a little longer, but Bob reminded her that the money didn't belong to them. It belonged to Ollie. Not envisioning Ollie ever living away from them, Cathy had innocently assumed that the money belonged to the family.

At this point in the conversation, which would continue on and off for several weeks, neither of them had realized the full magnitude of Ollie's blossoming finances. The galleries had been clamoring for ever more drawings, and Ollie had finally been paid—just over four thousand dollars—but that first round of checks only reflected the few days that had remained in the month after the galleries had received their first shipment. But then another round of checks, for a full month's worth of sales, came in and the numbers shocked

Bob and Cathy. In one month, Ollie made thirty-eight thousand dollars, not counting the money from the envelope, and not counting the deal Ollie's agent had just made with the city of Houston. Now, armed with this new understanding, Cathy went back to the beginning, back to selling the ranch, but this time with a couple of major tweaks: selling only part of the ranch, and selling it to Ollie.

She liked everything about it. She liked it for Ollie, who's soul thrived at the ranch, and for Cody, who, no matter how lost he might become, would know that his old home waited for him. She liked what it meant to the family, that they had saved the ranch for at least another generation. She liked it for herself, for a thousand little reasons that she hadn't understood until they had almost been lost. And then there was Bob, whose identity had been tightly and unusually bound to the ranch. His life's work had not been discovered in a college class or by an aptitude test. He had not stumbled into it. His business had been predetermined by a hundred-year-old family tradition. He had been born to be a rancher and, despite his scoffing swagger, losing the ranch would have been more than just a routine career change.

Cathy didn't hold back on the enthusiasm. Bob, on the other hand, stuck to the comfort of his skepticism. The thought of using Ollie's money as a bailout, and locking it into a long term investment that he may or may not have understood, didn't sit right with him. He also didn't like the idea of making this kind of decision based upon just a few months' worth of sales. What if Ollie's career hit a rough patch? And, most importantly, Bob pointed out that the plan didn't solve the original problem, the one that had forced the sale in the first place: a business that struggled to stay afloat.

He resisted, and had some valid reasons, but Cathy believed in this one. And she suspected that, somewhere deep down, Bob also believed. As a means to that end, she gently pointed out that the ranch had never actually lost money; it just had not made enough. What was the harm, she reasoned, in making at least some money doing what you love and supplementing it with money from the sale of some of the land?

In the end they agreed to move forward with subdividing the land but would wait a year—to see how Ollie's career progressed—before getting an appraisal and making the sale. They also agreed to make guardianship of Ollie's money their top priority and to pay him for grazing rights.

And when they asked Ollie what he thought, his simple response put a beautiful ribbon on the whole idea. He said, "I will never sell it. Never."

A year later, just after his eighteenth birthday, Ollie became the owner of seventeen hundred acres, one third of Buck Ranch. Sale of the mortgage-free land involved little more than a modest down payment, a title transfer, and an amortization schedule. Bob and Cathy didn't need to cash out; they needed monthly income, which Ollie easily had the means to pay. They carried the loan themselves at a bargain basement interest rate.

Only one loose end remained. They didn't know how to tell Cody. No matter what they said, to him it would look like Ollie had taken something that had rightly belonged to both of them. It would look like part of his inheritance had been stolen. So, Bob and Cathy did nothing. Except for a few dead-end remarks, they didn't even bother talking about it.

⋙⋙⋙⋙⋙⋙⋙⋙

The majestic old ranch eased into a long stretch of calm waters. The chronic money problems had been dispatched, and the nagging uncertainty that weighs down the day and stifles hope for the future, had been replaced with humdrum cares and everyday dreams. Even Cody's absence, sad in the way that it had unfolded, contributed to this much needed repose. If not happiness, everyone seemed to at least find a certain degree of peace.

Ralph Durbin continued to steer clear of Cathy, who showed no signs of ever forgiving him. He worked and sent money to his daughter, Rachel. Along with the monthly money order, he always included a note of love that asked for nothing in return, which is exactly what he got. The twenty-year-old photograph of Rachel faded. The photograph of Francisco, his grandson, still hung on the bunkhouse wall. In his spare time, Ralph helped Bob chase down Jubal's stolen treasure. They formulated theories, talked strategy, and dug holes, never coming away with anything more than rusty horseshoes and old beer cans.

Mariah Kelley blazed through college, got a good steppingstone job, and worked on her MBA. As the years passed, and as the milestones got checked off on her beloved roadmap, a certain degree of self-awareness also settled in. She realized that ambition has a price, and runaway ambition has a steep price. Though it would always be a challenge, this awareness helped her to slow down and to become more thoughtful and considerate. She thought about Ollie almost every day, and the way their friendship had ended. Some days she believed that she had simply moved on with her life. Other days she wondered if she had thrown Ollie overboard when he stopped fitting into her ambitions. She found videos on the internet. Some of them presented Ollie without any signs of impairment. Others made him look confused and deficient. Mariah wondered if a true friend would have cared either way.

Cody initially struggled in the minor leagues. He had too much money in the bank and too many tempting ways to spend it. But then the money ran out, the old feelings of want grabbed hold, and he buckled down. He made it up to triple-A by his fourth season, just a step away from the majors. During this time, he never went back home, and telephoned only twice, once to get a copy of his birth certificate, and once to check the date of his last tetanus shot.

Cathy tried to keep believing. Every family has a wild child who makes it out the other side. That's what she had to believe for Cody. But for her other son, the belief had weakened, especially in the area of communication. If Ollie didn't have a fear of conversation, he certainly had an aversion to it. And Cathy had run out of answers. A brain injury patient might be re-trained to pick up a pencil or to tie a shoelace. But how do you teach the many facets of conversation? How do you help them to decipher facial cues, body language, sarcasm, insinuation, and irony? And that's before you even get into the inconsistent hodgepodge that is the English language itself, or innumerable other obstacles such as accent, dialect, impediment, impairment, and the whole range of human emotion that is often unspoken but still part of the conversation. This minefield of confusing variables overwhelmed Ollie and, even as he transitioned from young man to grown man, he retreated back to the safety of basic communication. He stopped trying, he stopped practicing, and that effectively closed the one door that might have offered an escape. Art did give him true joy, and it really had made his life better, but then she'd see him flounder in a conversation or be saddened by the sight of a pretty girl, and she would feel the pain all over again. In truth, Cathy's emotions had never completely gotten off the rollercoaster. But, then again, she had slow and steady Bob to lean on, for which she felt very thankful. She loved Bob for his uncomplicated nature, unwavering codes, and the weary soul that tried so hard—the same traits that also made him hard to live with.

Bob built a big art studio for Ollie. Added onto the back of the house, it had all day sunlight and overlooked the two small mountains that jutted out of the miles-long hillside that gently sloped up to the end of the ranch. Unexpectedly, Bob also got something in return. Ollie started going on the treasure expeditions—not as a hunter but as an artist—and during these times together, over many hours on horseback and around the campfire, Bob came to realize that not every son has an eternal grudge against his father. For years Bob had accepted the guilty verdict handed down by the son who couldn't stand to be in his presence. But Ollie was different. The one who had every right to be resentful, who had been strong-armed onto that baseball field, said, in a way, "You're my father, I'm your son, so let's get going." And that's what they did. They spent time together and got to know each other. Conversation still came in fits and spurts—if it came at all—but together Bob and Ollie built the strong bonds of a father and his adult son.

Ollie got his driver's license. It took help from his father and some practice on the dirt roads around the ranch, but he did it, and the family celebrated in a manner befitting such a major milestone. His artistic talents continued to open interesting doors, sometimes involving travel to faraway places. Accompanied by his mother—who did most the talking—he completed a series of big city panoramas for Houston, Seattle, and Tokyo. Every project and exhibition saw new admirers added to Ollie's growing list of fans. His world had expanded in so many ways, but that didn't change the fact that he still only had half of a life. And he knew it. His parents didn't know that he knew, or at least didn't know how much he knew. And Ollie preferred to keep it that way. Their sadness would have only made it worse. He thought about Mariah every day. She represented what had been lost. She embodied wonderfully normal afternoons where the possibility of abnormality didn't exist. And they had had dozens of those afternoons. So, Ollie thought about Mariah. And he filled the void of a half-life as best he could. Mostly he filled it with art.

All voyages, even peaceful ones, must come to an end at some point in time. This one ended in 2001, four years after Ollie graduated from high school and five years after Cody left home.

Part Two

Backward & Forward

Chapter 13

The knock on the door surprised Cathy. Santa Anas had been howling all day, and she hadn't heard the car drive up the dirt road. A quick look through the peephole showed the face of a woman that Cathy didn't recognize. She cracked the door and a gust blew it open. A frail, nothing of a thing shuddered against the wind while holding the hand of a little boy. Her other hand held a small suitcase. Dark purple blotches covered the skin around her nose and forehead. It was Rachel, gaunt, ashen, and barely recognizable. Cathy grabbed her arm, pulled the pair inside, and closed the door. The suitcase, which had a picture of Winnie the Pooh on it, fell to the floor, and Cathy feared that Rachel might go down next. Cathy pointed toward the living room, a place to sit, but Rachel didn't move.

Instead, she steadied herself, caught her breath, and said, "This is Francisco. He's come to visit his grandfather." The words, spoken with force, had a practiced, unnatural sound to them. Then she turned away and stifled a wheezy hack with a handkerchief. The boy alternately stared up at his struggling mother and at Cathy. He had perfectly combed black hair that had barely been touched by the wind.

"Uh...ok, Rachel. Does Ralph know? He never said anything."

"No...he doesn't know."

"OK…Come in and sit down…please…I'll try to get Ralph on the radio. Have you had lunch?"

"I can't stay." Once again, the words had a bite to them, like a general who will not be distracted. She nodded at the suitcase and said, "There's an envelope in there with his birth certificate."

And now Cathy started to understand. You don't bring a birth certificate for a week at grandpas. This was something else, something more than a visit. And Rachel clearly didn't like it.

"His medical records are in there too…but he doesn't have nothing bad. The doctor checked." She searched Cathy's eyes with a pleading, mournful intensity.

Cathy heard a noise in the living room. She turned and saw Ollie standing in the doorway to his studio.

"Hi, Rachel. I remember you," said Ollie.

After another coughing spasm passed, Rachel looked over Cathy's shoulder and said, "Hi, Ollie. I remember you, too. This is Francisco. He's here to visit his grandfather, but maybe you can hang out with him, too. Maybe he can stay here in the house sometimes…." Her voice trailed off, and tears began streaming down her bony face. She repeatedly wiped at them and tried to sniffle them away, but they continued to flow. She took a deep breath, and then another, and then she kneeled down to her little boy, held him by the shoulders, and said, "OK, sweetie, mommy has to go now, but grandpa will be here pretty soon."

"But you're coming back, right?"

"After I get better, I'll come get you."

"Promise?"

"After I get better. Now listen to me, sweetie, I need to tell you something important."

"OK."

Rachel fought for breath and for composure. With a broken voice she said, "Mommy loves you. If you get sad, just remember how much I love you. Will you do that?"

"OK."

"And you love mommy, too. Don't you?"

"Uh huh."

Rachel hugged her son tightly, desperately. Then she released him, rose to her feet, and left the house without looking back. Cathy followed for a step but then stopped. She had a hundred questions but intuitively realized that she already knew the only answer that really mattered: Rachel wasn't coming back anytime soon, probably never.

Cathy cleared her mind and refilled it with the thoughts of a scared five-year-old who, like most children, probably knew much more than anyone could guess. She casually said, "Are you hungry, Francisco?" He started to answer but suddenly stopped, and became noticeably rigid. Something had scared the child. Cathy looked around and saw that their dog, Bongo, had roused his feeble old bones and had come to investigate. He stood in the hallway, to the left of the boy.

"It's ok, Francisco. That's just old Bongo and he likes kids," said Cathy, but the words didn't hit the mark. The boy had started to panic. His body shook and he fought for breath. He repeatedly looked back and forth between the dog and Ollie. By the time Cathy figured out that the boy saw Ollie as some kind of rescuer, it was too late. The boy had made the dash. "No! No! Francisco stop!" yelled Cathy.

Even after all these years, Ollie still had serious limitations, and that included strangleholds from panic-stricken children. Cathy remembered the Mariah incident, and how a simple embrace had turned her son into a trapped animal. Now she saw it happening all over again, and could do nothing to stop it.

The boy charged through the living room and plowed into Ollie like a ragdoll shot from a canon. He attached himself with a death grip to the back of Ollie's legs, and cast a wary eye at the dog. Cathy froze. Bongo yawned. The boy stared...And Ollie laughed. He gently patted the boy's head and said, "It's ok, little one, Bongo won't hurt you. Do you want me to show you?"

"No."

"OK. Maybe tomorrow. Do you want to see the pictures I drew?"

"OK."

Ollie took his hand and led him into the studio.

<hr/>

Ralph got called to the office but didn't think anything about it. Something needed to be fixed, or a cow needed to be rescued, or the calving barn needed a nightshift midwife, something along those lines. Even the sight of Cathy, who rarely said boo, didn't mean too much. Wearing a confused smile, she stood next to Bob, who sat at his desk. And then she shocked the hell out of Ralph. She said that Francisco was in the house at that very moment. And Ralph, after some disbelief, responded with a big smile. He showed his happiness, even if Bob and Cathy looked strangely reserved.

He turned to leave, eager to see his grandson and daughter, who he assumed was also there, but Cathy called him back. She had some things to explain.

When she finished, Ralph said, "Rachel's not here?"

"No."

"And Francisco has a suitcase?"

"Yes."

"A come to visit kind of suitcase?"

"I think it's more than that," said Cathy.

Ralph sat down and Cathy told him the rest of the story. He listened with complete understanding and didn't question Cathy's assessment of Rachel. Bad news had a natural ring of truth for Ralph. He understood the world of the might-have-been. It also made inevitable sense that his daughter had joined him in this world. His admittance had been caused by self-sabotage, and not in a million years did he think the same of his daughter, but, by whatever means, she still belonged. And it felt familiar. As devastating as it might have been, he understood dashed potential and a life cut short. He didn't, however, understand a small child with a suitcase. That had too much possibility attached to it, too much hope.

He looked at the door and then back at Bob. He said, "Gomer's still tied down...."

"I'll put him away," said Bob.

"He needs to be brushed and picked."

"OK."

Ralph stood but still didn't move toward the door. He said, "In prison the shrink said I'm what you call an absentee father. That means I didn't do nothing for Rachel...so I don't deserve nothing, and I don't know nothing...."

"It doesn't matter," said Cathy. "It's on the job training. You're as qualified as they come. Do you have extra sheets and blankets?"

"No, but I have an extra sleeping bag."

"That will work for now. You'll have dinner tonight here at the house, and I'll watch him tomorrow while you're at work," said Cathy. And then she pushed him out the door with her eyes.

Lost in a fog of uncertainty, Ralph walked down to the house and slipped through the back door. He listened for a second and heard the voice of his grandson for the very first time. He followed the sound of that voice until it led to the doorway of Ollie's studio, where he quietly stood and watched. The boy sat next to Ollie at the giant drawing table. He still had the same shiny black hair and chubby cheeks as in the picture in the bunkhouse. He wore little boy jeans, a nice button-down shirt, and red cowboy boots that dangled playfully from the stool where he sat. The boy noticed Ralph in the doorway. He turned to look and Ralph got a full view. And an image of Rachel as a little girl instantly popped into his head. The boy had a darker complexion but the shape of the face, and the mouth, and the thoughtful eyes looked the same.

"Are you my grandpa?"

"Yes."

"My mom says you have a horse."

"Yes, I do."

"Do you have two horses?"

"Yes…yes…uh…would you like to see them?"

"OK."

He hopped off the stool and said goodbye to Ollie. On the way out of the house he said, "I have cowboy boots, too."

With just enough sunlight, and winds that had packed up for the day, Ralph gave Francisco the grand tour. And, like a brand-new grandfather, he tried a little too hard. They scooped feed into the coop and called the chickens home for the night. They visited the giant calving barn, and the curious little boy said hello to a curious little calf. They rolled open the towering barn door, and Francisco climbed up onto the big John Deere. They went to the arena, and Francisco sat on the big wooden horse with the mechanized roping dummy where Ralph had spent countless hours learning to be a cowboy.

And when the twilight had almost slipped away, and the show had begun to fizzle, Cathy called everyone to dinner. She served macaroni and cheese, hotdogs, and apple pie, everything a kid loves, which Ralph appreciated because in his current state of shock he probably couldn't have boiled water with any reliability. Ollie and Francisco did most the talking that night at the table, with Bob and Cathy chipping in once in a while. Ralph pretty much sat there like a guy with a time bomb strapped to his chest. And then it ended and the time came to drive up the hill to introduce Francisco to the peculiar charms of his new home away from home.

The bunkhouse had rudimentary electricity, outdoor plumbing, and not much of anything else. Francisco's eyes got big at the sight of the outdoor shower and very big at the sight of the outhouse. Of course, he liked the wooden bunkbeds, two pair of which still remained from the early days, and wanted to sleep on the top bunk. Ralph convinced him to try the bottom for the time being.

The boy seemed to like the place, and when he had been successfully zipped into his sleeping bag, and when Ralph's head had finally hit the pillow, he congratulated himself for making it through the first day. But the day hadn't ended because Francisco almost immediately started to cry. He wanted his mother. Ralph didn't know what to do. It was this emotional stuff that bewildered him the most. He tried talking, and reasoning, and making promises, but the words didn't work. He pointed out the sound of a hooting owl and said that they should listen for other animals. Francisco gave it a try until a nearby pack of coyotes made a kill and celebrated a little too loudly. Then he started crying louder than before. Ralph told himself to think like a mother, but his brain didn't stretch that far—he had barely been a father…but, then again, maybe that was enough. He said, "Francisco, can I tell you a story about your mother when she was a little girl?"

He stopped crying and said, "OK."

More than anything else, Ralph knew stories about his daughter because that's all he had had for the last two decades of his life. Since his days in prison, he had continually been retelling and reliving them. Little did he know that all of that cultivation, and embellishment, might someday come in handy. He told his stories beautifully and they proved to be more than enough to comfort a little boy who missed his mother. At the end, just before sleep, Francisco said, "My mom calls me Cisco. You can too if you want. Goodnight, grandpa."

"Goodnight, Cisco."

The red-nosed manager poked his head through the locker room door and said, "Hey, Buckmeyer, pack your bag and get your ass over to the motel. Mr. B. wants to see you."

At first the guys hooted and threw out smartass jabs. And then they took turns slapping him on the back. They knew what it meant. Everyone knew. Cody had been tearing up the league for three months, and the call had finally come in. He was going up to the bigs.

"And lose the plug. He hates that stuff," said the manager.

Cody pulled the tobacco from his mouth, held it up, and said, "Yeah, here you go coach. You can borrow it for a few hours and save yourself a nickel."

The guys laughed. Cody had a way about him. He got away with things because nothing fazed him. Not a drunk, volatile manager, not a ninety-nine mile per hour fastball with the season hanging in the balance. Cody didn't care and that was a powerful weapon.

He had to grab his stuff from the same motel so he didn't mind a quick meeting with Mr. Bruggerman, but it was strange. Normally, this transition involved a phone call, a quick celebration, and an even quicker flight to wherever the major league team happened to be playing, not a meeting with a rumpled suit who owns a podunk baseball team. But, then again, maybe the guy was a glad hander who wanted to get in good with somebody on the way to the top. Whatever the reason, Cody didn't sweat it.

Back at the motel, the pea-green door opened and Mr. B. greeted Cody. He had a piece of lettuce stuck to his tooth and a mustard stain on his ugly tie. Cody looked past him, into the small banquet room, and saw a handful of other men. They wore nice suits. Cody figured that some bigwigs had come to town to get his signature on something. He strolled into the room and flashed a smile.

Nobody shook his hand. The most distinguished of them, an older man with a tan and neatly cropped salt and pepper hair, pointed to a chair at a round table and asked Cody to sit. Another man sat at the opposite side of the same table. He had his eyes locked onto the screen of a laptop computer. Bruggerman also sat, off by himself, and grumbled about something. Everyone else stood in a semicircle, surrounding Cody, and they looked serious, like someone had stolen Christmas. It didn't bother Cody. They probably wore stern game faces every time they tried to sucker some dumb jock into signing something that maybe he shouldn't sign.

"My name is Edward Yarnouth," said the older man. He had an honest face, the kind that sells hemorrhoid cream on TV. "I'm general counsel for Major League Baseball." He pointed to another guy and said, "This is Brady Buckner, general counsel for the Players Association. And this is Denate Jackson, general counsel for the Atlanta Braves." This last one, a muscular black man, looked angry.

Cody shrugged and said, "Yeah, so what do you want?"

The older man faced Cody head on and said, "You have violated your contract, Mr. Buckmeyer."

No way. It had to be a joke, a little hazing to celebrate his promotion, the pencil neck version of itching powder on a jockstrap. A sly smile crept across Cody's mouth, and he waited for the guys to break out laughing. It didn't happen. The dead seriousness never fell from their faces. This army of idiots hadn't come to town to escort him to the big time. They had come to bust his chops over some gibberish in a contract. And that made Cody mad. He deserved better. He was their top minor league prospect, king of the new crop, and that meant big money for these leaches. The kind of money that pays for Italian suits and fancy haircuts. He stared the old man down and said, "Unless a three-ninety average and forty-seven stolen bases is a violation, I say you're full of shit."

Unfazed, the man said, "We are aware or your accomplishments on the field, Mr. Buckmeyer. Unfortunately, that same excellence has not been demonstrated in the rest of your life." And then he just stared, the dramatic courtroom glower that's supposed to make the sniveling suspect jump up and confess everything.

"What the hell are you talking about?" said Cody.

"You've been betting on baseball games, Buckmeyer!" said the angry muscleman.

In a million years Cody never expected to hear those words because the bets had been completely anonymous— no ID, no signature, no nothing—just cash on the counter and a ticket in his pocket. The risk had been so low that it didn't even qualify as anything particularly interesting, other than a fun day at the casino. But now, like a snap throw to first, he'd been caught with his thumb up his butt. His brain scrambled for an answer but never got past an image of Pete Rose beating out an infield grounder. Rose had been kicked out of baseball and kept out of the hall of fame for betting. And Cody realized that if they had the power to do that to Charlie Hustle, they had the power to wipe a minor leaguer like him off the face of the earth. He had nowhere to go. They had him by the balls. But, of course, he lied anyway.

And they weren't having any of it. The guy at the computer turned the screen toward Cody. It showed casino security video of Cody placing a bet, and a screenshot of the exact bet between the Dodgers and the Diamond Backs. Then someone slapped down a copy of Cody's casino players card and a copy of his ID. And that's how they had done it. The bets had indeed been anonymous, but they had learned his identity by comparing that video with the video of him getting a players card—a completely harmless perk, but not anonymous. Aggravating little shits like this always did their homework.

They gave Cody one minute to decide between two bad options: Sign a confession, leave baseball forever, and the Braves don't go after the quarter million dollar signing bonus; or, fight the allegation, lose, and pay back the bonus plus legal costs and possible damages. Cody signed the confession.

Chapter 14

Jubal Wainwright had stashed twelve hundred gold coins somewhere on the ranch. And Jubal was a weird man. This combination of facts created problems at the time of the robbery in 1887 and continued to create problems down through the years. Which of Jubal's bizarre behaviors in the days before and after the crime pointed to the treasure, and deserved to be chased down, and which of them had simply been the meaningless meanderings of a strange duck?

The sheriff's account of the robbery contained a laundry list of oddities, but one in particular stood out from the others. A few weeks before the robbery, Jubal slid his line shack onto a makeshift sled, hitched it up to his horse, and dragged it four hundred yards down the hill. And, after setting up the shack in the new location, he covered up every indication that it had ever been in the previous location. Was this something, or was it nothing? The sheriff and the insurance company thought it was something. They believed that Jubal had hidden the treasure somewhere up the hill and had tried to deflect attention away from it. The theory had sideways logic with a touch of crazy, and it fit Jubal perfectly. But after a hundred years of futility and ten thousand holes in the ground, Bob had his doubts.

That's not to say that the shack still didn't have something to say—if the listener could just open his ears and clear his mind. Sometimes Bob and Ralph rode up to the site of the old shack, parked their butts for an hour or two, and tried to think like strange stagecoach robbers. During one of these sessions Bob remembered that something besides the shack had been removed all those years ago: Jubal had chopped down a sycamore tree to build the sled. This fact had been noted in the sheriff's report, and a police photograph from the time showed a single tree stump on an otherwise bald hilltop. From these few simple observations Bob developed a wild theory (by then most theories tended to be wild because all of the practical ones had been used up) which he bounced off of Ralph one day after work while they rode side by side back to the barn.

"Why do you suppose he chopped down the whole tree when he only needed a couple of good sized branches?"

"Maybe he needed firewood."

"He limbed it, scattered the leftover branches, and rolled the trunk down the hill. He never chopped firewood."

"Maybe he just didn't think it through," said Ralph.

"Or maybe he needed to get rid of the tree."

"Why?"

"Because if someone climbed the tree, they would have seen something they weren't supposed to see," said Bob.

"Uh...OK. But then why did he move the shack?"

"Same reason. The shack sat up off the ground, on top of the hill...maybe you could see things...." Bob's voice petered out.

"Umm…it's a little thin, Buck, but at least it's not hard to test. There are trees up there now."

"Think you can climb them?" asked Bob.

"Yeah…I could do it…might end up at the back cracker…but I could do it. You should get Ollie to do it. If anyone's gonna spot something, it'll be him. And you'll get a detailed drawing to boot."

Bob's eyes lit up. "Ralph Durbin, sometimes I think you're smarter than you let on."

It didn't take much to get Ollie on board. He heard the word "tree" and was hooked. Ollie liked chasing after drawings, and over the years had done it by foot, by horse, by car, by airplane, and by helicopter. But he had never climbed a tree to get a drawing. On the next excursion Bob and Ralph put down the metal detectors for a few hours and took turns hoisting Ollie up into the three trees that now lived on top of the hill where the line shack once stood. And then they whisked him back down to the studio with some simple instructions: "Draw what you see and look for hiding places."

Ollie created twelve drawings, four from each tree. The first set, taken from a tree located fifty yards from the site of the old line shack, didn't produce anything interesting. The second set, thirty yards from the old site, yielded one drawing that contained the mere wisp of a hint, which Bob didn't notice at first. This hint grew more pronounced on one of the drawings from the last set, captured above the very ground where the shack had stood but, once again, Bob almost didn't notice. It just looked like a shadow on the face of the cliff that rimmed the mountainside…but maybe it looked too dark and unusually shaped to be a shadow. And why would there be a shadow there anyway? He shuffled back through the drawings. And there it was again, the same dark spot captured on one of the drawings from the second tree.

"What's this?" asked Bob.

Ollie, now fast at work on something new, looked up from his drawing table and said, "That's the hiding place. You told me to find it. I found it." He smiled contentedly and submerged himself back into the work at hand.

"What kind of hiding place is it, Ollie?"

"It's a cave."

Five generations of Buckmeyers had ridden countless times past this cliff. They had repeatedly scanned its face. But they came up short, even on horseback, and didn't scan what they couldn't see. If they had had a tree to climb, or a line shack, they would have seen a teepee shaped crack where the cliff face met a protruding ledge. And by the time new trees grew back, nobody remembered that a tree had been removed in the first place. They remembered very little, except for an undecipherable hypochondriac named Jubal Wainwright.

※※※※※※※※※※※※※

Ralph heard Cisco talking about Rachel. He paused at the doorway of the studio and listened.

"She doesn't call me on the phone anymore."

"I know," said Ollie.

"Grandpa tried to call her, but she didn't answer. And then grandpa looked sad but pretended to be happy."

160

"Sometimes big people try to hide things," said Ollie.

"Do you hide things?"

"Sometimes."

"Do you hide things from me?"

"No, because you already know. Your mom stopped calling on the telephone, and your grandpa looks sad."

"And she didn't come get me."

"No, she didn't."

"But she promised."

"Maybe she didn't get better."

"That's what I think, too."

The conversation paused. Ollie continued drawing. Cisco worked on his homework at a small desk next to Ollie's. Then Ollie said, "Sometimes sad things happen, but it doesn't make all the good things go away."

"Did something sad happen to you, Ollie?"

"Yes."

"Are you still sad?"

"Yes, but mostly I'm happy. And that's what will happen to you, too. The sadness will get smaller and the happiness will get bigger. I promise."

"Ok."

"And if your mom doesn't come back, you can stay here with us. I'll be your big brother. You'll have your grandpa, and you'll have me. Does that sound good?"

"That sounds good."

Ollie and Cisco had been getting close ever since Cisco came to the ranch six months before. Because of the age difference it didn't make much sense. But in other ways it made perfect sense, and Ralph realized it before anyone else.

Up to then Ollie had pretty much given up on conversation, but that didn't mean he didn't want to talk. And the little snippets that Ralph heard every day when he came into the house to pick up Cisco after work proved it. Little five-year-olds don't talk like adults. They use simple words and don't know much about sarcasm or slang or body language. And this seemed to make a difference for Ollie. When Cisco talked, Ollie didn't get lost. Instead of understanding fifty percent of the conversation, and giving up, he understood ninety percent, and figured out the rest on the fly. It kind of seemed like Ollie had gone back to the beginning to learn the basics. He learned at the pace of a child. And because Cisco spent every afternoon after school at the house, and because he talked like a magpie, Ollie got a great deal of practice.

And Cisco got something out of the deal, too, something that made Ralph feel grateful. He got stability at a time when he needed it the most. He got it from Ollie. And nobody had more stability than Ollie. He religiously lived by his routine and fought against any and all change. The brain injury had made him that way. It had become his strength and his weakness. And even though Cisco's world had been turned upside down, he still knew that when he got off the school bus every afternoon, the big person who drew pictures would be waiting for him. And Cisco clung to his new friend like a frightened boy clings to his father.

If Bob and Cathy recognized this special relationship, they never said anything about it. Ralph didn't think they saw it. Maybe they didn't want to see it. After too many hard years, they had settled into roles that offered some peace.

They were the faithful parents, Ollie was the special child, and that's the way things would remain. But Ollie wanted something better. Ralph saw it, but he didn't say anything. With his track record he really didn't have the right.

SSSSSSSSSSSSS

Bob held up Ollie's drawing for everybody at the dinner table to see.

"You know that ledge is a good forty feet up the cliff," said Ralph.

"What, you don't think I can climb it?" answered Bob.

"I didn't say that. I'm just wondering how?"

"How would Daniel Boone do it? How would Lewis and Clark do it?"

"You're going to use an extension ladder, aren't you?"

"Exactly. Pass the salad."

They laughed. Cathy laughed, too. Bob liked seeing that. They had laughed more in the last six months than in the previous half dozen years combined. The ranch felt the way it used to before the accident and before the money problems. The recent discovery of the cave had added even more lightness, no doubt, but it hadn't been the source, and that was important to Bob. He wanted to find the treasure, but he didn't want to cross the line. He didn't want to be the feverish guy who can't see the best treasure in life because he's too busy searching for the second best. It wasn't always easy, but on this Friday pizza night, Bob knew the difference.

"Can I go?" said a little squeak of a voice. It was Cisco, looking up from his slice of cheese pizza. Nobody answered the question until Ollie said, "He can go. I'll watch him."

Fearing that Ollie had overstepped himself, Bob shot Ralph a glance and saw that no offence had been taken. So, Bob looked down at the boy and said, "Are you getting good at riding the horse?"

"Yes," said Cisco.

"Have you fallen off yet?"

"Yes."

"Did you cry big tears or little tears?"

"No tears," said the boy, with some five-year-old indignation.

"Well...that's good enough for me...except that there's no one to partner up with Cisco 'cause we need Ollie's help on this trip."

"I'll go," said Cathy. "Cisco and I will set up camp and maybe I'll show him how to use Ollie's old metal detector."

"What's that?" asked Cisco.

"That's how you find gold, my boy," said grandpa.

Cisco's eyes got big, a happy grin formed, and then he sheepishly accepted congratulations for being included in the upcoming treasure hunt.

Only one thing could have made the evening any better, but, even on that account, Bob had reason for optimism. Cody had been doing well in triple A and, while the impressive statistics made the father happy, the real satisfaction came from some unmistakable signs that Cody had at last started to grow up. The old Cody, the one who had been kicked out of the house, floundered during his first two years in the minors because he didn't possess the necessary maturity and self-control, not in his personal life, not in his baseball life. But in the last two years he had begun to change. He started to grow as a baseball player. He became more disciplined. Bob had to believe that the growth and discipline demonstrated on the field had been made possible, at least to some degree, by growth and discipline in his personal life. It happens all the time. People grow up. Bob had no reason to believe anything different for Cody.

The plan had sounded reasonable at the time. Truck the extension ladder up the hill, drop it off as close as possible to the cliff, and then carry it by hand the rest of the way. And the cool March day provided perfect weather for it. Bob quickly realized, however, that carrying an awkward load across a half mile of mountainous terrain is much different than a half mile on flat land. He dropped his end of the ladder and took another breather. The alternative had been to ditch the ladder and rappel from the top of the cliff, a skill which both Bob and Ralph had learned in the Marine Corps, but that had been many moons ago, when they had muscles, and when they didn't know about bunions and senior discounts.

"Let Ollie take it, Bob. What's the use of having a kid if you can't put him to work? We'll just strap his pack onto the ladder," said Ralph, who held the other end.

"I'm good. Nothing but weakness leaving the body," said Bob, quoting one of their favorite Marine Corps sayings.

"Looks like a few too many burritos, if you ask me," said Ralph.

When they got to the base of the cliff, Ralph, who seemed to have energy to burn, pulled the entrenching tool from Ollie's backpack and began leveling the ground at the base of the cliff. Almost immediately the blade struck something and made a funny noise. Bob and Ralph knew all about funny noises because they spent countless hours with metal detectors, dirt fishing and digging holes. This didn't sound like a rock. Ralph gently rocked the blade to loosen the object and then reached into the hole. He pulled out a long, rectangular green bottle. "Is that what I think it is?" said Bob.

Ralph rubbed dirt off the side of the bottle and said, "God bless you, Doctor Cooper."

Bob grabbed the bottle, saw the words "Cooper's New Discovery" molded into the glass, and began pumping his fist like a walk off homerun hitter. He said the word "Yes" over and over. Ralph danced a jig. Ollie laughed at the crazy old people. This clue specifically tied Jubal to this spot and, almost certainly, to the cave above their heads.

<hr/>

Cathy appreciated the bottle, and her husband's enthusiasm, but the same could not be said for little Cisco. The boy had been dreaming about bandits and buried treasure, not Doctor Cooper's secret formula for the treatment of gout, baldness, and general malaise. And it had also been a very long day for him, starting before sunup with a quick breakfast, followed by helping to tack and pack the horses, a two-hour trail ride to the base of the cliff, helping set up camp while the men fetched the ladder, watering and feeding the horses, and helping to make lunch. The kid looked like he needed to have some fun, and Cathy had a few ideas in mind. First, while he ate lunch, she snuck out to the area where they had found the bottle, poked three holes into the ground, and inserted a shiny half dollar into each hole. She salted the mine, so to speak. And then, after lunch, she told him a suspense filled version of the robbery, half of which may have been true. Then she set him up with the child sized metal detector and turned him loose to go find the "treasure."

The ladder had been positioned and extended to its full forty-foot length, but it came up about ten feet short of the ledge. And if Bob had said that he didn't seriously think about scurrying to the top of that ladder and engaging in some impromptu rock climbing, for which he was imminently unqualified, he would have been lying. They finally had some momentum. One clue had led to another, which led to another. It felt like an adventure movie with mummies and a catacomb full of gold. The word, "wait," almost sounded cowardly. But Bob took pride in his levelheaded discipline and didn't plan on letting a little bit of momentum cloud his good judgement. Besides, Cathy was watching.

So, they played it by the book and secured the base of the ladder to metal stakes and ran guywires to the middle section, approximately twenty feet up. These precautions took time to complete, but they added the reasonable assurance that if Bob fell during the rock climb, the ladder would have enough stability to hold the safety rope and possibly save his sorry ass. The final part of the plan called for the placement of a wire ladder spanning the gap between the ladder and the ledge, thus eliminating the need for any future rock climbing, but by the time the other work had been completed, the sun had slipped down low to the horizon. Bob figured he had just enough time to make the initial climb to secure the wire ladder—and maybe take a quick look inside the cave.

Outfitted with a body harness, a safety rope, and a backpack that held the wire ladder and a flashlight, he climbed to the top of the ladder and tied off to the top rung. Before starting the rock climb, he gave a thumbs up to the guys below and glanced over at the campsite. Of course, Cathy had him in her sights. She stood on the edge of camp, hands on hips, wearing a scowl that could fluster a titan. Bob smiled and waved. She jabbed a finger at him, her way of saying stop acting like an idiot and pay attention to what you're doing. But Bob couldn't resist. He hugged the ladder and spastically dangled his feet in the air. Cathy stormed off. Moments like this made marriage especially precious. Unfortunately, that's where the excitement ended because a multitude of hand and footholds turned the rock climb into a complete nonevent, roughly on par with an upper middle-aged man having a go on the local playground equipment—ugly but not deadly.

The whole theory hinged on the cave, and what might be inside it, but when Bob's head first popped above the ledge his eyes didn't go in that direction. They got distracted by something that didn't belong. And Bob said "Bingo" at the sight of it. A giant pulley rested on the ledge, not even three feet from his face. It felt like the clues had started falling from the sky. This latest one, comprised of cracked and weather-beaten wooden wheels sandwiched between a skeleton of rusty steel, stood out like a UFO hovering over the White House. But nobody had ever seen it because, just like the cave itself, it was obscured by the ledge.

Reenergized, Bob planted both forearms onto the ledge and hoisted up the rest of his body. As he got up to his knees, he saw the steel carcass of another pulley resting against the rock wall at the back of the ledge. A hundred years' worth of rust had stained the wall blood red.

The discovery of one pulley proved that someone had been there. This second pulley meant even more. Two pulleys create a mechanical advantage that can be used to lift heavy loads, and that's exactly the kind of help Jubal would have needed. He had found the perfect hiding place and needed to fill it with enough provisions to ride out the manhunt that he must have known was coming. Bob scrambled to his feet, untied the safety rope, and eyed the entrance to the cave. They finally had the bandit cornered. Bob felt it. He walked cautiously toward the entrance, saying, "Come on, Jubal, you've had a good run. It's time to give it up."

He kneeled before the small opening and, before even turning on the flashlight, saw Jubal's unmistakable calling card: Cooper's New Discovery. Twenty-four of the rectangular bottles, turned green from age and covered in dust, rested on the ground just inside the cave. The corks had withered away, and the magical potion had long ago been sucked dry by the arid climate, but otherwise they sat undisturbed in four perfect rows, exactly as Jubal had put them a century before. And, strangely, it made Bob pause.

Those perfect rows had been part of Jubal's perfect plan, and it had failed, just like so many other perfect plans that men and women have labored over since the beginning of time.

But Bob didn't have time for philosophizing. The wire ladder had not been set up, which he needed to safely get back down. So, he told himself that it would be just a quick look. The problem with one look, though, is that it sometimes turns into a second, and then a third, and before you know it, your wife is at the base of the cliff cussing at you and banging on a frying pan.

He shined the light into the cave and, a few feet past the bottles, saw a blistered and rust-worn rifle leaning against the wall. Another rifle lay on the ground next to it, the muzzle propped up on a mound of some kind. He crawled into the cave to get a better look and found the mound to be a pile of ammunition. From the looks of it, the ammo had been stored inside a stack of steel cases that had rusted away to nothing, leaving behind the contents in surprisingly good condition. The brass casings had turned green and the lead bullets had turned dusty white.

Bob sat back and shined the light around the rest of the cave. It looked to be about fifteen feet from wall to wall and maybe forty feet in length, but the blackness at the back of the cave devoured the light and made it difficult to judge. The solid rock floor slanted downhill, front to back and, despite the small entrance, the cavity itself offered enough room to stand and freely walk about. He rose to his feet and continued searching. On the opposite wall from the bottles and rifles, he found another mound. This one, about three feet high, consisted entirely of canning jars, dozens of them, most unbroken, all lidless, and covered in brownish orange dust, probably the rusty remains of the steel lids. Knowing Jubal, the jars had originally been neatly stacked, perhaps in cardboard boxes, but, as the decades passed, the boxes crumbled, and the jars started to tumble. Except for the grunge that lined the inside of the jars, the ones on top had given up their contents. Bob dug down through the pile and found some jars that still had something in them. He took one and shook it back and forth. It made a faint rattling sound. He rested the flashlight on top of the pile and poured out the contents of the jar into the palm of his hand. He got a heap of tan colored dust, but when the dust sifted through his fingers, it left behind a rectangular lump of who knows what, probably the petrified remains of a portion of beef or pork. This had been a cache of food, no doubt, but Bob kept digging, just in case other things had been stashed away. He didn't find anything.

Next to this mound, towards the entrance, he found a well preserved large wooden tray with four rusty eyebolts secured to its four corners. This looked like it belonged to the pulley system and most likely had been used to carry supplies—and twelve hundred gold coins—up the side of the cliff.

The cave had a lot of Jubal in it, just not the valuable part. Bob shined the light toward the back and saw the faint image of a wood beam leaning awkwardly against the wall. He walked toward it, but after only a few steps he hit a slippery spot and he fell hard onto his butt, landing like a circus clown in a pool of water. As he cussed and took inventory of his wet limbs, the sound of dripping water began to echo loudly throughout the cave. That sound had not been there before. A scan of the top and of the sides of the cave didn't reveal anything that looked like water. He shined the light down into the pool where he sat and saw a little rivulet of water running downhill toward the back of the cave. That's where the sound came from. His body had displaced the water, pushing it out of the pool, sending it trickling and dripping to a new location.

It didn't take a hydrologist to know that water makes a dripping sound when it falls from a height. The height might be five inches or it might be fifty feet. How far did this water fall? Not wanting to find out the hard way, Bob began scooting backward until he hit dry ground, where he rose to his feet.

Smartened up by a hard fall and some soggy britches, Bob used the dwindling light by the entrance to make a fresh evaluation. And he saw the chamber in a new way. It might have looked like a cave but a better description would have been to call it a channel or a watercourse. And, judging by the clean swept, U-shaped rock floor, it carried a fair amount of water every time it rained. This concave floor also explained how Jubal's supplies, stacked along the edges on the high sides of the floor, had not been swept away. And this watercourse also included the ledge outside that caught the surface water from the top of the mountain and channeled it into the cave. Where the water went from there, Bob didn't know, but he intended to find out.

Slowly walking back into the darkness, hugging the wall and staying out of the water, he found the pool where he had fallen, and the wet mark from the rivulet that flowed down to the back of the cave. He kept walking, aiming the light at the floor, not sure exactly what to look for but certain that the water had to have gone somewhere. And it had. And when Bob saw it, a shot of adrenaline flooded his heart and a shudder coursed through his body. Right there at the back of the cave, less than ten feet from where he had fallen, a gaping vertical shaft hid in the darkness and waited to devour whatever came its way. If he had not slipped and had kept walking, or if he had slipped closer to the hole, he very easily could have fallen down that shaft. He picked up a fist-sized rock, dropped it into the shaft, and counted two full seconds before the sound of splashing water echoed back up through the chamber. That amounted to a sixty foot drop and, depending on how many rocks you hit on the way down, was probably more than enough to do the job. Death didn't scare Bob, but dying like an idiot did.

He turned his attention to the wood beam wedged between the wall and the ground. Even though it looked as if it had fallen from its original position, the beam still traversed the space over the top of the five-foot-wide shaft. And it had an interesting groove cut across it. No doubt that groove at one time held a rope that had been tied off to the beam. The beam had secured the rope and the rope had been used to repel down the shaft. No other explanation made sense. Someone had gone down this hole.

Compared to the meagre progress of the last hundred years, the progress of the last two weeks had been like a ride in a rocket ship. The treasure hunt used to be pie in the sky silliness that you didn't mention in public. It didn't have a finish line. Now it did, and Bob expected to cross that line at any moment. He had no choice. He had to keep going. The idea of getting off the cliff before nightfall had now been officially abandoned.

Bob knew that another stupid mistake might end with something worse than wet underwear, so he carefully checked the ground all around the hole. He kicked the beam. It didn't budge. While maintaining a safe distance from the shaft, he eased down to his knees, planted his hands onto the rock floor, and lowered his body until he lay flat on his stomach. The ground under his left hand felt wet and slippery. His right hand, which also clutched the flashlight, felt coldness radiating through the rock. He slid his body under the beam. Water began soaking again into his clothes. He slowly inched toward the hole. The whistling sound of a stiff wind pulsated out of the shaft. His head cleared the void. The wind blew against his face. He saw nothing but blackness. He aimed the flashlight. And, not more than fifteen feet away, the remains of Jubal Wainwright stared right back at him. "I've been looking for you, my friend," said Bob.

If there had been even a remotely safe way to keep going, Bob probably would have taken it. But that way didn't exist, so he backed away from the shaft, and out of the spell. Just as he had gotten up onto his knees, though, a series of clicking, chirping noises caught his attention. He held up the light and saw some things flying out of the shaft, first a few at a time, then a steady thin stream, and then a black swarm. The clicking sounds quickly multiplied in intensity until the echoing cave sounded like a hundred popcorn kettles reaching climax all at the same time. Bob scooted back, sat against the wall, and watched as thousands upon thousands of bats darted out of the shaft, into the cave, and out into the nighttime hunting sky.

∞∞∞∞∞∞∞∞∞∞∞

Cathy put on a good show—for about five minutes—but she couldn't stay mad at Bob. He had gotten caught up in the excitement and, really, who could blame him? For the first time in forever he actually had something to get excited about. It might not have been *the* day he'd been dreaming about all these years but, judging by the sparkle in his eye when he came down off of the cliff, it came close. So, she called him an idiot and let it go. And then, after serving up heaping plates filled with steak and baked beans and garlic bread, she sat down on a log and listened along with everyone else to a good old fashioned campfire story.

Bob described the cave, its contents, and the sixty-foot shaft in a workman like way. When he talked about Jubal, though, his voice became quiet. He revealed that Jubal didn't die at the bottom of the shaft, as one might have expected. He died on a harmless looking perch just below the cave. His remains lay slumped against the wall with his face pointed up, as if looking up at the cave. The wispy remnants of a rope lay next to him and dangled impotently over the side of the perch and down into the shaft. That rope, along with the beam in the cave that looked as if it had fallen out of place, made Bob wonder if perhaps there had been an accident where the rope had come off of the beam and had left Jubal mortally stranded on the perch, possessor of a stolen fortune but forever imprisoned by just one wrong step. They say that

175

there's no such thing as a perfect crime, but, if this was indeed what had happened, it seemed like Jubal's mistake had an especially tragic bite to it.

Of course, everyone wanted to hear the G word, but Bob didn't have anything for them...except an interesting observation. The perch where Jubal died may have been something more than just a perch. Bob called it that because of the way it had looked from his limited vantage point up at the top of the shaft. It was possible that the perch extended beyond what Bob had been able to see, and that Jubal had actually found another cave within the system, a deeper, more difficult one that offered an even better place to hide the gold. After all, he had been down there for a reason.

During the course of this account, Cathy detected a hint of sadness in her husband's voice, and she thought she understood. The mystery of Jubal Wainwright had been a part of his life since the day he had been born. This same mystery had tightly bound Bob to his father, to his father's father, and right up the line through five Buckmeyer generations. It had also united Bob and Ollie. And even though the gold had not yet been found, and part of the mystery still remained, the human part of it had been solved. The quirky, scheming, funny, desperate part that connects one frail human heart to another had been laid to rest. The ever-present Jubal had been laid to rest. And maybe in some strange way it felt like the funeral of an old friend.

While this might've been mere speculation on Cathy's part, she often understood her husband's emotions better than he did himself. And in her book, this lack of emotional awareness didn't make Bob less human. He possessed all the emotions that mattered and showed them in his own way. A good example of this unfolded right there at the campfire when Bob remembered what she had told him about Cisco and the hidden silver half dollars. With no intention other than letting the boy bask in a little sunshine, he asked if he'd had any luck with the metal detector. Cisco, who had been completely engrossed in Bob's story, looked embarrassed. Uncle Bob had just told a great story about a spooky cave with a deadly shaft and the bones of a desperado. All Cisco had was a few measly coins. So, Cathy encouraged him. And so did Grandpa Ralph. With a healthy pat on the back, he said, "Come on boy, show us what you got."

Cisco, not really a shrinking violet, readily obliged. He put down his soda can, stood up from the log that he shared with his grandpa, and pulled the coins from his pocket. He held them out next to the light of the campfire. Everyone cheered. Ollie whistled loudly. Grandpa smiled proudly. Cisco looked like a proud tomb raider.

"Well, my boy, I think you got me beat," said Bob. "I found a few empty bottles and you found three silver coins."

A new round of cheers ensued.

Cisco interrupted. "No, I found four coins, but the other one isn't very good. It's not shiny."

The revelry sputtered to a stop. Ralph looked quizzically at his grandson. Bob shot a glance at Cathy. Ollie suppressed a smile. Cisco reached into his other pocket and pulled out a ten dollar gold eagle.

And that's when the celebration really started. The first piece of Jubal's elusive treasure had finally been found…by a child.

The next day, Sunday, everyone climbed the ladders and took a tour of the upper cave, including Cisco. He wore a safety harness and grandpa manned the safety rope from atop the cliff. They also gave the ground where Cisco had found the gold coin another scan but didn't find anything else. And, after some debate, Cathy managed to persuade the gung-ho men to put off exploration of the shaft and lower regions of the cave system until they came up with a proper plan with the proper equipment.

∭∭∭∭∭∭

When they got back on Sunday evening Bob popped into the office to take care of some paperwork. Other than being unusually tired—probably from all the excitement—he felt good. These little expeditions had been a part of his life since childhood, but none had ever been as enjoyable as this last one. Having Cathy along for the first time since the boys had been little made it feel like a family event. It also meant a major chuck wagon upgrade. And the way Cisco knocked over the whole gang when he pulled the gold coin from his pocket still made Bob laugh. It just didn't get any better than that. Self-diagnosis can be tricky, but Bob could honestly say two things: The treasure still had not been found (except for Cisco's little breadcrumb), and he felt as satisfied as ever.

The latest edition of *Baseball America* sat on top of the stack of mail and, upon seeing it, Bob's mind shifted gears to Cody. After his performance during the previous baseball season, Cody stood a good chance at making the Braves' roster for the upcoming season. At the very least he would be invited up to the big club for spring training. Bob opened the magazine, expecting to have to do some digging before finding out Cody's status, but almost immediately stumbled upon a picture of his son accompanied by a full-length article. The title read, "Atlanta Bombshell." The blurb underneath the title read, "Top Braves' Prospect Banned from Baseball."

And in that instant Bob's world collapsed. The heaviness of lost hope, from which he had only recently been freed, once again landed hard upon his heart. The sense of wellbeing that had so cautiously been flowing back into his life, drained off like water from a pierced radiator. And the happiness that had just been carried down the mountain, that had almost felt transcendent, withered in the face of overwhelming grief. He never saw it coming. Bob had believed in Cody's ongoing rehabilitation. He had believed the age old wisdom that sees maturity on the other side of wild oats. He had been comforted by the inevitableness of it, soothed by the normalcy of it.

But Cody's problems went deeper than wild oats, and now Bob knew it. Maybe he had always known it. Maybe he had clung to that homey Rockwellian explanation because he didn't have the courage to take a hard look at his own son. And he still didn't have the courage.

A few hours later, after Bob had made a quiet trip to the liquor store, Cathy came out to the office to see why he hadn't come to bed. She saw the bottle on the desk and the sadness in his eyes, but he didn't tell her about Cody. He didn't have the heart. So, like a good alcoholic, he made up a story about a bottle of Scotch and a promise he'd made to his father to crack it open when he found gold. She could always tell when he lied, but she seemed to appreciate the effort. He followed her into the house, feeling wearier than ever before, like his clothes had been dipped in cement.

〰〰〰〰〰〰〰〰〰〰

Razor wire surrounds the fire support base, reflecting the glaring, oppressive afternoon sun. Raw sewage flows in channels on the other side of the wire, rejected by the soggy ground, simmering in the heat. The second lieutenant follows a corporal from the landing zone to the company command post, passing through a hillside pockmarked with foxholes and tattered hooches. The grunts take notice. Their mocking, incredulous stares are not subtle. The lieutenant wears new boots and cammies with perfect press marks. He removes his cover and bends into the command post hooch.

The captain, sitting at a lopsided, makeshift desk, looks tired and unimpressed. He says, "Straight out of Basic and good to go. Is that right, Lieutenant?"

"Yes, sir."

"Maybe even a little eager."

"Yes, sir."

"Well, this isn't TBS, and you don't know shit. You shadow Hunter. You might outrank him but he knows how to save your ass. You don't make a cup of coffee without his nod, got it?"

"For how long, sir?"

"Until I figure out if you're gonna get anybody killed."

When the lieutenant climbs out of the hooch, everything is different. He's no longer at the company support base. He's alone with his platoon in the jungle. He sees Maloof, Reynosa, and Hochlichtner. They look filthy and half dressed. They stare blankly, knowing what he's going to say because he has already said it in a thousand previous nightmares.

He can't unsay what has already been said. Maybe back when he really said it, there might've been a way out, but not now. It's too late, and everyone knows it. "Get your gear. We're going after Durbin," says the lieutenant. They don't protest, not even a cuss word.

"Who's that over there?" asks the lieutenant.

"That's Cody, the new guy."

"Go get him. He's coming, too," says the lieutenant. He then looks down at his new boots and freshly pressed cammies.

This time Bob didn't wake up.

Chapter 15

Cisco and his grandpa made their routine morning drive down to the house and saw a gray van parked in the driveway. Grandpa whistled and said, "They sure don't waste any time."

Cisco had trouble sounding out the word on the side of the van. He said, "What's a coro...coro—"

"Coroner. That's who you call when someone dies."

"Did somebody die, grandpa?"

"Oh, no, just Jubal, the guy in the cave."

"But that was a long time ago."

"You still have to call the coroner. That's how they keep track of things. The hospital keeps track of everyone who is born, and the coroner keeps track of everyone who dies."

Grandpa parked in his usual spot, and the two walked down to the house. All the lights were on. Aunt Cathy met them at the backdoor. She gave Cisco a hug. Her eyes looked red and she still had on a bathrobe.

"You eat your breakfast now. Your grandpa and I will be right back," said Aunt Cathy, as she ushered Cisco to the table.

They left him alone in the kitchen. And he didn't like the look of things. When big people pretend like they're not crying, bad things happen. Cisco threw his backpack onto the table and went searching for Ollie. He found him in his studio, on the floor, rocking back and forth, banging his head against the wall. Bongo lay nearby, head down, staring at Ollie. Cisco walked up slowly and sat down next to the two.

"What's wrong, Ollie?"

Ollie didn't answer. He kept rocking and moaning and banging his head.

"Please don't hit your head, Ollie. It scares me."

Ollie didn't say anything.

Cisco started crying. And then Ollie stopped doing it. He wrapped an arm around Cisco. He said, "My dad died last night."

"Uncle Bob died?"

Ollie nodded. Cisco started crying again, and so did Ollie.

<hr />

Cody put down the phone and, without saying a word, went to the bedroom. The beautiful young cleat chaser who he had shacked up with, and who hadn't figured out that his career wasn't worth a bag of peanuts, knocked on the door. But Cody had locked it. He sat down on the bed, closed his eyes, and saw the face of the man who had dominated every day of his life. He began sobbing.

Love is an easy cry, but Cody didn't have that luxury. And he didn't have the reprieve of simple love and hate, where love is diluted and the pain is cut in half. He had love, hate, estrangement, and, most of all, the crushed hopes of reconciliation where the man was supposed to finally come to his senses and start loving his son like a real father. That's what Cody had, and it overwhelmed him.

Ralph rode hard that day. He drove the cattle with anger and cut them without mercy. Bob didn't have to die. And stress didn't kill him. And neither did diet or personal demons or Vietnam.

Ralph and his horse didn't come close to making it to the end of the day. When both had been spent, reduced to a foamy sweat and a slouching shell, Ralph finally broke down. In the middle of the range, teetering in the saddle, with uninterested cattle as the only witness, Ralph bellowed, "You stupid son of a bitch! You saved the wrong guy and look what it got you! Look what it got you!" And then he cried bitterly. A couple of cows looked up, but then went back to chewing their cud.

Cathy had started her day with just a touch of irritation. Bob had forgotten to start the coffee maker and had gone off somewhere. After looking out the kitchen window and not seeing a light on in the office, she went back to their bedroom and found him still in bed, lying on his back, with a white face and open, lifeless eyes. She immediately knew the worst, and that terrible understanding exploded out of her body like a riot whistle. Her scream shattered the morning grogginess and sent old Bongo charging to the scene. She fell onto the body and yelled her husband's name, as if her sternness had the power to rouse him into action, as it had so many times before. She put her face next to his, cheek to cheek, searching for the intimate warmth that she knew so well. She felt only coldness. She called his name over and over, calling him back, hoping that he hadn't gone far, and might still heed her call. She felt someone touch her arm. It was Ollie. She fell into his arms and cried.

186

C ody slipped into the front row pew and sat next to his mother. She stifled a tearful gasp and pulled him into a desperate hug. She looked different, older and frailer, not the same hard charger he had always known. Ollie sat on the other side of mother. He had grown up. Cody said hello.

With lifeless organ music playing in the background, Cody and mother whispered back and forth about the shock of father's sudden death. A few times she broke down, and Cody tried to change the subject, but she didn't follow along. She wanted to talk about him. Cody nodded solemnly at every sentiment. The subject of baseball didn't come up, but when it did Cody had a story ready and waiting.

A couple of times during the conversation mother looked toward the back of the church. And then, after a few minutes, she stood up, squeezed past Cody, and said, "I'll be right back."

She moved up the aisle a few rows and stopped to talk to Ralph Durbin. Cody hadn't seen him on the way in and didn't welcome the sight now, or what happened next when mother led Ralph and a little Mexican kid down the aisle to sit with the family. Cody, dumbfounded, stood up to let mother back into her seat. His eyes met Ralph's. They nodded coolly to each other. Then everyone slid over to make room for the intruders.

Change happens and Cody didn't usually care. But he cared about this one. Somehow the murderer had wormed his way into mother's heart, and it felt like a betrayal because she had always been an ally in his hatred for Ralph Durbin. And where the Mexican kid fit into all of this, Cody didn't have a clue.

After a few hymns and a fill-in-the-blank eulogy, the minister offered the microphone to anyone who wanted to say something about the dearly departed. Cody, a member of the grief-stricken family, figured he got a pass on this, so he sat back and concentrated on being the dutiful son. But then that awkward moment—when everyone wonders if anyone is going to get up and talk—didn't happen. It didn't happen because Ollie immediately jumped out of his seat. Mother gasped. Ollie walked quickly up to the podium. *Oh shit, this is going to be painful*, thought Cody.

Ollie held a piece of paper in his shaking hand and started to read. "When I was eight years old, I told dad that I wanted to ride a calf in one of those little kid rodeos. He said Ok, and for the next month I wore a cowboy hat to school and told everyone about the rodeo. But when the day came, and we got there, and I saw the kids getting thrown to the ground, I got scared and wanted to go home. Dad took me over to the man with the microphone and said that a boy who brags in front of everybody better have the guts to chicken out in front of everybody, too. I still have the trophy from that day, and it reminds me of all the hard things that dad helped me to do.

"When I injured my brain nothing else mattered except getting back to the way I used to be. Most people said that I could do it, but not dad. He said that you don't go forward by looking backwards. I didn't want to hear this. I just wanted him to say that I'd be like the old me.

"Now it's been eleven years since the accident, and, just like dad said, looking backward didn't help at all. He told the truth because he knew that I needed to hear it. He made me do hard things because he knew that I needed to be strong. My dad didn't talk very much about love, but he showed it to me every single day." Ollie began walking back to his seat.

Alright, that wasn't too painful, thought Cody. The kid sitting next to Cody started clapping. Everyone else started clapping. Cody clapped along.

Unfortunately, this also meant that he had to go up there, too. He hadn't prepared anything, hadn't even thought about it, but even at his worst, Cody knew how to captivate. And he did. He said all the right things, with all the right inflections, touching all the right emotions.

※※※※※※※※※※※

After the service Ollie and Cisco went back to the ranch to help Ralph set up for the reception, and Cathy stood at the back of the church greeting the guests. Sometimes, though, her eyes wandered over to Cody as he mingled with people he knew. She couldn't help it. The things he had said at the service had been so thoughtful and kind. Bob had said that Cody was coming around, and now she had seen it with her own eyes. If only Bob had been there to see it too.

A surprise guest soon presented herself and, even though it had been many years, Cathy never could have mistaken the almond shaped green eyes. It was Mariah, all grown up, and very beautiful. She wore a modest black tea party hat over wavy reddish blonde hair that had been pinned back on the sides. The hat and the hair style accented her enchanting, nymph like features. A simple black mid-cut dress with elbow sleeves complimented a slim figure. And Cathy immediately thought of Ollie, and how he had never gotten over Mariah.

"Mariah. Thank you so much for being here."

"Oh, Mrs. Buckmeyer, I had no choice. Your family meant so much to me as a child. It seems like a day doesn't go by without some special memory of the ranch popping into my head. And when I think of Mr. Buckmeyer, this is exactly what I see." She held up the memorial program that showed a particular picture of Bob. "I see him with this fluffy chef's hat, standing over his giant barbeque."

"Yes, Bob and his perfect world: fire, smoke, and red meat. Of course, if we don't have a barbeque today, I'll hear all about it when I get to heaven. I hope you can make it, Mariah. I know Ollie would love to see you." Cathy studied Mariah's response, which seemed hesitant.

She said, "Yes…I'd like to come, but I'm wondering about Ollie. After the accident I feel like I let him down."

"Not at all, dear. Ollie didn't have room for friends back then. He got put in a strange place, and it took a long time to figure it out. But I know for a fact that he has only the best memories of you."

Mariah smiled and said, "OK, I'll be there."

Cody had been back for only a few hours and with every passing minute he liked less of what he saw. At the ranch Ralph Durbin had taken charge of the reception and had taken over father's position at the barbeque. If anything, out of common courtesy, that honor should have gone to Cody, the eldest child, not to the ex-con goat roper. And the Mexican kid still didn't make sense. He ran in and out of the house like he lived there. And he had a change of clothes waiting for him in the laundry room.

Just now the kid had taken a plate of food to an empty picnic table. Cody, still curious, grabbed a beer and sat down next to him. The kid studied him out of the corner of his eye. Cody took a long, loud swig of cold beer. And then he said, "That's a good looking plate of food you got there."

The kid said something that got muffled by the food in his mouth.

"I go for the hotdog, myself," said Cody. "After a steak, two hamburgers, and three pieces of chicken. I eat a lot. Do you eat a lot?"

"Not that much," said the kid with wide eyed amazement. He wore jeans, a dress shirt with pearl snaps, and red cowboy boots.

"I sat next to you in the church. My name is Cody."

"I know who you are. You're Ollie's brother. You play baseball."

"That's right, I do."

"Uncle Bob said that you stole the most bases last year."

"Uncle Bob? Who's that?"

"That was Ollie's dad...and your dad, too, I think."

"And who's that over there?" said Cody, pointing at his mom.

"That's Aunt Cathy."

"And who's that working behind the barbeque?"

"That's my grandpa."

Now Cody understood. The door gets slammed on felons but not on their cute grandsons. That's how sly old Ralph had done it. The ranch was becoming just a bit more complicated than Cody had expected.

The kid continued working on his plate. In between mouthfuls he said, "I found a gold coin."

Cody took another long swig of beer and said, "Oh yeah. Where'd you find that?"

"Up the hill where we went looking for Jubal's treasure."

"Then you're the lucky one. I wasted half my life up on that hill. Where's the coin?

"At the bunkhouse. Grandpa doesn't like me showing it to people."

"That makes sense. Did you find anything else?"

"Yeah, we found Jubal's—"

"Cisco!"

The voice startled the kid. It was Ralph. He stood just a few feet away, looking more troubled than usual. He said, "I need you to run up to the barn and grab another box of hotdogs from the freezer."

The kid got up from the table and the two walked away.

Interesting. The grandson said he'd found gold and had been right in the middle of saying something about Jubal when grandpa abruptly cut him off. It kind of looked like dear old grandpa had something to hide.

~~~~~~~~~~~~~

Mrs. Buckmeyer scanned the crowd of people but didn't see Ollie. "I know where he is," she said. "Sometimes when it gets noisy or crowded, he likes to go to his studio."

Mariah smiled politely but didn't find this information to be particularly comforting. It reminded her of the Ollie from high school who didn't know how to cope. Mrs. Buckmeyer must have sensed the apprehension because, just before they got to the house, she turned and said, "He's easy to talk to, Mariah. He just has difficulty understanding body language and talk that is vague or indirect." And then she smiled sweetly, like a little mystery had just been solved. But, in truth, Mariah already knew this much from the websites she had visited that dealt with brain injuries.

They went through the backdoor, through the kitchen and dining room, and into the living room. The house looked just as it had when she and Ollie used to run around as kids, except for a double doorway that now led to Ollie's studio. Mrs. Buckmeyer pointed to it and then disappeared.

Mariah stepped into the doorway and saw Ollie sitting at a tilted art table. He looked like the grownup version of the sweet boy she had met at her seven-year-old birthday party which had been held at the ranch. He had the same thick blond hair with the rebellious cowlick in front and the same honest looking face, accented by his mother's blue eyes. As he concentrated on his work, a slightly strained expression crept across his face just like when they used to do homework together. Behind the desk she saw the same lanky frame that used to have to burn a massive number of calories to keep up with an overactive imagination. He looked like a handsome young man. He looked like her Ollie...and this was where she always stumbled because the brain injury had not changed Ollie's appearance. It had spared the outside and ravaged the inside, leaving behind a mismatch that Mariah had been unable to accept. She did not doubt her response if it had been solely a physical condition because a decent person doesn't drop a friend just because they look different. But what about a friend whose personality has been stolen, and they are no longer the person they seem to be? That question didn't have such an easy answer, and Mariah eventually stopped trying, preferring, instead, to get on with the business of life, which she took very seriously.

In typical fashion, Mariah had finished high school with a 4.0 grade point average, had ticked off the B.A., the MBA, middle management, and, most recently, V.P. of marketing at a Silicon Valley startup. But memories of Ollie followed each step of the way, as did a growing realization that the joy of success felt a little hollower than she had anticipated. Eventually the complicated past began to look less complicated, finally boiling down to a simple question: Had Ollie ever done anything that warranted the withdrawal of her respect and admiration? Now she stood in his doorway, and she knew the answer. He was Ollie. He had always been Ollie. And the biggest change that had come between them had not been a brain injury or passing years or diverging paths. It had been her confused understanding of what it means to be a friend.

He looked up, stared quizzically, and said, "Mariah."

"Hello, Ollie."

He slid away from the giant table and came over to where Mariah stood by the doorway. He smiled at her. Mariah knew better than to give him a hug, so she extended her hand. Ollie pushed through the hand and wrapped her up. After this greeting he stepped back, stared at her some more, and said, "I'm so happy to see you." He then whisked her across the studio to a sitting area where they sat together on a sofa.

Not wanting to neglect the sad occasion that had brought her there, Mariah said, "I'm sorry for your loss, Ollie."

Ollie didn't understand. He repeated the words to himself but didn't respond.

Good job, Mariah. And you've only been here for ten seconds, thought Mariah. She tried again. "I'm sorry about your dad."

The confusion cleared and Ollie said, "Me too. I never thought about him dying because he was always so strong. I wish I had said something really nice to him on that last day, or maybe I could've drawn him a picture of his horse. Then maybe he would've gone to sleep with a smile."

This expression of kindness caught Mariah off guard. She appreciated the love that Ollie had for his father, but it was more than that. She hadn't really talked with Ollie since way back in the cafeteria when he had been a stammering mess. The time before that, in the park, he had been downright frightening. And more recently, videos on the internet often showed that while his artistry had improved, his struggles had not. But now, for the second time that day, she had seen something that seemed to contradict this lopsided image. At the memorial Ollie had spoken to a large gathering and had been surprisingly articulate, if not a bit childlike. And now he had just shown a degree of empathy and thoughtfulness that, in her book, could have only come from a healthy intellect. She saw the impairment, no doubt, but she also saw that he essentially was all there. And this mattered to Mariah. It mattered more than she had allowed herself to admit. She had promised to accept Ollie as she found him, but she was also only human. Tears began to form. She brushed them away and said, "Maybe your dad did go to sleep with a smile. You're a good son, Ollie, and that's enough to make any father smile."

Ollie saw the tears and said, "I'm sorry I made you cry, Mariah. Let's talk about something that won't make you cry."

"That's going to be hard, Ollie. I'm crying because I'm so happy to see you."

"Then I think we're in trouble," said Ollie. They both had a good laugh and that launched them into a two hour chat that felt like two minutes. In the middle of it they made an appearance at the reception, loaded up some lunch plates, and retreated back to the privacy of Ollie's studio.

While outside, Mariah had caught a glimpse of Cody as he stood in a circle of friends. With beer in hand, he exuded coolness. Mariah wondered if he had ever graduated past the high school kegger. She clearly remembered "the date" and how he had used her to attack his own brother. Thankfully this unpleasant shadow quickly disappeared when she caught sight of another member of the Buckmeyer family. She saw Mrs. Buckmeyer tracking her and Ollie from a distance. And, in the midst of undoubtable grief, she smiled. Mariah didn't know what caused it, and she didn't care. The day was beautiful and all goodwill was welcome.

Just like in the old days, Mariah could have easily let the Saturday barbeque stretch into Saturday's supper, where the whole gang pitches in, cleans up the party mess, and then makes a meal out of the abundant leftovers. But she still hadn't visited with her parents and had a long drive the next morning up to the Silicon Valley.

As she stood up to leave, Ollie said, "I have something for you." He went to a nearby dustcover and removed it to reveal a large collection of matted artworks leaning against the wall. He pulled out the front piece, a watercolor, and gave it to Mariah. She instantly recognized the hill and the oak tree with the plank swing where she and Ollie had spent countless hours together. But she also noticed that the next picture in the stack looked like the one he had just given her.

She asked about it and Ollie said, "I've drawn it twenty-seven times, but I think this is the best one."

Ollie probably didn't know it, but this simple statement meant a lot to Mariah. It showed that Ollie still thought about those times, just as Mariah did. She looked more closely at the version he had chosen for her. It depicted the oak tree and the two-person plank swing enveloped in the radiating warmth of an orange sunset. The scene easily evoked a flood of cherished memories but it also elicited a certain wistfulness. The tree looked lonely. The swing sat empty. And the day had ended. She wondered why Ollie had allowed this sadness to creep into his drawing, but maybe she already knew the answer. Maybe the empty swing represented the last ten years of their friendship.

"Ollie," she said.

"Yes."

"Is the swing still there?"

"Yes."

"Do you think I could see it before I go?"

〰〰〰〰〰〰〰

How was it possible that Ollie Buckmeyer walks away with the prettiest girl at the party? But that's exactly what Cody had just seen. And the girl, who Cody remembered from high school, gave him a strange smirk when they passed by. Feeling like a stranger in his own home and no longer in the mood to mingle, he wandered into the house. Except for the few seconds it had taken to drop off his suitcase, Cody hadn't really checked out the old homestead, especially Ollie's new workroom, the exterior of which he had spied from the back yard. Father had built it for him.

After finding the entrance—located somewhat awkwardly off of the living room—Cody stepped through the double doorway and saw a surprisingly stylish art studio with a sitting area. The studio, on the left side of the room, had a big slanted desk, a smaller child's sized desk, a giant work table, and a number of cabinets. In the sitting area on the right, Cody saw a sofa, chairs, a coffee table, and more cabinets. Cody took it all in, but mostly he noticed the size of it. Their penny-pinching father, who considered cable TV an extravagance, had built a studio for Ollie that easily took up a quarter of the house's total square footage. In the Buckmeyer world this amounted to a tidal wave of generosity, and Cody certainly had never seen anything like it. He had gotten continual disappointment etched into his father's face and not much more.

He snooped around, opening drawers, looking into cabinets, and flipping through artwork. Ollie churned out the stuff like a copy machine and then sold them for a thousand dollars a pop. Judging from the multiple stacks leaning against the walls, Cody figured there had to be an easy seventy or eighty grand just lying around. He wandered over to the drafting table and saw the current project, a pencil drawing of some cave. The ranch had a few caves but this one didn't look familiar. On the corner of the drafting table a nice looking cell phone caught his eye. He looked closer and recognized the model, one of the best on the market, with all the bells and whistles, including a built-in camera. He picked up the phone and looked at some of the photos, typical Ollie stuff mostly, buildings, landscapes, and cityscapes. He found a picture of the cave that Ollie was currently drawing, and a picture of a cliff with a ladder which looked like it led up to the same cave, and then, interestingly, a picture of the kid posing with a coin in his hand. He also found a snapshot of his father standing by the ladder and looking unusually happy.

And then it clicked. The kid with the coin, Ralph Durbin breaking up the conversation, pictures of the cave, father's big smile. They had found something. Cody quickly emailed the pictures to himself and left the studio.

Chapter 17

The numbing whirlwind had run its course. The funeral parlor had been visited. The burial checklist had been completed. The mourners had gathered and dispersed. Bob was still dead. And Cathy waited for the grief to pull her under, to pull the breath from her lungs. She didn't want to find a rainbow on the other side of grief, like a drugstore sympathy card. She wanted to embrace the pain because it proved that Bob still lived in her heart.

After robotically putting away a pot that had been left in the strainer and wiping down a counter that had already been wiped down, she slipped into the family room and sat on the empty couch. She saw an indentation where he should have been. She saw the pile of remote controls that only he knew how to operate. She thought about the thousands of movies they had enjoyed…and how she inevitably fell asleep on his shoulder.

After a while Cody came in and the trance ended too early. But Cathy didn't mind. Cody had made peace with the world and she looked upon that as a big going away present for her husband. The last worry, the one that had dominated their midnight whispers for the last five years, had been laid to rest right alongside her husband.

He sat next to her and they quietly talked about nothing in particular, the memorial service, the beautiful things he had said about his father, the different people they had seen at the reception. Then Cody changed the subject. He said, "Mother, I need to talk with you about something."

"OK."

"I'm thinking about coming back to the ranch. You need someone to run this place, and I'd like to do it for you."

These words surprised Cathy because Cody had never shown any interest in becoming a rancher. Perhaps the emotion of the day had gotten to him. She said, "That means a lot to me, Cody, but I know how much you love baseball, and it would be selfish to take that away from you."

"I know, and I never thought I'd say this, but today I realized that I love the ranch more than I ever knew."

"And it will always be here for you. But now you have the other thing that you love. And you're doing so well. You're so close to the top."

"Well...that's the other thing...I got cut."

"What? Cody! What happened?"

"The game has changed. When I got drafted, they wanted speed and batting average from the middle infield, so I fit the mold. But now everyone wants a power hitting shortstop. I'm the odd man out, and my agent hasn't found anything else, except for maybe South America. But, to tell the truth, today when I saw you and Ollie, I realized that it doesn't even matter. I'm ok with it."

Cathy didn't understand. Bob knew baseball inside and out, and if there had been a fundamental change such as this, he surely would have said something. But, on the other hand,

Cody didn't easily admit defeat, yet here he sat, as humble and honest as Cathy had ever seen. He at least deserved to be heard out. "But how would it work, Cody? You don't know anything about ranching."

"Ranching is only one possibility. You know you're sitting on land that is selling for twenty thousand dollars an acre? That's a lot of money. Maybe ranching doesn't make sense anymore."

Cathy wondered how her son knew about local land values but then figured that someone at the reception must have said something. She said, "I know. Your dad and I went round and round about that, but now things are different because…." She stopped short just before blurting the news about Ollie owning part of the ranch. She wanted to tell Cody, but just now the timing didn't feel right. She scrambled to recover, "…because…uh…I love the ranch and…now, with your father's life insurance, we'll have more than enough money to keep the place going."

"OK. Then maybe Durbin can teach me the ropes for a few months."

"It takes longer than that, Cody. And you know how it is between you and Ralph. If I tried to put him in that position, I think he would leave."

"Mother, I don't mean to sound cold, but I don't understand what's going on around here. That guy is a convicted murderer who got a job that he didn't deserve at a time when no one else would have ever hired him. He was a charity project and it wasn't supposed to become anything more than that."

"But it has, Cody. Your father helped Ralph, that's true, but Ralph also helped your father."

"But he's not your son."

"Of course, Cody, I know that, but it's not that easy. And now Cisco is here and that makes it even more complicated."

"I need this, mother. I failed at the one thing that dad wanted for me. And I never fixed things with him like I should have, and now it's too late. I have to live with that every day. But if I come back and take care of this place, he'll know that I'm sorry...and that I love him." He began to cry.

"Oh, Cody, he knew all that. And he didn't hold anything against you. He bragged about you every day. You just got unlucky, that's all. He died too soon and you didn't get a chance to talk. It's not anybody's fault." She gave him a hug.

Cody wiped away the tears and said, "I guess all this has been eating at me for a while."

"Well, that's got to stop. And don't you worry. I'll figure out what to do about Ralph. Just give me some time. Okay?"

"OK. I just want to be here for you, mom, that's all," said Cody, as he stood up.

"I know you do, Cody."

He started to leave, but when he got to the door he turned and said, "Oh, there was something else. Cisco said something about a gold coin. What's that all about?"

Cathy hesitated for just a moment before saying, "Oh that silly boy. He was dying of boredom so I planted some coins in the ground—like I used to do for you and Ollie—and now he can't stop talking about it. That's all it is." She smiled weakly.

"Oh," said Cody.

And then he left, leaving Cathy to wonder at the lie she had just told...and at her own fickleness. Just moments before she had been admiring Cody's growth and maturity, and then, out of the blue, she felt the need to lie to him about a stupid coin. She didn't understand it, and she didn't like it. Her son deserved better.

Sleep didn't come easily that night for Cathy. As she lay on her side of the empty bed, a handful of worries held her captive. The lie still bothered her but so did the rest of the conversation. Cody wanted to run the ranch, but this meant taking the job from Ralph and asking him to train the one who had taken his job. This sounded like a good way to lose a key employee. And then there was a matter of trust. She thought back many years to the terrible fight that she and Bob had had when he brought Ralph home from prison to live at the ranch. She wanted to murder both of them that night, but to this day she still remembered something her husband had said: I trust Ralph with my life, and you can too. And now, all these years later, Cathy knew that Bob had been right. She did trust Ralph, even more than she trusted her own son.

But that still didn't solve any problems because Ralph had proven himself only because he had been given a second chance. Didn't her son deserve the same kindness? He had just lost his father *and* the career to which he had devoted his life—all in the space of just a few weeks. If he didn't get a lifeline soon, he might never recover. Cathy owed it to him. It didn't make sense. In fact, it looked foolish, but she had to do it.

But then her mind circled back around and she thought about the collateral damage that came with this mess, to Ralph trying to find work as a convicted felon, and especially to little Cisco. He had lost everything, but by God's grace the ranch had been there to catch him. It broke Cathy's heart to even think about taking it away from Cisco. And yet, Cody had to come first.

For all of the sleeplessness, Cathy got nothing but bad answers to hard questions. And she wasn't done. Another question had been gnawing at her since the day Bob had died: Why did he get drunk? His lapses happened so infrequently. And those few days before his death had been so absolutely wonderful. He had said it himself. Something must have happened on Sunday night after they got back, after he went into his office.

The nightstand clock read two a.m. Not in the mood to clock watch for three hours, Cathy got up, put on slippers and a robe, and went out to the barn and into Bob's office. After turning on the light she immediately saw one of Bob's baseball magazines on his desk, opened, resting face down. *That's it,* she thought, *it's just what Cody said. The game had changed and Bob had read about it in the magazine.* She flipped over the magazine, saw Cody's picture, and, just like her husband, everything came crashing down. But, unlike her husband, she didn't feel just the weight of her own sadness, she also felt Bob's. She realized that he had not died with the peaceful knowledge that Cody had finally turned the corner, as she had assumed. Just the opposite. He had died with a broken heart. Maybe he had died *because* of a broken heart.

Ralph saddled up Gomer and began the long ride up the hill. Two hours later, as he approached the base of the cliff, Ralph pulled up the horse and stared at the old campsite. Bob had just been there, telling his story at the campfire. Everyone had been so happy. Now he was gone and that happiness felt like a faded picture in a forgotten drawer.

Ralph looked over at the cliff with the ladder and searched for any signs of disturbance. He didn't see anything. He dismounted and covered the last thirty yards by foot, still carefully looking for signs of recent human activity. He climbed the ladder, searched the cave, and found everything just as they had left it, including the ropes and safety harnesses that had been left behind.

Ralph didn't care about the gold. In every way he already had more than he deserved. And he had it because of Bob and Cathy. If Cathy never wanted to set foot in that cave again, he didn't care. If she wanted to mount an expedition tomorrow, he'd be right there with her. But for now, until she told him otherwise, he had a duty to protect her interest.

While standing at the base of the ladder, he pulled three wooden matchsticks from his pocket. He broke off the flammable bulbs and discarded them. He then wedged the remaining sticks into three separate rungs of the ladder in a manner so that the exposed part only stuck out by half an inch. Now anyone who tried to climb the ladder would unknowingly leave behind the evidence of a broken matchstick.

Ralph didn't lay this trap for just anybody. He laid it for somebody who had already shown himself to be a thief. And until this person proved otherwise, that's exactly how Ralph intended to treat him.

On the way back down the hill Ralph's mobile phone rang. The annoying contraptions had replaced the clunky and annoying shortwave radios that they used to carry, so it had probably been an upgrade, but Ralph still didn't like them. He pulled it out of the saddlebag and answered the call. It was Cathy. She said that they needed to talk, but she preferred to do it in person. Her words sounded clipped and strangely formal. They set up a meeting for later that afternoon.

⚞⚞⚞⚞⚞⚞⚞⚞⚞⚞⚞

Cody had just pulled his old enduro motorcycle out of the barn when Ralph Durbin rode into the stable and started untacking his horse. The guy didn't have a clue, and Cody couldn't resist the temptation, so he wiped the oily grime off his hands and strolled over. Ralph, always on guard, stood on the other side of the horse and tracked Cody's approach.

"Hey Durbin."

Ralph nodded and continued loosening the cinch. His old man's face looked like a bad case of wood rot.

"I'm trying to fire up my old bike. Do you know where we keep the starter fluid?"

"Yeah, there's some in the cabinet by the compressor."

"Thanks, appreciate it—oh, just so you know, I'll be taking over my dad's job—to help my mom out, you know—so she's probably going to be talking with you pretty soon."

The watery eyes looked Cody up and down, but he didn't say anything. Cody said, "I'm just trying to give you a heads-up, Durbin, that's all."

"Yeah, your mom called. We're meeting this afternoon, but she didn't say what it's about."

"Now you know," said Cody matter-of-factly. "Like I said, just giving you a heads up. Don't want you to get caught off guard by the changes I'll be making."

Ralph stared. Cody smiled pleasantly.

※※※※※※※※※※※

In the late afternoon, several hours after Cody sprang the news, Ralph sat rigidly on the living room couch and waited for his meeting with Cathy. When she had called that morning to set up the meeting, the tension in her voice had puzzled him. Now he understood perfectly, and it scared the crap out of him. He had an axe hanging over his head, a set of skills that nobody needed, and a six-year-old grandson to take care of. And he was an ex-con with nothing in the bank. The old Ralph would have popped a beer and laughed it off. The new Ralph cursed his stupidity for not being more prepared.

He heard Cody's sports car pull into the driveway. A minute later the front door opened and Cody breezed into the house. Ralph watched from the living room. Cody had played it perfectly and, as he looked into the entryway mirror, had that certain air of self-assurance to prove it. He strolled into the living room, said, "Hey Durbin," and plopped down on the other couch.

"Hello, Cody."

Cathy came into the room a few seconds later and, if the pain on her face meant anything, she had bad news to deliver. Over the last ten years Ralph had seen Cathy in almost every light, but he had never seen this kind of anguish. Her blue eyes swam in pools of bloodshot sadness and her shoulders slumped in total defeat. And Ralph knew that no matter what his problems might be, he had to make it easy for her. He owed her that much, and a great deal more.

She pulled a side chair into position and sat down, with Cody to her left and Ralph to her right. She kept her eyes averted until she started speaking. Then she looked at Ralph and said, "Before we talk about anything else, I need to say something to you, Ralph. For the last ten years, I didn't trust you, and I didn't like you. And at every turn I made sure that you knew it. But I was wrong, and you proved it, not with words or promises, but by the way you lived your life. I owe you apology, Ralph, and I hope that you will accept it."

"No, Cathy, you don't owe anything because you had good reasons to feel the way you did. But I thank you just the same. It means a lot to me," said Ralph with sincerity, even though he had a feeling that her kind words had been part of a Dear John termination that would now follow.

But it didn't. Instead, Cathy turned to Cody and said, "I'm sorry, Cody, you're not ready to run the ranch."

"What! What are you talking about?"

"I saw the article in the baseball magazine. You might love the ranch, but you're here because you have nowhere else to go."

"No way. With a halfway decent lawyer, I could be back in baseball by next season. I'm here because I want to help you."

"Then why didn't you tell me the whole story?"

"There's nothing to tell. That article is bullshit, and I assumed that you'd think better of me and want to hear what I have to say. But I guess I was an idiot, wasn't I?"

"Cody, I love you and will do everything I can to help, but you always have an explanation for the trouble you cause. I don't want to hear your explanations. I want to see it in your life. This is still your home, and there's a job here anytime you want it, just not the job you want this time. I'm sorry." She then turned to Ralph and said, "I need a ranch foreman, Ralph, and I'm hoping you'll take the job."

Ralph took the job, and Cody stormed out of the meeting, but not before smashing a chair to pieces.

※※※※※※※※

Cody sped down the two-lane highway a full thirty miles over the speed limit and didn't care if he got a ticket or, even better, if he crashed and died. That's what she deserved for her betrayal, to be eternally saddled with guilt and remorse. This juvenile fantasy provided some comfort but the relief quickly disappeared as the rage reasserted itself and the ambush played over and over in his mind. He pushed on the accelerator, the turbocharger spooled up, and the Viper whipped up a storm of dust.

She had chosen a lowlife scum over her own son. And then she had the nerve to dress it up with phony professions of love. The screaming muscle car topped out at the redline, and Cody wanted more. If only it had been fueled by hatred.

He flew fast and far and never wanted to return. But even as he left his family in the dust, some small thread held him back. A thread of opportunity tugged on his mind. It was that coin in the photograph. The kid had called it a gold coin, mother had called it a worthless nothing, and the difference between these two stories might make all the difference in the world. He eased up on the gas pedal and the car slowed. His anger slowly subsided and shrewd commonsense rose back to the top. If they had found one coin, who's to say that they hadn't found all the coins, and Cody had just walked out on his fair share of the treasure? Or, at the very least, maybe the one coin had put them hot on the trail of all the others?

A half hour later the sports car drove tamely back up the dirt road, but it didn't go all the way up to the house. It veered to the left and took the bumpy road up to the bunkhouse where, from a hundred yards out, Cody didn't see Ralph's truck. He continued past the bunkhouse and parked the car in a secluded spot behind a stand of deer weed. He then walked back down to the cabin, all the while listening for sounds of life. He heard nothing. He knocked on the door. No one answered. He pushed his way into the unlocked home, surveyed the place, and quickly found his way to the kid's dresser. In the top drawer he found a little decorative wooden box. He opened the lid and found the coin—a gold coin—easily identifiable because it looked just like the gold coins hidden in his bedroom, the ones he had stolen back in high school.

A good athlete always knows where he's at in the game. He knows if there is one out and he has to play shallow, or two outs and he can play deep. He always knows the score, and Cody knew the score at Buck Ranch. His own mother had lied to him. And she had lied for a reason. Now he needed to figure out that reason, and he needed to do it while attracting as little attention as possible.

He apologized to both his mother and Ralph that very hour. He didn't agree to work for the man because that wouldn't have been believable, but he got himself back into the game.

A few days later he cornered Ollie and, in five seconds flat, figured out that the treasure had not yet been found. Father had been close, maybe even real close, but then he died and everything stopped. Cody didn't find out any information about the cave, but that didn't matter because he had the photos from Ollie's phone, and he recognized the strange ribbon of rock shown in the photos. He knew exactly where to start looking.

<hr/>

Ralph accepted the apology but didn't believe it. Something about the way Cody had gone from violent rage to fuzzy bunny begging forgiveness in barely an hour didn't sit right. It felt psycho. The next morning, he took the revolver from the office safe and started carrying it wherever he went on the ranch. He just didn't trust the guy.

Chapter 18

Cisco had never met his grandmother, but she still felt like a real grandma because of all the pictures and stories that his mom used to share. They had been happy stories, but Cisco knew that there had been a sad one, too. One sleepless night, after the owls and crickets had gone to sleep, Cisco asked his grandpa about that story.

"Grandpa, are you awake?"

"Yes."

"Can you tell me about Grandma Durbin?"

"What do you want to know?"

"What happened to her?"

"She died, Cisco."

"How did she die?"

"Because of something I did."

"Is that how come you went to jail?"

"Yes."

"But didn't you love grandma Durbin?"

"Yes."

"Then how come she died?"

"You deserve to know the answer to that, Cisco, but now isn't the right time because you're too young to hear it, and it would be hard to understand. I can tell you some things, though. I drank too much beer back then, that's for sure.

And that can make a person do bad things. And I was selfish, too. That's probably the biggest thing really. Instead of thinking about your grandmother and your mother like I should have, I only thought about myself."

"Do you miss grandma Durbin?"

"Yes."

"I miss my mom, too, but I don't think about her as much as I used to."

"That's Ok, Cisco, that's kind of how it works. You loved her, and she knew it, and that's the important thing."

"Ok," said Cisco. And then he started to fall asleep, but Grandpa said something else.

"Cisco, I need to tell you something. I did bad things, but now I try to do better. I try to think about the people I love. And do you know who I think about the most?"

"Who?"

"I think about you."

"You do?"

"Yep."

"I think about you too, grandpa."

∞∞∞∞∞∞∞∞

In the course of his troubled life, Ralph had received hundreds of letters from lawyers, but none of them hit harder than the one he got just a few weeks after Bob's death. From a lawyer in San Bernardino, it contained his daughter's death certificate. Under cause of death it said, "HIV disease resulting in multiple infections." The envelope also contained her last will and testament, naming Ralph as Cisco's legal guardian, and a cover letter from the lawyer telling Ralph that his guardianship needed to go before the court, but that he didn't expect any problems getting it approved.

It was now safe to say that death had taken an unusually firm grip on Ralph's life. His best friend had died suddenly and unexpectedly. His daughter had been taken decades too early and had died with a heart still full of hatred, taking a father's dream of forgiveness into the grave with her. But death also consumed Ralph for another reason. He wondered about his own death and worried about what it might mean for Cisco. The boy didn't have any family to speak of. He didn't have money or a good name. In all likelihood Cisco's safety net consisted of an overworked social worker and a crapshoot foster home. And that didn't cut it.

Chapter 19

The boss had a question, and Mariah had an answer. And it was a good one. It also happened to be calculated and self-serving—just like the good old days—but she couldn't help herself. She said, "Have you heard of Ollie Buckmeyer?"

"Ollie Who?" asked Vijay Kaur, founder and CEO of Book It Now, Inc. which provided scheduling and reservation software for a variety of businesses, including some major airlines and hotels. Just now the CEO, along with the director of marketing, had come into Mariah's office for an impromptu meeting. They wanted ideas on how to draw attention to their little guppy of a company that swam in the same Silicon Valley fish tank as some of the biggest companies in the world.

"He draws giant skylines. Several companies have used him for their promotions," said Mariah.

"Yeah…I saw him on TV," said Judy, the director of marketing. "He's a…what do you call it…a savant. It's really pretty incredible. He goes up in a helicopter for thirty minutes, memorizes what he sees, and then for the next week everyone gets to watch him create a giant drawing of your city's skyline. A Japanese geothermal company brought him in to do Tokyo and it turned into a pretty big deal."

Mariah kept the momentum going. "And the nice thing is that it turns into a community event so not only do we build brand awareness as the sponsor of the event, but we also foster community pride. And then you have the national and international exposure from the internet. He's completed five of these projects and each of the online videos has over three million views."

Now a faint smile started to form on the CEO's face. Mariah continued, "Maybe we could fly him North to South along the bay. We've got Golden Gate Bridge, the financial district, Candlestick, the airport, Foster City Canals, Bair Island, Redwood Shores, and Dumbarton Bridge. Then we bring him back to a giant tent set up right here on Redwood Shores Parkway. We can make it fun, like a carnival, with street food, and attractions for the kids. We'll show the big boys how to run a promotion."

"I like it. How much does it cost?" asked Vijay.

"I'll find out. He's a friend of mine…uh…which I…uh…probably should've mentioned earlier…."

The bosses stared at Mariah. Then Vijay said, "I still like it. Let me know what you find out."

<hr/>

Cathy heard voices in the studio. She poked her head through the doorway and saw Ollie sitting behind his desk with Ralph facing him in a businesslike manner from a chair that had been pulled up from the sitting area. She said, "Hi boys." And they returned the greeting, but Cathy got the impression that she had just walked in on more than a casual conversation. She said, "I'm sorry, I didn't mean to interrupt."

"Oh no, you're alright, Cathy. I was just leaving," said Ralph. He returned the chair to the sitting area, picked up his black cowboy hat from a nearby table, and fiddled with it for a few seconds before saying, "Like I said, Ollie, it's just an idea…just something to think about."

"I think it's a good thing to think about," said Ollie.

"Yeah, I think so too," said Ralph, smiling strangely. And then he left.

Now Cathy's curiosity had been piqued. She hovered, hoping to glean some information, but Ollie went back to work. Cathy said, "I don't usually see Ralph here at this time of day. He must have had something important to say."

"Yeah, I guess so," said Ollie, without looking up.

"Nothing bad, I hope."

"No, nothing bad."

"Something good then?"

"Mother, sometimes I just like to think about things and not talk about them."

"Oh. Ok. Sorry." And then she left, feeling hurt and confused. Ollie had never shut her out like that.

Over the following weeks Ollie and Ralph had more meetings. And on at least two separate occasions Ralph came to the house with a file folder tucked under his arm, and then the two of them drove off together. Of course, Cathy pried, quietly, and got nothing from Ollie and a vague cliché from Ralph about Ollie growing up and needing some space.

A few months after all of this began, Ollie announced that he had accepted an out-of-town commission that had just popped up in the Bay Area, and that he planned to make the trip without Cathy. And then, in the same breath, he said that Cisco would be going with him. Cathy didn't like the idea but, once again, Ollie and Ralph seemed to have everything all worked out.

Intellectually, Cathy knew that Ollie deserved the privacy of a twenty-three-year-old adult, but he had never cared about it, and those boundaries had never been part of their relationship. But now, practically overnight, it seemed that Ollie had changed his mind.

∾∾∾∾∾∾∾∾∾∾∾

A fashionable new hairstyle had been procured, and a slinky little black dress had been added to the wardrobe. The calendar had been cleared, and nighttime entertainment had been lined up, including orchestra seating for *La Bohème* at the Curran Theatre and a very special surprise at the end of the week. Mariah felt good. She stood under the giant arched entryway to the Garden Court Hotel in Palo Alto, eager to see what possibilities the upcoming week might reveal. Then the limousine pulled up, and out popped a little kid carrying a *Winnie the Pooh* suitcase.

Transfixed by the unexpected sight, Mariah barely noticed when Ollie gave her a hug and said, "This is Cisco. He's going to be my helper this week."

The boy, still clutching his suitcase, stared at Mariah. She mumbled a greeting, but her mind had disconnected. Ollie had brought a child...and not a self-sustaining kind of child either. He brought the kind that needs hand holding and bedtime stories and little bags filled with fish crackers.

222

Mariah's plans sometimes fell flat. She knew it. And when her ambitious calculations misfired, she knew how to gracefully accept the consequences. But this was something else. If Ollie had doubts about their relationship, he only had to say it. He didn't need to bring a child for protection. Now he had ruined all of her plans.

She could have easily pulled Ollie aside and talked it out, but she chose to indulge her hurt feelings instead. She chose the cold shoulder. When Ollie and Cisco got back from dropping off their luggage in their suite, Mariah met them with a stony face and a disposition that barely qualified as socially acceptable. On the ride over to the campus to inspect the tent, she ignored Ollie's small talk and only answered questions that pertained to the event. And she felt satisfied with the chill that radiated from her affronted being. Cisco certainly seemed to feel it, judging by the uneasy glances that he repeatedly cast in her direction. Ollie, on the other hand, happily chatted away and looked out the window. So, when they got to the tent, and Ollie asked about replacing the swivel chair with a taller one, Mariah added sarcasm to the campaign. She said, "Yes, we can do that. Or maybe you can just borrow a booster seat from Cisco." Ollie laughed. And so did Cisco. They loved the joke. Her plan obviously wasn't working.

An hour later, after arriving at a bustling, noisy restaurant, a couple of things happened and Mariah began to understand the situation a little more clearly. They had just been seated when she heard a distinct low pitched, monotone humming sound. It came from Ollie, who sat next to her in the booth. Then, just a few seconds later, the waiter filled their water glasses and Ollie, still quietly humming, took an index card from his shirt pocket, wiped both sides of it with a napkin, and placed it over the top of the water glass. And that's when Mariah woke up because savantism, for all its beauty and awe, is always accompanied by a downside, most often in the form of autism or characteristics of autism. One such characteristic is the inability to understand social cues and body language. And yet Mariah, who knew better, had chosen to deal with her hurt feelings with nothing but social cues and body language. The humming and the business with the water glass related to other common characteristics, and had been the clues that nudged Mariah back to reality. The humming, a soothing behavior, had started when Ollie became anxious in the crowded restaurant. And the index card, which had been ready and waiting in his pocket, seemed to be part of a routine. Ollie apparently had a water glass routine. And he probably had others.

Mariah had discovered the cause of the glitch in their communication but, more importantly, she had also discovered a myopia that had affected her view of the relationship. She had been so caught up in the discovery of Ollie's progress, and in the joy of having him back in her life, that she had neglected to open her eyes to the whole picture. But now it had come into focus. She had begun to see limitations. It made her feel sad to think about it, but she naturally had to wonder how those limitations might affect their relationship. Maybe it wasn't such a bad idea to take a step back from the candlelight and soft music and see how things looked after a week of no expectations. Thankfully, nothing special had been planned for that abbreviated first day.

Early the next morning she hitched a ride in the limo before it went to the hotel. Besides wanting to make sure that the event got off to a smooth start, she also wanted to push the restart button with Ollie. She wanted to communicate in ways that he understood. As the car pulled up, she saw him standing alone under the archway with his trusty artist's case in hand. He got into the car and, before Mariah had a chance to say a word, he said, "I'm sorry I made you mad, Mariah. I hope you'll tell me what I did so that I can make it better."

"How do you know that I was mad?"

"Cisco told me."

Mariah busted out laughing. Ollie looked confused. She gave him a hug and said, "You know, I think you're pretty wonderful."

The driver took them to the airport for the skyline flight across the Bay, and they had a nice conversation along the way. Mariah told Ollie exactly what had made her mad. And he told her all about Cisco, and how he had come to live at the ranch, and how his mom had just died, and he didn't have a father. After hearing all of this, Mariah's anger from the previous night began to look rather small. And the cause of it turned out to be a nonevent because Ollie had arranged childcare through the hotel for the entire week, and they ended up having plenty of time together, including all the rides to and from the event and a week's worth of leisurely lunches. In the evening Cisco joined them, and the ad hoc family did fun things up and down the San Francisco Peninsula.

꧁꧂

Ollie and Cisco had something to talk about—part of the same discussion that Ralph had started several months earlier—and thanks to the door-to-door limousine service provided by Mariah's employer, the conversation had gotten off to a good start during the drive up north and continued on and off throughout the week. And they talked about other things, too, including Mariah, a topic on which Cisco didn't feel bashful about giving advice.

One night after a visit to Paramount's Great America amusement park, the two exhausted travelers lay in their beds and made plans for the next day, which happened to be the final day of the event.

"Do you want to come to the tent tomorrow to see me finish the drawing? I'll be busy working, but Mariah will be there," said Ollie.

"OK."

"But tomorrow night you'll be back here with childcare because I'd like to spend some time alone with Mariah. Sometimes grownups like to do that."

"I know," said Cisco. And then he giggled mischievously and said, "Are you going to tell her you love her?"

"I don't know. Maybe."

"I think you should. My mom used to watch movies where the man tells the lady that he loves her like a million times and then she starts crying. And then he takes off his shirt and shows her his muscles and she cries some more. It's pretty icky but I think you have to do it. It's like a rule or something."

Ollie laughed, and for some reason the funny thing made him think of a question. He said, "Cisco, is it better to have a friend or a father?"

"Um…maybe a father, 'cause sometimes he can be your friend and then you get to have two things."

"That makes sense. Goodnight, Cisco."

"Goodnight, Ollie."

❊❊❊❊❊❊❊❊❊❊❊❊❊❊❊

After Cisco had spent the day bouncing and crawling and sliding his way through the assortment of kid's attractions, and after he had eaten two snow cones, a hotdog, and an unknown quantity of popcorn, he and Mariah took their seats in the tent to watch Ollie finish the drawing. The crowds had been steadily growing throughout the week and now, thanks to an especially captivating segment from the previous night on one of the local news programs, the five hundred seats in the tent didn't come close to being enough for the grand finale.

In the segment the reporter had shown a photograph of the Golden Gate Bridge that had been taken at the exact moment when Ollie's helicopter flew past. She counted out a total of eleven big rigs in the photo. She then showed that section of Ollie's drawing, which had already been completed, and counted the same eleven big rigs, all of them in the same spots as in the photo. Mariah had heard people talking about it all day. She managed to find space for the surging crowd by removing the back and side panels of the tent and creating a large standing room only section.

When Ollie got to the very edge of the drawing, and had only the smallest sliver to go, the already lively crowd became even more energized, including Cisco. He stood on his seat and watched every pen stroke. And when Ollie finished the drawing, and signed his name with a flourish, nobody cheered louder than little Cisco. Mariah gave him the VIP treatment by ushering him up to the stage to greet his friend. Ollie's face lit up, he picked up Cisco, and made him part of the celebration.

Mariah's boss, with microphone in hand, pulled Ollie to center stage to offer his congratulations, and probably get in a few plugs for his company as well. After this Ollie had some interviews lined up so Mariah used the time to escort Cisco back to the hotel and into the evening childcare program. Of course, Cisco, who hadn't slowed down all day, fell asleep before the car turned out of the parking lot. She looked down at his face, mouth still stained pink from the last snow cone, and thought about how all her plans had been thrown out the window, and the week had still turned out pretty great. And it wasn't over yet. They still had one night left, and Ollie had taken charge of it.

When she got back to the tent about an hour later, Ollie had just finished the last interview, and the place had mostly cleared out. He smiled at her, said he had a surprise, and herded her straight back into the car. This time, instead of sitting on the opposite seat, he sat next to her. The car pulled away and Ollie, still smiling, opened his art case and took out a neatly folded hotel hand towel. He held it up and said, "I hope I do this right. I watched a video on my laptop."

He opened the roll top refreshment center and retrieved a bottle of champagne that had been chilling in a sunken bucket of ice. After unwinding the wire cage, he placed the towel over the top of the bottle, popped the champagne, and poured their glasses.

"What a nice surprise. Thank you, Ollie," said Mariah.

She started to take a drink, but Ollie held up his hand and said, "Not yet. The video said that I can make a toast if I want to, and I want to." He held up his glass and said, "Let's have more tomorrows just like today." He gently touched his glass to hers and said, "Just like today."

This little toast meant so much to Mariah because things like that didn't come easily to Ollie, but he had cared enough to figure it out. And if this had been the extent of their evening, it would have been more than enough. But it wasn't because after two glasses of champagne, the limousine entered the little wine country town of Yountville and pulled into the parking lot of The French Laundry. It took a few seconds before Mariah connected the dots. Somehow Ollie had found out about her big surprise—which she had cancelled—and had turned it into his big surprise. She said, "How did you know?"

"Your boss. He told me how much you had been looking forward to it."

Mariah didn't have words for this thoughtfulness, but she did have something else. She kissed Ollie. And Ollie kissed her back. Together they cautiously strayed from the boundary of mere friendship.

A few wonderful minutes later, just as they were about to enter the restaurant, Mariah realized something important.

She grabbed Ollie's arm, pulled him to a stop, and said, "Ollie, you know the food is going to be different than what you're used to, right?"

He smiled innocently, pulled something from his jacket pocket, and said, "That's Ok. I have this just in case." He held a PB&J, halved and neatly tucked into a sandwich bag.

Mariah had begun the week under a romantic spell. She broke the spell by standing the new Ollie right next to Ollie of her memories. The new Ollie still liked people even though they confused him. He still liked conversation even though he easily got lost. And, most noticeable of all, the new Ollie had routines. They told him when to get up in the morning, what to wear, what to eat, what utensils to eat it with, and how many ice cubes to put in the water. They started in the morning and didn't stop until he closed his eyes at night and went to sleep. Mariah got a close look at this one day when she had been delayed for their lunch date. She got to the tent and found Ollie paralyzed by anxiety. He stood in the middle of the stage, humming loudly, and staring catatonically at the entrance to the tent, oblivious of how strange he looked to the people in the audience. When he saw Mariah, his face brightened and his body relaxed, ready to be swept back up into the safety of his routine. She had only been ten minutes late.

Mariah had seen the challenges. They hovered over the relationship, and she didn't know the answers. But she did know that she loved Ollie Buckmeyer.

Phineas Mardikali barely remembered being anything except old. That's how long it had been. For the last fifteen years of his career, he had been the archetypical ancient professor who is seen shuffling across most every university campus in the land, resuscitated daily by the youthful vitality that whizzes around at a million miles per hour. But five years ago, even that failed to get him going, and he had no choice. He retired and moved up to Palo Alto to live with his younger sister. He became a kept old geezer.

Other than the loss of dignity that this new station naturally bestowed, Phineas also suffered in other ways because while his sister, Berenice, had the heart of a saint, she also had a certain zealotry for his welfare. She threw out the walking stick without even the pretense of debate, and put Phineas into a walker, complete with tennis ball pegs and a little seat to rescue him during the arduous journey to the mailbox.

There are setbacks in life, but few of them rival the fall from the walking stick to the walker. A good walking stick has style. They are ornate and convey artistry. They can be used as a weapon or a dignified prop. You can raise it to the air and say things like "Tallyho!" or "To the manor!" or "Bring me my brandy you scallywag!" Try doing that with your walker and all you'll get is a cozy seat by the fire and a nice bowl of mush. Walking sticks are also used to transport contraband such as cigars and whiskey and daggers. What do you carry in the walker except for maybe a spare diaper or a blanket, or some other token of your decline?

And then, unless you opt to go straight to the grave, the next stop is the electric scooter, which, comparatively speaking, isn't half as traumatic as the walker because you go faster and have the power of the motor to mask your feebleness. And this is where Phineas now found himself. He had graduated to the senior scooter. And, besides that upgrade, he also had to admit that even though Berenice hovered like a goose, she also treated him, a mere brother, like an honored guest. On this beautiful summer evening in 2002 she had surpassed even her own generosity, and had brought the two of them to The French Laundry.

The meal had begun with the iconic salmon tartare cornets. Both Phineas and Berenice had artistic backgrounds and enjoyed nothing more than experiencing and talking about culture and art, and these imaginative little cornets promised to be the launching pad for a long evening of inspiring conversation. But then something happened that threatened that prospect: Phineas began to cry.

Admittedly, it didn't take much these days to get the tears flowing, but he usually knew better than to allow such a thing in front of his sister because it inevitably sent her protective propensities into overdrive. It made her ask questions like an ER doctor. And the answers didn't matter because she always bumped him up the triage hierarchy, and started talking about ambulances and how she had graduated at the top of her Red Cross CPR class. The tears could have been caused by a beautiful sunset and she'd be putting gel on the paddles.

And this time her eagle eye had caught the tear before it had barely formed.

"What's wrong Phin? Do you need a pill? Is something stuck? Can you breathe? If you can't breathe, I want you to tap your finger three times."

Phineas partially composed himself and said, "I can breathe, Bee. I'm ok, really."

"Good. Tell me your symptoms and I'll tell you if you are ok or not. Is it your heart?"

"No, Bee, I don't have any symptoms."

"I'm calling an ambulance." She pulled a phone from her purse.

"No, please. It's nothing. I just saw one of my students, that's all."

She looked him over for a moment, and then surveyed the dining room. Her three-alarm countenance relaxed. She nodded toward a young couple that had been seated just a few minutes before. Phineas nodded back.

"Do you want to tell me about it?"

"I told you, it's nothing...it's just that I was supposed to be the teacher but sometimes they taught me more than I taught them."

"Yes, Phin...I know. Tell me about this one, won't you?"

She had heard it before, and now Phineas told her again. He wanted to hear the words, too, even if they came from his own broken voice. "That boy faced terrible obstacles but he had a weapon that I didn't understand. He had his mind. He showed me every day what a beautiful gift it is. He taught me that if you have your mind, you have something to live for. And when...." His words became choked and the tears flowed freely. "And when he walked in with that young woman, holding hands and looking so happy, I remembered all of it. I remembered the lesson that I had foolishly forgotten. That's all. See, I told you it was nothing."

"I understand, dear. It's not easy being human. Wouldn't it be so much better if we were just robots?"

Phineas laughed through the last of his tears and said, "Most definitely, Bee, most definitely." And then he took a deep breath and resolved to get the evening back to where it belonged—starting with a particularly grand idea. He said, "I'm going to send a nice bottle over to that fine young couple. What do you think of that?"

"I think it's going to cost a fortune, is what I think."

"Good. Anything less would be an insult."

When the bottle arrived, the young man looked around until his eyes locked on to his old professor. He quickly rose from the table, crossed the room, and the two old friends shared a beautiful reunion. This time the tears flowed all around.

Chapter 20

Ralph didn't like keeping secrets from Cathy, but he understood the reason behind it: Ollie wanted to take charge of his life. Everyone has to fly the coop some time but, because of the accident, Ollie had never gotten the chance. He had needed his parents too much. Now, a few years late, he had fixed this lopsided balance in a big way. Just the same, Ralph wished that he hadn't been caught in the middle. The good news, though, was that Ollie had put down his boundaries and everything would soon be getting back to normal.

And that's what Ralph expected in late summer 2002 when the family got together for Friday night pizza. Everyone at the table seemed to be in good spirits. Ollie and Cisco had had a great trip. Cathy had everyone back under her wing. Cody sat cordially, showing no outward signs of resentment. And Ralph, for his part, couldn't have been more content. He honestly had hope for the future, especially Cisco's future.

Ollie had everything in hand, and so far, he had done it in a way that sidestepped the unnecessary hand wringing. Instead of making a big announcement and being buried by fear and second guesses, he decided to lure his mother to the adoption hearing under the pretense of a lunch date. He wanted the judge to do the talking, so to speak. At the very least Cathy would have time during the hearing to think about things and maybe hear the answers to some of her questions. It sounded like a solid plan. Unfortunately, when one of the conspirators is six years old, even the best plan can quickly fall apart. In this case it crumbled before the second slice of pizza, just after Cisco told everyone about the fun things that he and Ollie and Mariah had done up in the Bay Area.

Cathy, who seemed to enjoy the account, said, "Do you like Mariah?"

"Yeah, I like her," answered Cisco. "I hope Ollie gets married to her 'cause then I'll have a daddy and a mommy."

Cathy looked confused, then suspicious, and then went searching for an explanation, first zeroing in on her son. "Is there something you're not telling me, Ollie?"

He froze like scared rabbit. She turned to Ralph. He looked down at his plate.

"Somebody say something," said Cathy.

"Something very interesting is going on here," said Cody with a grin.

Cathy went back to Cisco. "What do you mean, sweetie? Is Ollie going to be your for real daddy?"

Cisco started to answer but suddenly cut himself short and got a fearful look on his face.

"It's ok, Cisco. You didn't do anything wrong." said Ralph.

Cisco smiled and said, "Ollie's going to be my new dad. The judge is going to tell him to do it. But we're not supposed to tell anyone 'cause it's a secret."

Cathy's body stiffened, like she'd just eaten a rotten anchovy.

Cody busted out laughing.

Cathy took turns shooting daggers at Ralph and Ollie.

Ralph wanted to jump in but held back. This battle belonged to Ollie and, after a few uneasy seconds, he came through as best he knew how. He said, "Mother, this is my decision. I'm not a kid anymore."

No! You're not a kid! But you're not a father either!"

"This is too good," said Cody, between bellows of laughter. "The widow mother takes care of the very big boy, the very big boy takes care of the very little boy, and the very little boy goes to the shrink."

"Watch yourself, Cody," said Ralph.

"Come on man, you know it's a joke. Ollie doesn't have a clue about being a father."

"Yes, he does!" said Cisco. "He's a good father! And he doesn't get into trouble like you! And he owns this ranch so he gets to do what he wants!"

A hard silence fell onto the table.

Cody's eyes, filled with suspicion, studied the faces at the table. He said, "What's he talking about?"

Nobody answered.

Ralph comforted his confused grandson, saying, "It's ok, Cisco. We're just talking, that's all."

"Ralph, maybe you and Cisco can finish your dinner out on the patio. The boys and I have some things to talk about," said Cathy.

The move to the patio didn't erase the sounds that followed. Cody barked loud, rapid fire questions. Cathy tried to explain but Cody repeatedly cut her off. And when Ollie defended his mother, Cody trampled over his brother's words like they didn't exist. It sounded bad, but for these brief few seconds it didn't sound any worse than any other really bad family argument. Then Cody heard how many acres Ollie had bought, and the scene exploded into chaos, dominated by the pitifully ugly sound of a grown man throwing a temper tantrum. Ralph moved his grandson up to the stable, away from the obscenities but with a line of sight through the window in case Ralph needed to run down and jump into the middle. As with most tantrums, though, Cody ended up storming to his room in pretty short order.

Ollie had purchased his share of the ranch over four years earlier, and Ralph had no idea that Cody didn't know. Otherwise, he wouldn't have said anything to Cisco. It had been an innocent mistake, but Ralph still felt bad. The next morning, he parked his truck at the stable as usual, but instead of watching Cisco run down to the house by himself, Ralph went with him. He wanted to apologize to Cathy. Before they had gotten half way to the house, though, he saw Cathy marching up the hill in the opposite direction. When their paths intersected, she greeted Ralph with four sternly spoken words: In the office, now.

He followed her back up the hill and into the office where the two squared off, Cathy standing behind the desk, Ralph just inside the doorway. Ralph saw the anger in her red, swollen eyes. He said, "I'm sorry, Cathy. I didn't know that Cody hadn't been told. It's my fault."

"You're apologizing for the wrong thing, Ralph."

Ralph stared. He didn't want to fight with Cathy. She didn't deserve it. But he didn't have the stomach to betray what he believed. He said, "I have nothing else to apologize for."

"You manipulated my son for your own selfish purpose!"

"Absolutely not."

"Then tell me, Ralph, why did you do it in secret?"

"That was Ollie's call, and I had to respect it."

"And what exactly does Ollie get out of your scheme? I'll tell you. He gets a commitment that he doesn't understand and that will never go away!"

"He gets to help someone he cares about."

"He can't even help himself! And you know it! And you used it against him to get what you want!"

"That's not how it happened. The three of us have talked for months about this. And your son is way more capable than you give him credit for. That's the real problem here."

"He's twenty-three years old, has brain damage, and knows nothing about being a father! How much stupid does it take before you realize that an idea is really, really stu—" She stopped mid-sentence. Her eyes got big.

Ralph heard someone behind him. He turned and saw Ollie standing just outside the doorway.

"That's why I didn't talk with you about this, mother. Because you don't think I can do anything except draw pictures," said Ollie. He turned and left.

Cathy slumped into the desk chair, covered her face with her hands, and began to cry.

"I'm sorry Cathy. I didn't mean for it to happen like this," said Ralph. He then left her in peace.

Illusions of the perfect father didn't plague Ralph Durbin. He had been around too many bad fathers, and had been way too imperfect himself, to ever consider such a notion. Because of this lowered expectation, and because of the bond he had seen since day one between Ollie and Cisco, Ralph didn't see the same limitations that Cathy saw. He saw a fighting chance. He also believed that over time Cathy would come around. She loved Cisco too much for any other outcome. And two days later she started moving in that direction. She apologized to Ollie and Cisco. Two days after that she went to the adoption hearing where Francisco Durbin officially became Cisco Durbin Buckmeyer. On the drive home she joined in the celebration and invited everyone to a special dinner in honor of the occasion.

This left only one part of the plan still undone, the part that hurt. The next morning Ralph started packing. As he boxed his few possessions, he saw signs of life scattered all over the bunkhouse, life that had not been there before. For nine years the place had been dark and cheerless. And then little Cisco dropped his suitcase onto the wooden floor and everything changed, for the old bunkhouse and for Ralph, starting with the terrifying realization that he had been selected as the last person standing in someone else's life. The boy didn't have another soul on earth. And that sink or swim ultimatum had been the medicine that Ralph needed. It gave him the strength to stand up and finally learn what it means to love someone more than himself. Cisco gave that to him. Thankfully, Ollie came from a better place and didn't have the same kind of baggage that Ralph had had. But Ollie still needed to be set up in the best possible way. He needed to be the new last person standing in Cisco's life. That's why Ralph had to move, even if it hurt more than he could have imagined.

He loaded the last of his belongings into the truck and drove to his new place—three hundred yards away, in a vacant trailer that had been used by a ranch hand and his wife. On the way down the hill, he ran into Ollie and Cisco as they drove Ollie's stuff up to the bunkhouse. Ralph waved. As the cars passed, Ralph heard Cisco yell, "Hi grandpa!" And those simple words, which he never tired of hearing, put his sadness into perspective. He still had Cisco in his life and that was more than he deserved.

∾∾∾∾∾∾∾∾∾∾∾∾

That land should have been part of Cody's inheritance, and Ollie had taken it. With nothing but a measly $136,000 down payment he had taken property worth over thirteen million dollars. And in the last five years the land had exploded in value. Ollie had become a mega millionaire without lifting a finger! Cody could have done that deal himself! He had had some money back then. But not really; he had gotten a one-time signing bonus. Ollie, on the other hand, made serious money month after month. He had a way to make the big monthly mortgage payment. Cody had had prospects of someday making that kind of money, but now he didn't even have that. Now he didn't have anything.

And the real joke was that Cody had been the one that had turned Ollie into a money machine in the first place. If Cody hadn't written that letter to the news station his brother would probably now be sitting in some adult care program

241

playing with a box of crayons. Cody had done it. He had set him up for life. And he had been repaid with a knife in the back.

But Cody's regrets and reminiscences didn't stop there. He went way back to the baseball game. Why did Ollie live when other people die every day from lightning strikes—and they're not wearing metal cleats and leaning against a metal pole that towers a hundred feet into the air? Everything could have been different. Cody's life could have been different. But instead, Ollie gets banged on the head and walks away with everything, while Cody works his ass off in the minors and gets shit.

Cody had never entertained these kinds of thoughts before and, like the thoughts that come from most fits of anger, they quickly disappeared, at least in part because he had something more important to think about.

The very next morning he began gathering equipment. Two days after that he strapped a duffel bag to the back of his motorcycle and raced down the dirt road. At the highway he turned right, but stayed on that road for only about a mile before turning right again onto the fire road that abutted the western boundary of the ranch. He rode up this dirt road for thirteen miles, making as little noise as possible. At the very top of the hill, he made another right turn onto another fire road and slowly rode along the back side of the ranch, all the while looking for a way onto the property that didn't involve cutting barbwire. He found it in a rickety old gate that had been used when the cattle used to graze on the surrounding land. He rode through the gate, pointed the bike at the first of the two small mountains that jutted up from the hillside, and coasted down the hill on the side of the mountain that had the different colored ribbon of rock that he had seen in Ollie's photograph and drawing. He found the cave in less than an hour. The forty-foot ladder made it hard to miss.

Chapter 21

Ralph drove up to the bunkhouse to pick up Ollie and Cisco, and then the three of them coasted down the hill to the dinner Cathy had planned in honor of Cisco's adoption. After rounding the final bend in the road, they saw the house lit up by two rows of tiki torches. Cisco jumped out of his seat with excitement. Ralph pulled up to his usual spot by the stable and saw that the torches formed a pathway that led over to the barn. They followed the pathway, entered the barn through the partially opened giant rolling doors, and a sight greeted them that looked like it had come out of some old-time English movie where they drink rum punch and listen to the pudding singing in the copper. On the left side of the barn, where they stored heavy equipment and had a workshop, flickering lights had been strung everywhere, over the big John Deere and the little Bobcat, over the tall band saw and through the grids of the wide panel saw, and all over the workbench and cabinets. A dozen or more eucalyptus wreaths hung from the rafters and gave off the aroma of a freshly trimmed lemon grove. Fresh straw had been laid down to form another pathway that led through the barn and over to a candle lit dinner table that had been set up near the entrance to the office. Bob's cowboy hat hung from one of the chairs at the end of the table, and his picture had been placed on the table in front of the chair, along with his own honorary place setting. Cathy stood next to that chair, smiling warmly.

"Hello everyone. You're just in time. Cisco, since you're the newest member of our family, why don't you take the place of honor right there at the end of the table," said Cathy, as she pointed to the opposite end of the table.

Cisco scampered up to his chair.

"Ollie, you sit there next to your son, and Ralph, you sit on the other side next to your grandson. Cathy sat between Ollie and her husband's chair.

Ralph had been to dozens of ranch barbeques, and that pretty much summed up the depth of his culinary expertise. You sear it, slather it, and cook it slow. Throw on some baked beans, and you're done. No mystery. But this one looked different, out of his league. He'd seen his fair share of chicken breasts but never any cloaked in orange slices with little sprigs of edible finery popping up like a ladies Easter hat. And he knew rice just as much as the next guy but didn't have a clue where you get rice that comes in so many different colors. And sauces, those always cause problems, because if you accidently put the lemon sauce on the potato, everybody looks at you like you just drew a mustache on the Mona Lisa. Fancy dinners have fancy rules, so he sat on his hands and tried to stay alert.

After some brief chitchat about everyone's new living arrangements, Cathy gave thanks for the meal and for the ones who couldn't be there with them, and then she took a few seconds to explain the spread, which Ralph appreciated. She said, "This is orange glazed chicken, this is mac and cheese, just the way Cisco likes it, this is rice pilaf with cherries and pistachios, this is peanut coleslaw, and this is orange sauce for the chicken, if you want it."

And, in a blizzard of activity, everybody started scooping and passing and reaching and talking and eating. After a few minutes, Cathy interrupted the chaos and said, "By the way, before I forget, Cody sends his regards and wanted to be here tonight but had to go out of town for a few days to visit some friends."

Ralph had seen Cody take off on his motorcycle earlier that day, and now Cathy had filled in the rest of the picture. But something about it seemed strange. Cody lived for his cool man image, and the expensive sports car had become a big part of that show, even if the thing had started to show its age. And now that he had been booted from baseball, what else besides that car did he really have? It didn't make sense that he had left it behind. Also, his motorcycle only had a small engine and while it might have been street legal, it wasn't the most practical for "out of town" travel.

Besides this little puzzle, which may have been nothing more than Ralph's suspicious nature, the evening went off beautifully, topped off by an unexpected surprise from Ollie. He announced that he had hired an architect and planned to build a house for himself and Cisco on his property. Everyone liked the idea—Cisco instantly had a dozen questions—but Ralph noticed a hint of concern in Cathy's smile and in her eyes. After a few minutes he found out the reason when she quietly asked Ollie if she could be the one to tell Cody about the house. She obviously had concerns about how Cody might handle the news and, judging from his last explosion, Ralph didn't blame her.

∞∞∞∞∞∞∞∞∞∞

With the duffel bag slung over his shoulder, Cody had just begun climbing the ladder when he thought he heard a snapping sound. He looked down but didn't see anything. He stepped back down to the ground and looked again. He found two tiny twigs wedged into the bottom rungs of the ladder and, after closer inspection, found a third one, the one he had broken, on a different rung. He said, "Good try assholes, but you're gonna have to do better than that." He removed the broken twig, which turned out to be a matchstick, and separated the partially attached sections. He then reinserted the longer of the two sections back into the rung and resumed the climb, carefully avoiding the matchsticks, and carefully looking for other lame detective tricks.

At the top, feet firmly planted on rock, he surveyed all of the items that Jubal had left behind, both inside the cave and out. They formed a kind of pristine time capsule, which Cody all but ignored, calculating that this easily accessible section had already been gone over by his father. He opted instead to begin his search at the vertical shaft where somebody had tied a red warning flag around a giant beam. Cody reasoned that his old man might have hesitated at that shaft—which had to be a good five feet wide and who knows how deep— and might have retreated back to his office to obsess over details and draw up plans. Cody, on the other hand, had two-hundred-fifty feet of rope and a strong, athletic body, the

248

only plan he needed. Having peeked down the shaft, he also had seen the skeleton and figured that if Jubal had had anything to say about his own death, he would have chosen to die as close as possible to his treasure. The gold could even be right there with him now, just fifteen feet away. With more than enough room on the perch, it looked like the perfect place to begin the search. But, just so he knew the score, he picked up a good sized rock and dropped it into the shaft. After a few seconds he heard a splash. OK. A splash was better than a thud.

Cody exchanged his flashlight for a headlamp and went to work on the beam. He raised one end of it—which looked like it had fallen out of place—by wedging it into some boulders, so that the entire beam now traversed the shaft some four feet over the shaft opening. He then tied two ropes around it, one seated in the groove that had been carved into the wood and the other spaced about three feet away. With one of the ropes, he lowered the duffel bag down into the shaft. It contained the metal detector, backup headlamps and flashlights, and some basic survival gear. He grabbed the other rope with his bare hands, gave it one last test tug, and then pulled himself off of the ground, letting his body swing out over the shaft. While he waited for the swinging motion to ease, he noticed a whistling noise in the shaft and felt a breeze on his face. Using only the strength from his hands and arms, he began lowering himself. As he got closer to the bones, he got a bigger picture of where they lay. From above it had looked like a perch that had been carved into the wall of the shaft. Now it looked like another cave altogether. Cody welcomed this sight because it gave him more room to maneuver, and because it looked like a good place to hide a treasure.

When he had lowered himself down to the level of the entrance, and while he continued to dangle from the rope, he pointed his head toward the newly discovered cave. The headlamp filled it with light. His eyes searched expectantly. He saw nothing except for the bones.

He reached out with one hand and grabbed the other rope. Now, with a rope in each hand, he initiated a swinging motion by alternately pulling on one rope and then the other. It took just a few seconds before the swinging motion brought his body next to the lip of the cave, and he stepped right onto it, not much harder than stepping off a bus. Still holding the ropes, he wedged one of them underneath a boulder, and then started pulling on the other until he had dragged his gear up and into the cave.

A quick look showed this cave to be similar in size to the other one, but Cody preferred to concentrate on something else first. He pulled the metal detector from the duffel bag and started scanning the area around Jubal's skeleton, which rested on the floor of the cave. And he instantly got a hit—a strong one. He dropped the detector, pulled a trowel from the bag and carefully excavated the area. But when the trowel disturbed the pelvic bone, the upper half of the skeleton, which rested against the wall of the cave, came crashing down. Jubal's skull bounced loudly onto a rock, hit Cody's leg, and bounced a few more times downhill toward the other end of the cave. Cody gasped like a frightened child.

After catching his breath and telling himself to get a grip, he resumed the search, this time without the gentleness. He knocked the pile of bones out of the way, scooped up a layer of sediment, and brought the scoop up close to his headlamp to be inspected. He ran his fingers through the clumpy, dusty stuff and felt something hard and flat, roughly the shape of a large coin. He grasped it and it felt like it had the right weight. He wiped away the grime and saw symbols and writing and…a hole drilled near the edge. Gold Eagle coins don't have holes drilled into them. It was a piece of worthless jewelry, probably some kind of a talisman, judging from the weird symbols and all the stories that Cody had heard about Jubal and his various paranoias.

Beginning with this first rush of adrenalin, Cody would feel many of the same emotions that his father had felt when he searched the upper cave—expectation, confidence, impatience—but unlike his father, Cody would also experience frustration and anger because after an exhaustive search that included two days of darkness and two nights of shivering sleeplessness, he found nothing. Except for the bones, he didn't find a single clue that anyone had ever been down there.

Beyond the frustration and anger, this failure also meant that Cody now had to search the next section of the system, the more dangerous section. He had to lower himself some fifty feet down to the bottom of the shaft. He didn't like this for several reasons. Other than water, he didn't know what waited for him down there. He knew that the cave had bats because they turned the place into a creepy echo chamber two times a day, but what other creatures might be down there lurking in the dark? And once he got down there, would he be able to find a suitable ledge or bank that could be used to get his body out of the cold water? And would he have the strength to pull his body, plus twenty pounds of soaked clothes, back up a fifty foot rope to get to the lower cave and then another fifteen feet to the upper cave?

Cody had more questions than answers, but it didn't matter. He had to do it, and he wasn't going to wait around for all the answers. He began by tying knots, spaced about five feet apart, all along one of the ropes. Physically, he had the ability to easily climb twenty or thirty feet. These knots provided handholds and footholds that would hopefully extend that range. As a precaution, he also extended the other rope down the shaft but didn't tie any knots into it. He left most of the supplies and gear in the cave, packing the duffel bag with only the detector, the trowel, a jacket, and a backup flashlight.

He put his arms through the straps of the bag like a backpack, grabbed the rope just above the first knot, and let his body swing out into the middle of shaft. As expected, the knots made the descent a breeze, taking less than five minutes.

At about fifteen feet above the waterline a bleak reality began to reveal itself. The shaft had opened up into what looked like a very large cavern. He spun his head all around, and in every direction the size of the chamber, and the blackness of it, swallowed the light from his headlamp. Cody didn't want anything large, especially if half of it lay underwater. He wanted compact and easily searchable.

He continued the descent, now pointing his headlamp to the bottom, looking for a landing spot that would let him keep the metal detector dry. Depending on the depth of the water, he thought he saw several possible options. He shined his light into the water, looking for shallowness, and was struck by what he saw. The water had a brilliant turquoise color with an incredible sparkling clarity. It looked like a National Geographic photo of some luminescent Polynesian lagoon.

He also saw, just a few feet from his line of travel, what looked like an underwater shelf that extended up and out of the water. Using the same technique as before, he grabbed the other rope and swung himself over to the shelf and safely into the shallow water. Just a few easy steps later he found himself on dry rock.

Cody stood for a few seconds staring out over a massive natural reservoir. The majesty and beauty of it meant nothing to him. The unsearchable size of it meant everything. He dropped the duffel bag to the ground and, without thinking about any particular direction, began hiking and climbing along the jagged edge of the reservoir, looking for the end of it. At one point the chamber narrowed dramatically, a hopeful sign, but after reentering the water and floating through a small opening, it opened back up with no end in sight. After fifteen minutes, he stopped and looked back over the ground that he had covered, and at the ground on the other side of the reservoir, and at all the underwater nooks and crannies. He saw ten million hiding places and a never-ending search for the gold. He saw himself failing every day of his life but still boring the shit out of people with talk about clues and theories and meticulous calculations. He saw himself becoming a replica of his father.

He hiked back the way he had come and, without even bothering to get the duffel bag, climbed up the rope and out of the cave.

∞∞∞∞∞∞∞∞∞∞

After the adoption, and after the brief turmoil caused by rearranged households, life at the ranch settled down to a familiar pattern. Ollie still went to work every day in his studio, Cisco still came down to the house for breakfast and to catch the school bus, Ralph still worked the ranch, and Cathy found out that her son still needed his mother. She made this discovery one day when Ollie came to her and said, "I haven't told Mariah about the adoption."

"OK…Are you worried about what she'll say?"

"I just don't know the best way to tell her. I know that it's the right thing, and I want her to know it too."

"I'm sorry, dear, you can't control what she thinks. She's either going to be ok with it, or not, and if you try to get fancy with the words, it's just going to cause confusion. Better to just come out and say it, I think."

"But what if I tell her, and she gets mad, but I don't know that she's mad?"

"She'll tell you…She does know that she has to tell you those things, right?"

"Yes, we talked about it."

"OK. You tell her, and then you give her some time to think about it. That's all you can do."

"You're right, mother. That's what I have to do."

Not long after this conversation Ollie returned to his drawing table with a smile on his face, and Cathy knew that all was well on that side of the house. She couldn't say the same for the other side, though.

〰〰〰〰〰〰〰〰〰

Other than opening his bedroom window to give the smoke somewhere to go, Cody didn't bother to mask his activity. He put on the tunes, got comfortable on his bed, and lit up one joint after another until blessed distortion filled his head, turning the seconds into hours and small thoughts into profound ones. And today the pinpoint focus of the Maui Wowie mind wanted to think about water. Every detail. Cody smelled the mustiness that permeated the rock, and tasted the cold, flavorless purity. He heard the echo of a thousand water drops from a thousand stalactites, and saw himself standing over an undiscovered sea like a new world explorer from a grade school history book.

He also saw a stupid man begging for the stuff when all the while he had an underground lake sitting right under his nose. Cody started laughing. He remembered the nonstop dinner table bitching about the cost of water. He saw the buck-up sternness on the hardened face. The guy bucked himself up alright, and for no good reason at all. The laughter now flew from Cody's chest in one continuous spasm, unhinged, uncontrollable.

Someone knocked on the door. The funny thought wiggled away from the grip of the distorted mind. Cody thought about the door. He put down the joint and answered it. It was mother.

"Hello, mother."

She looked at him and into the room. She put on the special look of longsuffering disappointment and said, "Cody, you are better than this."

"No, I'm better *because* of this. You should try it sometime."

"You have so much potential. Why do this to yourself?"

"Uh…because it feels good?"

She gave him the stare and said, "I'm not talking to you when you're like this."

"Excellent idea. I don't like talking to me when I'm like this either."

He closed the door. She pushed it back open. "Your brother is building a house on his property. The permits are being pulled and construction will start in a couple of months. I just thought you should know."

She turned and left. Cody closed the door, lay back on the bed, and tried to remember the funny thing that had made him laugh.

Chapter 22

Construction began in mid-December and so did the incessant drumbeat of his brother's success. It echoed without mercy. He heard it in the jobsite chatter and in the stale boom box music, in the reverberation of the hammer and in the shrill of the circular saw. Different sounds said different things. The parade of diesel belching cement mixers announced the laying of the foundation. The framing gun that echoed like a sniper's rifle proclaimed that the monument had now begun to rise to the sky. The staccato wheeze of the screw gun declared hanging drywall and the birth of impressive new living spaces in the impressive new mansion. He kept time by the twice daily migration of the workers' rattletrap pickup trucks. He knew when deliveries arrived by the screeching sound of the vehicle back-up alarms. He knew when the roof went up by the revving oscillation of the construction crane. Every day he endured a never-ending construction cacophony composed and performed in honor of his brother's success. He had no way to escape it because he had nowhere to go.

〰〰〰〰〰〰〰〰

Mariah took two weeks off at Christmas, spending most of that time with Ollie at the ranch. And, as their relationship progressed, she learned new things about him. When in his element, and feeling comfortable, he liked to laugh and have fun, but finding that level of comfort wasn't always easy. He had a tendency to focus on the present moment, not because of a carefree personality like he used to have, but because he didn't trust the moment and seemed to feel that it needed to be watched. Mariah accepted this because she tipped the scale in the other direction by constantly looking at the future. She told herself that maybe the two unbalanced tendencies made for a balanced couple.

As she considered their prospects, Mariah noticed other people doing the same thing. She saw it in little ways, like the way Cisco's grandfather carefully watched as she took Cisco by the hand and led him to the chicken coop to collect eggs. The grandfather didn't look unhappy or worried. He looked like someone evaluating a horse that might be added to the team. Same with Mrs. Buckmeyer. Instead of the casually polite demeanor of a lady who has a guest who will soon be gone, she had the expectant, almost effusive demeanor of a matchmaking mother on the home stretch. Mariah understood. They each had expectations and wanted the best for their loved ones. She herself had been working through her own set of evolving expectations.

And that's where she came face to face with the one big detraction. If Mariah could have changed one thing about Ollie, she would have drawn a red X through a certain member of his family. Arrogance and selfishness are almost understandable in a star athlete, but now Mariah also

258

detected menace and anger. He had been kicked out of baseball and everyone knew it. Instead of being the big man in town, he had become a humiliated washout, and the weight of that knowledge seemed to be taking a heavy toll.

A couple of times Mariah caught him staring at her. When she looked back at him, he threw out the dashing smile that had opened so many doors for so many years. But now the smile looked forced and didn't match the shadow of sadness that hung from his face. Mariah kept a careful distance from him.

※※※※※※※※

In her beauty he saw a perfect picture of all that he had lost, and he couldn't help staring at it. He saw the admiring eyes of the cleat chasers that used to line up in front row box seats like a collection of shoes in a rich man's closet. He saw for sale signs on tantalizing faces, clothes on the floor, and countless bedroom victories. They had played for commitment. He had played with counterfeit chips. But now he had lost it all. Now he stared at a picture like a jerkoff in the basement.

※※※※※※※※

The cloying smell of marijuana smoke seeped nonstop from his bedroom. Except for bathroom breaks and trips to the fridge, he rarely showed his face. A couple of times, though, the power of the drug inspired energetic visits with the family, where he acted strangely and made others feel uncomfortable. Regardless of his condition, Cathy used every encounter to try to engage him, to cast a gentle net and drag him out of the darkness. She showered him with praise and made his favorite meals. Her desperation only made him laugh.

At the end of the holiday season, just before Mariah had to head back up north, Cathy invited the gang down to the house for a New Year's Eve party. With the food and beer and music, she had hoped that he might also join the celebration, but the door stayed closed. Then, just before midnight, when everyone stood ready with full champagne glasses, Ollie turned down the volume on the New Year's Eve television program and announced his and Mariah's engagement. Cathy's shriek of joy may have broken some glassware. It also roused him from his bedroom.

Looking haggard and unwashed, he stood just inside the doorway and stared. Little Cisco stared back. Ralph looked wary. Mariah stood close to Ollie. And Cathy jumped into action, putting down her glass and scurrying over to the table to make him a plate of food.

He walked up to Mariah and said, "Can I see the ring?"

She held out her hand. He took her hand into his, inspected the diamond, and said, "It's nice. I guess everything is perfect now. Congratulations."

"Thank you," said Mariah, quietly.

He turned and left. The clock hit midnight and the sound of his closing bedroom door echoed through the house. The New Year's revelers stood in silence. Cathy stood with a heaping plate of food and no one to give it to.

The transition from jealousy to revenge happened fast, like a four-six-three double play. He didn't entertain questions of right and wrong. His conscience didn't become a battleground. He knew how to make everything right and how to get back everything that had been stolen, and he immediately started marching. First, he grabbed a small box from a hiding place in his closet. It contained the gold coins he had stolen back in high school. He needed them. Next, he stowed the weed, put away the zig-zags, and threw open his bedroom door. After a shower and a fresh set of clean clothes, he found his mother in the kitchen and gave her a kiss. He told her that he was going to be alright. She believed him.

Chapter 23

"Ollie! Ollie!" yelled Cody, as he bull rushed the studio.

Ollie jumped in his seat. Cody charged around the big desk. "I found it, Ollie! Do you hear me! I found it!" He threw his arms around his brother and hugged him tightly, purposely violating his space and inflicting the maximum degree of emotional discomfort.

"What? What are you doing? Don't do that. Don't do that," said Ollie.

With one arm still wrapped around his brother's shoulder, Cody presented his other hand, in the form of a fist, for closer inspection. Grinning wildly and staring into his brother's eyes, he then slowly opened his fingers to reveal a handful of gleaming gold coins. "I found the treasure, Ollie, I found it."

"You found it?" said Ollie, carefully measuring each word."

"Yes, Ollie, yes!"

"Oh my gosh! I can't believe it!"

"They're real, man. Here, see for yourself." Cody thrust the coins into Ollie's hand and smiled as he fondled them.

"Where did you find it?"

"In the cave, just like you said, but I had to go down to the lower section, and there they were, barely ten feet from where Jubal died."

"I didn't even know you were looking. Did you tell mom?" asked Ollie, as he handed back the coins.

"No, no, not yet. I want to surprise her but I need help getting them down the cliff. There are thousands of these things and I need your help, Ollie. And then we'll surprise mom together. A hundred years after we started, the Buckmeyers will finally finish the job. You and I together. Will you help me do it?"

"Yes, I'll help you, Cody. But you're the one who did it. You took the last step that father couldn't take. You did it for him."

"Yeah, I guess I did, didn't I?" Cody gave his brother one last uncomfortable hug and then started to leave. At the doorway he turned and said, "Oh, I forgot. We need Cisco's help too. You and I will lower the gold down the cliff and he'll unload it for us. But don't say anything to him yet. And don't tell anyone else. We want this to be a surprise for mom."

"OK, Cody. I won't say anything."

"How about Saturday morning?"

"Yeah, Saturday is good."

<hr/>

Cody pulled right up to the front of the Radio Shack and gave the Viper a loud gulp of fuel before cutting the engine. Heads turned.

He liked this place. It made him feel like he had his own little team of super-nerds all boxed up and ready to be put to work at a moment's notice. He entered the store and saw a guy behind the counter that he remembered from high school. "Hey, how ya doing?" said Cody.

"I'm doing quite well, thank you for your inquiry."

Oh yeah, Radio Shack all the way baby, thought Cody. Then he plopped a caver's headlamp onto the counter and said, "I got this headlamp here and I need some kind of a thingy to turn it on and off without actually touching it."

"Are you asking about a remote relay switch?"

"If you say so, man. You're the expert."

"Let me take a look. May I?"

"Yeah. Knock yourself out."

He popped open the battery compartment, probed around for a few seconds, and said, "It's a bit tight, but you can do it. All you need is a single line DC remote relay module. It comes with a built-in receiver and a push button transmitter." He put down the headlamp and looked bored, as if the challenge had been beneath his expectations.

"And I'll be able turn the light on and off with it?"

"Yep."

"OK, I'll take it."

The guy leaned to his right, tapped a few keys on the countertop computer, and said, "We have seven in stock. How many would you like?"

"Just one."

"Do you need some butt connectors?"

"Well...uh...I don't know...but in general I'm a big fan of connecting butts," said Cody with a laugh.

Mr. Personality didn't laugh. "They are used to connect the wires. Unless you are planning on soldering, it's probably the way to go."

"OK then, throw them in."

The guy came out from behind the counter, snatched the items from the shelves, and returned. As he rang up the merchandise he said, "You probably don't remember me, but we went to high school together. My name is Marvin Darmlesch, but you called me Poodle."

"Yeah…OK…yeah…I thought I remembered you. Not that you look like a poodle or anything. Anyway…that was back in high school. You know how that goes. I'm…uh…sure things are better now."

"Yes, I cut my hair short now."

"There you go. Too bad you didn't figure that out in high school. You could've skipped all that shit," said Cody with a lighthearted laugh.

"Yes, too bad. That will be eighteen dollars and forty-three cents."

Cody paid, but before the guy handed over the bag he said, "Hey listen, I heard about what happened, and I want to let you know that I'm in pretty tight here with the owner and if you need a job or anything, I could put in a good word for you."

At first Cody thought that it had to be a joke. But then he saw the seriousness on the guy's face…and maybe even a bit of a smirk. "Yeah, right," said Cody, with a smirk of his own. On his way out he mumbled, "Geeky little shit."

It took a few seconds for Ralph's eyes to focus—the matchsticks blended in with the sandy tread marks on the ladder rungs—but then he found them, undisturbed, just like the last time he had checked...except this time one of them looked shorter than the others. He plucked out all the matchsticks and, sure enough, the one from the second rung came up a good quarter inch short. He didn't remember it being that way and wondered if someone had broken the stick and then tried to cover it up. But, then again, Ralph didn't have the best memory in the world. Maybe it had been shorter all along. He climbed the ladder, looked around the cave, and didn't notice any signs of a trespasser. He climbed back down, replaced the matchsticks, and went on his way.

⁂

Cody led the way from the house, chirping loudly to distract Ollie from any one of his many phobias that could derail the plan before it even started. They got up to the barn and Cody pointed to his brother's old dirt bike, which had been cleaned and freshly tuned. Cody hopped on the bike and gave her a kick. She started right up, but Ollie looked like he wanted to bail. Cody brought in some relief. He said, "Whataya say Cisco? Feel like going dirt bike riding?"

"Yeah!" said Cisco, with all the enthusiasm that Cody had expected.

"But I don't have a helmet for him," said Ollie.

"Got you covered, bro," said Cody, pointing to a shiny new helmet that rested on the nearby workbench.

"...And I haven't ridden in ten years. I don't think I even remember how."

"Sure you do. Just give it a try and it will all come back," said Cody. He knocked back the kickstand and wheeled the bike over to where his brother stood. "We'll wait here while you take it for an easy spin to the house and back."

"Come on, dad. You can do it," said Cisco.

Ollie strapped on his helmet, took a seat on the bike, and timidly revved the engine a few times. He then put her into gear and gingerly pulled away. Cody watched him ride down to the house, never getting the bike past second gear. On the way back, though, Cody heard a full cycle of gears, and the bike started moving with some style. Ollie pulled back up to the barn and said, "I think I got it."

"Just like I told you. OK, Ollie this red backpack is for you and, Cisco, let me help you with this helmet and then you can hop on the back with your dad, and you guys will follow me."

<hr/>

Ralph had just started down the hill when he thought he heard the sound of motorcycles. Local kids sometimes snuck onto the property with their bikes and Ralph had to always be on the lookout. He rode to a nearby peak, pulled out the binoculars, and followed a trail of dust down by the house until it led to the perpetrators, which this time turned out to be Cody and Ollie...and a little guy on the back of one of the bikes hanging on for dear life. And Ralph had to smile. Young fathers do fun things with their kids, fun things that broken down old grandpas never do, and Ralph liked that. His decision looked better every day. The fact that Ollie and Cisco had included Cody in the outing didn't sit that well.

But, in this case, it all looked harmless enough. Ralph gave old Gomer some rein and continued on down the hill.

⚟⚟⚟⚟⚟⚟⚟⚟⚟⚟

"Do you like surprises, Cisco?" asked Cody after they had parked their bikes and had walked down to the base of the cliff, and after the kid had asked a dozen questions about what they were doing.

"Yes," said Cisco. "I like surprises."

"Well, I got the biggest surprise ever. I found Jubal's gold."

"Wow! You found the gold!"

"Yep, and since you're part of the family now, part of it belongs to you. But you gotta help us get it down here. What do you say about that?"

"I'm good at stuff like that. I can help you."

"You betcha. Now your job is to bag up the gold, so you're gonna wait right here by the ladder, and when we lower the basket you put the gold coins in these bags, and stack the bags right here on the ground." Cody handed him a stack of pull-tie cloth bags.

"OK. I can do that," said Cisco.

"Cisco, why don't you wait over there in the shade under that tree," said Ollie. "And here's my phone in case something happens and you need to call grandma or grandpa."

"Nah, he's not going to need that, Ollie. He's just going to be putting coins into bags."

"I want him to have it."

Even if the kid knew how to use the phone, and ended up talking with someone, he really didn't know anything. Just the same, Cody didn't like the unexpected variable. He said, "OK. Maybe you're right. Better safe than sorry, like dad used to say. Here, let me check the phone to make sure you have reception."

Ollie handed over the phone, and Cody powered if off while pretending to check the reception. He then gave the dead phone to Cisco and said, "OK, you're all set. You hang tight here and the first load will be coming your way in just a few minutes. We'll holler from the top of the cliff when were ready. OK?"

"OK."

"And don't go anywhere, Ok?" said Ollie, as he escorted Cisco over to the shade, just a few feet away.

~~~~~~~~~~~~~~~~

Cisco waited patiently under the tree for at least a minute before he got bored. After two minutes he had his dad's mobile phone powered up. After three minutes he had started playing a skateboarding game on it.

~~~~~~~~~~~~~~~~

Ollie hugged the wall at the back of the cave and looked anxiously down at the shaft. He said, "I thought you already had the gold up here and we just had to lower it down the cliff. I can't go down that rope."

Cody pulled a big bundle from his backpack, held it up for Ollie to see, and said, "No worries, bro. I brought a rope ladder. You can go down a ladder, can't you?"

"How far is it?"

"Just fifteen feet, that's all."

"No. How far to the bottom?"

"Sixty feet."

"I don't know, Cody. What happens if the rope breaks?"

"This is what happens," said Cody. He dropped a rock down the shaft, it splashed into the water, and he said, "You go swimming, that's all. But this ladder can hold two thousand pounds so it's not going to happen."

"OK...alright," said Ollie, but he still looked nervous.

"I'll tell you what. I'll go down first, and you'll see how easy it is. How's that sound?"

"OK."

Cody secured the ladder to the beam, making a show of strenuously testing each knot, and said, "You just reach out like this, grab the rope on one side of the ladder, and then grab the rope on the other side. Then bring one foot over like this and then the other. See. Nothing to it. Just make sure your helmet is snapped and the headlamp is tight, because it's pitch black down there." Then, with a confident wink and a reassuring smile, he said, "See you in China," and started climbing down the ladder.

When he got down to the level of the lower cave, Cody paused and looked up through the shaft opening. Not seeing any activity, he said, "Remember, Ollie, we're doing this for mom...and for dad, too." A few seconds later a hand reached out and grabbed one side of the rope ladder. And then the other hand grabbed the other side. "Doing good, Ollie. Nothing to it," said Cody, who then grabbed one of the hanging ropes and swung himself into the cave. A short time later Ollie's body came into view as it descended the ladder.

Cody reached into his pocket and located the transmitter. He ran his fingers up and down and felt the contours of the button. Getting down there had been the tricky part. Now he just had to push a button.

"How do I get over there?" said Ollie, who dangled in the center of the shaft.

"Give me your arm and I'll pull you over here to the edge."

A few seconds later Ollie had his feet on solid rock and a look of relief on his face. He said, "I did it." Then he looked down at the messy pile of bones. "What happened to Jubal? He didn't look like that before."

"I don't know. Maybe he got mad and fell apart when I found his treasure," said Cody. He massaged the transmitter in his pocket.

"Where is the treasure? I don't see it."

"I got it hidden over here at the back of the cave. Follow me." He took two steps and pushed the button.

"Cody, Cody, my light went out. I don't have any light."

"OK, don't panic. I'm right here." He turned and faced his brother, who had started moaning like he used to. "No worries, bro. It's probably just a loose battery or something. Let me take a look." With his own headlamp still working perfectly, Cody flicked his brother's lamp with his finger a few times. Of course, nothing happened. He unsnapped the headlamp from the helmet, opened the battery compartment, and made a show of the investigation before giving up and saying, "I'm not sure what the problem is, but it's nothing to worry about because I have an extra up in the backpack. Just wait here, and I'll be right back."

"You're leaving me here in the dark?"

"One of us has to go. It's not going to fly down by itself. Do you wanna go?"

"No. I'll stay here, but please hurry. I don't like it here."

"OK, Ollie, It'll just take a minute." As Cody maneuvered toward the shaft, he looked one last time into his brother's eyes. He saw fear and helplessness. He didn't see terror. Not yet. But even that would have been OK because terror is all consuming and doesn't have room for blame. Sad eyes, though, are sad for a reason. They know something. They know who cuts the rope. Cody didn't want to see those kinds of eyes. And he didn't deserve it. Ollie had caused this, and had only himself to blame.

Cody climbed the ladder to the upper cave, where he braced himself against the beam and looked down the shaft. His headlamp illuminated the full run of it. He said, "Ollie, I can't find the other headlamp. I thought for sure that I packed it. I think we better call it quits for today. Are you OK with that?"

"Yes. I'm OK. Get me out of here."

"OK. I'll keep shining the light from up here, and I'll swing the rope ladder toward you. When it gets close, just grab it."

"OK, OK, I'll do it. Keep shining the light down here." His nervous moaning now echoed loudly throughout the cave.

While still bracing himself against the beam with one hand, Cody reached under the beam and swing the rope ladder back and forth. After a few seconds, Ollie snagged the ladder.

"I don't know. I don't know. I don't think I can do it," said Ollie.

"You have to do it, Ollie. It's the only way out, unless you want to end up like Jubal," said Cody. He reached into his pocket and pulled out a switchblade.

"OK. OK. I can do it. I can do it."

A few seconds later, Ollie's body swung out to the middle of the shaft. Cody said, "Good job, bro. You got it. Now just start climbing." He pushed the button on the knife. The blade popped out, making a loud snapping sound.

"What was that? What was that noise?"

"Oh, nothing, bro. You're doing good." Cody put the blade onto the rope and started cutting. This movement caused a shift in the position of his head and a shift in the direction of the light.

"Cody! I can't see! Where's the light!"

"Sorry. My bad." With a few more easy strokes, Cody cut through the final strands of the first rope. The ladder lurched violently and partially collapsed. Ollie's body slammed into the shaft wall, but he managed to hang on by clinging to the side of the ladder still secured to the beam.

"Cody! Help me! Please! Help me!" screamed Ollie.

"Hang on Ollie. I can fix this. The knot just came loose. Hold on."

"Hurry, Cody! Please hurry!" said Ollie.

With three swift motions, Cody cut through the other side of the ladder. The final cut caused the load bearing rope to whip out and smack against the wall of the shaft. Ollie gasped. He started falling. His head snapped back. Cody saw terror in his eyes. Ollie screamed all the way to the bottom. After the splash perfect silence reclaimed the chamber, except for the subtle sound of the breeze that always blew through the shaft.

Jubal had most likely died because he had had no way to get up the shaft and out of the cave. Ollie would be suffering the same fate—if the fall hadn't already done the job. But, unlike Jubal, no one would be finding Ollie's bones. And he would not be dying alone. Cody didn't have a choice. It didn't make sense to kill the thief just so the property could go to the thief's son.

∾∾∾∾∾∾∾∾∾∾∾

It had been a good half hour since the sound of the motorcycles had stopped echoing off the hillside and, being a worried kind of grandfather, that bothered Ralph. Maybe someone had gotten hurt or had broken down. He pulled up Gomer, pulled out the mobile phone, and called Ollie. He answered on the first ring.

"It's just me, Ollie. Just making sure everything is OK."

"Hi, Grandpa. It's Cisco."

"Oh, Hey, Cisco. How do like the motorcycle?"

"Guess what, Grandpa?"

"I don't know. What?"

"Uncle Cody found the treasure and I'm helping him get it out of the cave."

"Where are you, Cisco?"

"Right here by the ladder."

"On top of the cliff or down on the ground?"

275

"On the ground."

"And where's Ollie?"

"He went up in the cave with—I gotta go, Grandpa. Uncle Cody needs my help."

"Wait. Cisco. Listen to—" The line went dead. Ralph redialed. No one answered.

No way. It didn't make sense. Exactly when did Cody find the treasure? He had been holed up in his room for the last two months, doing nothing except smoking dope. It didn't add up. Ralph pointed Gomer back up the hill and rode him hard.

〰〰〰〰〰

"High five, big guy."

Cisco had to jump high to reach the hand, but he did it. Then Uncle Cody knelt down close and said, "There's just too much gold up there, big guy. We need your help. Your dad told me to come get you."

"OK. I can help you."

"Great. You climbed this ladder before, didn't you?"

"Yeah, I climbed it, but I'm supposed to wear the red thing with the straps."

"Oh yeah, that's right. Your dad told me about that. I'll go back up and get it." He stood up, put a foot on the first rung of the ladder, and looked back at Cisco. He said, "Hey, Cisco, what are you gonna do with your gold?"

"I don't know. What are you gonna do?"

"I don't know…maybe buy a ranch and build a beautiful house on it."

"Wow."

276

※※※※※※※※※※

With the rope in hand, Cody stood back a few feet from the edge of the cliff and kept the line tight as the kid climbed up the ladder. His dwarf legs moved painfully slow but Cody used the time to review the checklists in his head and to think about the next part of the plan. Finally, when most of the safety rope had been pulled up and coiled at his feet, he started throwing down some attaboys to keep things moving along. He then heard some grunts and breathing, and a face popped up over the rim. But it wasn't the kid. It was the kid's ugly grandfather, and he had the safety harness wrapped around his arm so that Cody had had something to pull against. Ralph had tricked Cody.

For a fraction of a second, before Ralph got onto solid ground, Cody thought about charging him and knocking him off the cliff. But he didn't do it because of the possibility that they'd get tangled and he'd end up at the bottom of the cliff along with Ralph. And, also, up until then Cody's plan had been perfect, and he knew one thing for certain: Ralph didn't know anything except what the kid may have told him, and the kid didn't know anything.

"Ralph, I'm glad to see you. Did you see Cisco down there?"

"Yeah. He said you found the treasure and need some help."

"Yeah, yeah, that would be great. Ollie's down in the lower cave but I think he's having some kind of episode because he's not saying anything. Maybe you could go down and help him out?" Cody stepped aside and motioned Ralph into the cave, but Ralph balked.

He said, "You first."

Cody led the way through the small opening and tried to make small talk. "Pretty crazy, all this, right?"

"Yeah. I'm surprised you didn't say anything," said Ralph.

"Well, we're trying to surprise mother but so far it's not going great."

Once inside the cave both men stood and Cody said, "Hey, listen, I don't have another headlamp, but Ollie has his and I can shine a light down the shaft for you."

"What's that?" said Ralph, pointing to the ground near the glass jars. Cody looked. His headlamp lit up the area and he saw a flashlight sticking out of the yellow backpack that he had dropped earlier that day.

"Yeah, yeah, we got flashlights. I was just talking about headlamps," said Cody, as he quickly grabbed the flashlight and closed the bag. Cody handed over the flashlight. Ralph looked at him suspiciously.

Cody turned and continued leading the way to the shaft. He had to think fast because Ralph had clearly gone on the defensive and didn't believe anything he heard. And with each step the freshly cut ropes became more and more visible. As he walked, Cody tried to position his body to block Ralph's view of them. When he got to the shaft, Cody quickly leaned against the beam, pushed the limply hanging stubs as far from view as possible, and grabbed one of the other ropes. He presented it to Ralph and said, "Ollie shimmied down this rope with the knots in it and didn't have any problem at all. I'm sure you could do it, too."

"I'm sixty years old, Cody. I'm not shimmying down anything," said Ralph.

Ralph shined his light on the beam and stepped to the side to get a better view.

Cody casually reached into his pocket.

The sound of a voice, pleading for help, began to fill the cave. Cody knew that voice. And so did Ralph.

"Ollie!" yelled Ralph.

Cody pulled out his knife and snapped it open. The long sharp blade shimmered in the light of his headlamp. Ralph shined his flashlight at it. He smiled contemptuously. Cody felt the familiar hatred smoldering in his chest. He brandished the knife and moved in for the kill. With his free hand Ralph reached behind his back and pulled out a gun.

"Drop it, Cody, or I will put a bullet into your forehead."

※※※※※※※※※※※

Ollie had felt the violent slap of the ice cold water and—after hitting the hard ground under the surface—a thud that reverberated through his legs and hips. When he kicked and clawed back to the surface, he also felt intense pain in his lower left leg. But he was alive. Even as he bobbed to the top and gagged out some of the water that had shot into his nose and mouth, he knew he was alive. But he didn't get a chance to think about this amazing fact because treading water with a useless leg in complete darkness has a way of diverting one's attention. And Ollie hadn't fallen into the everyday boogeyman kind of darkness. He got the underground kind that steals your breath and makes you freeze for fear of danger that might be just an inch away and staring you in the face.

He caught his breath, calmed his mind, and began a methodical one-legged swim in an ever-increasing circle. It didn't take long before his foot found a shallow spot and his hands bumped into a rock that jutted out of the water. He ran his hands along the rock until he found a low spot that allowed him to drag most of his body out of the cold water. Shortly after that he heard Ralph's voice and a light shined down the shaft.

"Ollie, can you hear me?"

"Yes, I can hear you," said Ollie, with as much strength as his shivering body could muster. "I need help. I think my leg is broken."

"Can you move?"

"Yes."

"I'm sending down a safety harness. See if you can put it on."

∾∾∾∾∾∾∾∾∾∾

"Get up Cody. You're going to help me pull Ollie out of the shaft."

"And what if I say no?"

"I shoot you, I call search and rescue, and they pull Ollie out. You choose."

Cody got up from the ground where he had been lying prostrate. Ralph motioned toward the shaft with his gun. "You're going down to the lower cave."

"Why?"

"Because I don't trust you. Now get moving."

Cody grabbed the knotted rope and disappeared down the shaft. Ralph then untied the other rope, the unknotted

280

one, draped it over the smooth groove that Jubal had carved into the beam, and fed the end of it down to Cody.

Ralph liked this method—one man below pulling down on the rope and one man above pulling up—because it didn't exert any sideways pressure that might unseat the beam from the boulders. The plan also made sense because it put Cody on ice while Ralph thought about something. He had to think about the thing that had ruined his life. He had to think about doing it again.

A beam of light shined down the shaft, and Ollie saw the safety harness dangling from the end of a rope. By this time the bad leg had started to throb and even the smallest movement sent a jolt of pain through the upper leg and into his lower back. He still managed to swim out to the harness and drag it back to the shelf. He put it on, hollered up to Ralph, and soon after that the rhythmic chant of "one-two-three" began filtering down the shaft. And with every chant Ollie rose out of the water and into the pitch black shaft, at first just a foot at a time, and then two or three.

When he got almost to the very top, he saw a light in the lower cave. It was Cody pulling on the rope. Ollie said, "What happened, Cody? I don't understand what happened."

Cody didn't answer, and he didn't look at Ollie.

Ralph grabbed onto Ollie's upper body and pulled him onto the floor of the cave. When his leg hit the ground, he grimaced with pain. Ralph took the knife that Cody had dropped and cut open Ollie's jeans. He saw black and blue markings on the lower leg but no blood.

With Ollie looking to be stable, Ralph went back to the shaft just in time to see that Cody had started climbing up the remaining rope. Ralph pointed the gun at him. Cody stared defiantly and then retreated. Ralph pulled the rope out of the shaft and dropped it onto the floor of the cave.

"You can't do that man! You can't do that!" screamed Cody.

"What's wrong with Cody?" asked Ollie.

Ralph tucked the gun out of sight and said, "Uh...I think he's mad...'cause he doesn't want to share the gold."

Ralph helped Ollie onto his feet and out of the cave. After propping him up against the wall at the back of the ledge, Ralph hollered down to Cisco and told him to get Gomer. Within a few minutes Cisco had the horse lined up in the right spot, and Ralph used a safety harness to lower Ollie directly onto Gomer's back. Ralph and Cisco then hopped on a motorcycle and slowly led Gomer and Ollie down the hill.

Chapter 24

At Ralph's trial the word premeditation had been talked about to no end. It meant the difference between ten years and the death penalty. That word had saved Ralph's ass. He knew it like a crack prosecutor. But it wouldn't be there to help this time because Ralph had crossed over to premeditation about five seconds after hearing Ollie's frightened voice. Ralph had premeditation stuck to him like cheap aftershave, and only a lack of courage had stopped him from finishing the job. Now he had the courage.

Right after Cathy, Ollie, and Cisco left for the emergency room, Ralph searched Cody's bedroom and found his car keys and wallet. He drove Cody's car up the hill, way farther than it had any business going, on terrain barely suitable for an ATV much less an aged sports car. When it bogged down near the top of a ridge, he cranked the wheel hard to the left, and got out. He released the parking brake and watched it roll backwards down into a small canyon where it crashed into a giant boulder. With the sun setting low in the sky, he then hiked the rest of the way to the cave.

〰〰〰〰〰〰〰

Cody heard noise up above. He picked himself up off the ice-cold ground, edged a few feet toward the shaft, and looked up through the opening. A light shined in his eyes. "Ralph, Ralph, you gotta get me out of here, man. I'm dying of thirst, literally."

"It takes a week to die of thirst, Cody."

"This is called kidnapping, Ralph, and you're going to prison for it. Do you hear me? You're going to lose everything if you don't get me out of here right this minute."

"I'm curious, Cody. I'm looking at what's left of two ropes up here and both of them have been cleanly cut with a knife. What's that all about?"

"I don't know, man. I've never seen those before. Ollie went down the knotted rope and made it safely, just like I told you. I don't know how he ended up at the bottom."

"And where's all this gold you're talking about?"

"I already told you! It's right here! You can come down right now and see for yourself."

"How about you just show it to me? I can see from here."

Cody mumbled some cuss words to disguise his cleverness. He'd gotten good mileage out of those old coins, and now they were about to get him out of the worst of all jams. Walking into the cave, out of Ralph's view, he pulled the coins from his pocket. He then walked back to the shaft, thrust out the palm of his hand, and said, "What do you say now, asshole?" Of course, Ralph didn't answer because he didn't have an answer. "Now get me out of here," said Cody.

"I want to see the coins first. Wrap them in this bandanna and tie it to the rope," said Ralph. A few seconds

284

later the large red cloth, dangling from the rope, came down the shaft.

"Man, don't you trust anyone? I told you what happened and everything backs it up. But you just don't let it go," said Cody, as he tied the wrapped-up coins to the rope.

Ralph pulled up the coins and shortly after that the apologies started pouring out. "I'm sorry, Cody. I made a mistake. You haven't come out of your room in two months so I didn't see how you could've found the gold. I'm sorry I put you through this."

"Fine. Just get me out of here."

Ralph let down the rope once again. Cody jumped onto it and started climbing while also keeping his eyes fixed on Ralph up above. And, unbelievably, he saw him reach out with a knife and start cutting the rope.

"What are you doing! Don't do that! Don't do that! Please! Listen to me! We can talk...."

<hr />

Ralph committed murder for the second time—maybe not instantaneous murder but murder just the same—and this time he didn't have any regrets. If he went to death row he'd go with a clear conscience and the satisfaction that for the first time in his life he had given everything for his family.

This come-what-may outlook didn't stop him from thinking like a courtroom veteran, though. To prove the culpability of the so-called victim, he took as evidence the two ropes that Cody had cut when he tried to murder his brother. To cover his own ass, Ralph also took the rope that he had cut. And then, after throwing the car keys and wallet down the shaft, he climbed down the ladder and rode the remaining motorcycle down the hill. He got back to the ranch before Cathy and the boys got back from the hospital.

Over the following days and weeks, he covered for Cody's absence with a series of lies that eventually sounded like a reasonable story. But he didn't just tell a story to cover his crime. He told a story that caused the least amount of harm to the people who really mattered, one that turned Cody from a cold-blooded murderer into an impulsive lost soul. Nobody wanted to hear the real story.

※※※※※※※※※※※※

Cathy asked questions, but some of the answers scared her, especially the ones from Ollie. Though shrouded in a fog of confusion and uncertainty, his chilling words hinted at a kind of evil that Cathy didn't have the courage to confront. Instead, she listened to Ralph. He spoke with sad assurance and said that it had all been an accident, and that Cody had felt ashamed, and that, on a bad impulse, he had run off with the gold. Ralph even had some of the coins to back up the story. And why would Ralph lie? If anything, he would have told the most damning story possible. But he didn't. He told a story that painted Cody as a thief, but one that also explained away everything worse than that. And even when Cathy found Cody's mobile phone on the floor in his bedroom and remembered that he never left the ranch without it, she didn't let this inconsistency draw her away from the comfort of Ralph's account.

Chapter 25

Cody saw darkness and death. And if he didn't figure out the darkness, he didn't stand a chance against death. He swam slowly with extended hands to keep his face from smacking into a rock, searching with his feet for the underwater shelf that last time had led him up to dry ground where he had dropped the duffel bag that held his gear—including extra flashlights. The duffel bag was still there somewhere.

But last time he had had a headlamp, and he had seen things, little markers that gave him his bearing and showed the difference between wet and dry, flat and jagged, safety and danger. Now he didn't see those things and it made basic survival feel helplessly out of reach. He swam and swam, but the reservoir might as well have been an ocean because every time he hit a rock he didn't know if it marked one end or the other, or if he had been swimming in circles and had hit the same rock fifteen times before. He found underwater ledges everywhere—or maybe the same ones over and over again—and he followed them. Sometimes they disappeared beneath his feet back into the depths of the reservoir, and sometimes they led to the edge, where he pulled himself onto dry ground and groped blindly for the bag. And where, after not finding the bag, he lay shivering like a dying fish.

This routine went on for what felt like hours until he stopped going back into the water even though he knew it offered the best chance to find the bag. Instead, he groped, frozen and wet, along the jagged rocks, never knowing if he was within ten feet of the bag or a hundred. After a while he stopped thinking about the darkness and started thinking about death, most likely caused by hypothermia. He sat on the rocks, knees tucked up to his chest, hands rubbing his arms and legs to generate heat. While doing this he felt something in his pocket. It was the transmitter he had used to turn off Ollie's headlamp. He got an idea, a crazy, stupid, one in a million kind of idea. With a violently shaking hand he reached into his pocket and pulled out the transmitter. He held it up over his head and pushed the button. And, just like flipping a switch at home, a light turned on and turned the water into a luminescent pool that reflected into the rest of the chamber. Cody had never seen a more beautiful sight. He stood up and saw things, faintly, even some of the little things, like boundaries and a safe path to the green duffel bag not more than thirty feet away.

In addition to the flashlights, the bag also held a thick winter jacket. He tore off his wet shirt, put on the jacket, and zipped it up tight, hood and all. And then, as his body slowly warmed, he took a new inventory. The darkness had been dealt with, but death still wanted to kick him in the teeth because even with this reprieve he was in worse shape than even Jubal had been. And everyone knew how that had turned out.

He looked around the chamber and saw something floating near the edge of the water. Using the flashlight, he recognized it to be the red backpack that Ollie had worn. He retrieved it and inside found three soggy sandwiches and water bottles. Next to where the backpack had been floating, he also found a tangle of rope. He recognized two of the sections. They came from the rope ladder that he had cut. The third, longer section, came from the one Ralph had cut. With those three pieces of rope, he had more than enough to reach the top of the shaft but, just like Jubal, the rope was useless until it got tied off overhead. And if that had been impossible for Jubal who had only needed to scale fifteen feet, it looked insane from forty feet lower. No. If he wanted to live, he had to think differently. He had to find the thing that Jubal had missed.

And before the last soggy sandwich had been eaten, he found it. But it really found him, repeatedly tickling his face and whistling in his ear, but never showing itself. And it only came out for a few hours at a time, during the day, judging by when the bats came back into the cave. It was the wind, the wind that had no business being there because the wind isn't supposed to blow through a sealed chamber. The wind proved that there had to be another way out.

After the bats had gone out and come back in three times, he strapped on the red backpack, coiled the rope over his shoulder, and marched into the wind. It took a grueling search that lasted many days but, in addition to overcoming the darkness, he eventually also cheated death. And then he had time to think about hatred.

Chapter 26

Ollie and Cisco moved back down to the house while Ollie recovered. Cisco quickly got back into the routine of the school year, but Ollie floundered. He spent nearly every waking hour glued to his desk, pouring out dozens of drawings depicting the terrifying plunge to the bottom of the shaft. If he had had the inclination to share the renderings, which he did not, the casual observer would have had a hard time discerning much difference between one drawing and the next. But Ollie saw the differences. He saw every splintered beam of light from Cody's headlamp and the frame-by-frame path of the whipsawing ropes that followed him to the bottom. He saw every crevice and crack in the wall and the way the unnatural light made them look ghostly and distorted. In rapid click succession he saw himself falling farther and farther away from the light, like a dying man witnessing the exact moment when the light goes out and his life is extinguished. As quickly as he finished a set of drawings, he started a new set, only interrupted by restless sleep and the occasional hobble to the kitchen for an unwanted meal.

One drawing, however, did stand out from all the others. It depicted just a fraction of a second in time, right before he hit the water, and actually showed something quite remarkable. But Ollie didn't like it. It didn't match the story that everyone believed. It didn't match the story that Ollie wanted to believe, the one that said his brother had not tried to kill him. Ollie wished he could make the image go away, but he couldn't. So, he tore it up. Every time he drew it, he tore it up.

After six weeks the cast came off, but sadness and confusion remained. Ollie felt himself slipping back into the old ways when the world had been locked out, and he had had nothing but pencil, paper, and fear. He wanted to fight back, for Cisco and Mariah's sake if nothing else, but didn't know where to begin. He didn't talk with mother for fear that she might find out about the special image in his head and that it might confuse what she believed and make her sad. And he didn't talk with Ralph because Ralph had the story that everyone wanted to believe.

On a cold morning in March shortly after the cast came off, Ollie saddled up a horse and rode up to the cave. He went there in search of any kind of evidence, no matter how small, that might back up Ralph's story and give Ollie something to hang on to. He didn't find it. He found the exact opposite.

⬥⬥⬥⬥⬥⬥⬥⬥⬥⬥⬥

Ralph sent one of the cowhands out to check salt blocks because some of the cattle had been licking at the dirt and eating plants that they normally didn't touch—possible signs of salt deficiency. A few hours later the cowhand came back and said that someone had taken a sledgehammer to some of the salt blocks, reducing them to rock and dust. It didn't make sense. Who gets their kicks like that? Or, if someone needs salt, who needs that much of it, and who goes to all that trouble to get it? The incident bothered Ralph, but it mostly confused him.

A few days later, during the monthly wrangler's barbeque, Ralph opened the big chest freezer in the barn and found that it had been raided. Twenty pounds of steak and a box of hotdogs had gone missing. He knew it without a doubt because he had stocked the freezer himself in preparation for the barbeque. Now, because of these two seemingly minor acts of vandalism, his mind wandered in a direction he didn't want to go.

Ralph had resolved to live with the consequences of what he had done and, if needs be, wanted to be the one who sips coffee on the front porch while the cops close in. But he didn't have just his own safety to think about. If he had somehow bungled the job and had left Cody free to plan some kind of twisted revenge, then the ones he really cared about had been put in danger. That's why his mind wandered. It lumped together the two acts of vandalism, tossed them around, and didn't like way they came out the other side. The way he saw it, the one person who needs that much salt is the same person who has meat to preserve, such as someone who is hiding out in the wild. He saw a connection...or a bad case of paranoia.

Whatever it was, the question of what to do next looked dicey. He couldn't very well pass out rifles to the family, not with the flimsy evidence he had, and not after telling them for the last two months that poor misguided Cody had committed no crime worse than theft. Even a casual conversation about Ralph's concerns had the power to knock the feet out from under the family, especially if they came to understand that in reality Cody was more coldblooded than any murderer Ralph had ever met. And he had met many. Other than staying vigilant and telling the cowhands to be on alert for unusual activity up on the hill, he had no options.

This uncomfortable limbo changed quickly two days after the barbeque when the smallest of sounds—a breaking twig—woke Ralph in the middle of the night. Reflexively, he reached under the nightstand for the revolver. He held his breath and listened. The sound of crunching gravel faintly echoed in the stillness. Skunks and opossums don't crunch gravel. He pulled back the hammer on the gun. The whispering footsteps got closer. He sat up and peeked through the trailer window. A shadow off to the left, maybe twenty feet away, crept toward him. He got to his feet and edged toward the window by the front door. The shadow crept closer, still on the left. In one fast motion, Ralph turned on the porch light, flung open the trailer door, and aimed the gun...at Ollie.

Ollie screamed.

Ralph screamed...then he yelled. "Ollie! What are you doing!"

"I'm sorry, Ralph! I'm sorry!"

Ralph uncocked the gun and, still agitated, said, "What is going on?"

"I have to talk with you."

"And you had to scare the crap out of me in the middle of the night?"

"I didn't want my mom to see us talking."

"And this is what you came up with?" Ollie didn't answer. Ralph continued, "Alright, I think I'm Ok now. Come in." He put the gun on the kitchen counter and pointed Ollie to the swivel chair by the door. Ralph sat at the nearby dinette table. Ollie held some folded papers, and he looked troubled—as he had ever since the incident. Ralph suspected, even hoped, that Ollie had information about Cody—even in the middle of the night, and even if it put a dent in Ralph's story. "You want some coffee or a coke or something?"

"No thanks."

Ralph motioned to the papers in Ollie's hand and said, "Alright, show me what you got—and it better not be some crossword puzzle that stumped you."

"I went back up to the cave," said Ollie.

"Ok."

"And I saw something."

"Alright."

Ollie handed over one of the papers, a drawing, and said, "I drew this the same night I got back from the hospital. It's from when you helped me out of the cave. Do you see the yellow backpack next to the jars?"

"Ok," said Ralph, not exactly sure where this was going.

"That's the big backpack that Cody wore that day."

"Yeah, I remember. It's probably still there."

"No, it's not. It's gone."

"Um...OK...that's right...Cody used it to carry the gold...now I remember," said Ralph, stammering and lying and trying to make sense of it.

"This is what I saw when I went back last week." He handed Ralph the second drawing and said, "It's the small red backpack that I wore."

Ralph took the drawing. He saw the red backpack sitting where the yellow one had been.

Ollie continued, "I had on that backpack when I fell down the shaft and it came off when I hit the water. I didn't bring it back up with me, but here it is. And I don't know how it got back up to the top unless Cody did it. But you said that you saw Cody run off with the gold."

Now Ralph had the proof he wanted, but he proceeded with caution, saying, "Yes, Ollie, I did say that."

"Then when did he go down the shaft?"

"I don't know the answer to that," said Ralph.

This answer didn't satisfy Ollie. He stared intently at Ralph, looking more agitated than ever, and then blurted, "I don't think Cody really found the gold."

Ralph didn't feel a desperate impulse to save the lie. If anything, he felt relieved at the prospect of having someone by his side that knew the truth and understood the danger. "And why would you say that?" said Ralph.

"Because I didn't see any gold when I went down to the lower cave…and because of something in my head."

Ollie had a mind like a surveillance camera and Ralph knew better than to doubt the things in his head. He said, "Ok, so what do you think it means?"

"I don't know, because you said that Cody found the gold…and that's what mom thinks, and what I want to think, but I can't make the other stuff go away."

"You don't need to make it go away because it's true."

"What are you saying?"

"I'm sorry, Ollie. I made up that story to protect you guys."

"To protect us?"

"Yes."

Ollie cleared his throat repeatedly and got tears in his eyes. He said, "Cody tried to kill me, didn't he?"

"Yes, Ollie. And when I got to the cave, he was trying to do the same to Cisco."

Ollie's tears now flowed strongly and his speech faltered. Ralph gave him some time and then said, "I liked what you said about your dad at the memorial, and you're right. He helped make you strong. And if he were here right now, he'd treat you like a man and tell you the hard truth. And that's what I'm going to do."

Ollie wiped away the tears, cleared his throat, and said, "Ok."

"Cody's still here and we have to get ready for him."

"What do you think he's going to do?"

"He loves his grudges. I hope I'm wrong, but I think he's going to try to finish what he started."

"Why don't we call the police?"

"Because I tried to kill Cody. I cut the rope, he tumbled down the shaft, and I left him for dead. If we call the police, they'll arrest me and there will be one less person to fight."

Ollie stared with big, disbelieving eyes.

"I'm sorry, Ollie. I didn't have a choice. And you may not have one either. I have a rifle in the office for you, but you have to decide if you're ready to use it."

"I'm ready," said Ollie.

"Ok."

"And we need to tell my mom."

"Well, I'm the one that lied to her. I guess I should be the one to tell her the truth. I'll do it this morning."

With several hours to go before sunup, and still needing to figure things out, Ralph quietly coasted the pickup down the hill with the lights off and deposited Ollie back at home. He then parked the truck and went into the office, where he pulled two rifles out of the case and loaded them full bore. He also grabbed a box of cartridges and went out to the ranch pickup where they kept another rifle. But when he looked inside the truck, the gun was gone. And Ralph knew what it meant. Too many bad clues had piled too high for it to mean anything else.

On the way back to the office, Ralph scanned the surroundings. Even in the moonlight, he saw a hundred tailor-made hiding places for a guy with a rifle and a bad attitude. The house, the bunkhouse, the stable, the barns, and all the walkways that connected them, sat exposed and vulnerable. He went into the office, pulled a chair up to the window that overlooked the house, and tried to come up with a plan. He also tried to figure out how to tell Cathy that he had tried to murder her son.

Two hours later, after the school bus had picked up Cisco, Ralph made the phone call. Cathy sounded happy. She said that a fresh Danish had his name on it. He grabbed one of the rifles, headed for the door, but then changed his mind. *Better break it to her slowly, and then give her the rifle*, he thought. He left it behind.

Once outside the barn, Ralph paused and looked through the morning mist at the surrounding hills. He took a deep breath and, just as he stepped toward the house, a loud gunshot split the morning calm. Ralph crumpled into a heap. When he tried to get back up the excruciating pain in his right leg overpowered him. That's when he saw blood spurting from the flesh just above the knee. He had only seconds to apply a tourniquet, but he also had to get out of the line of fire. Using his arms and one leg, he crawled back into the barn, across the barn floor, and into the office. He rolled onto his back and pulled off his belt. As he threaded the belt and pulled it tight around his leg, the silhouette of a man appeared in the barn. The hazy daylight spilling into the entrance hid his appearance but Ralph had a pretty good idea. With the blood loss slowed, he kicked the door shut, pulled himself onto a chair, and grabbed the rifle. He had a lousy position but just needed one shot. He cocked the rifle and waited. Then the big John Deere roared to life, and Ralph knew that Cody had chosen a different option. That tractor, parked just on the other side of the wall, had a thousand pound spiked bucket aimed right at Ralph. And it had the power to tear through the wall like a bulldozer.

The engine revved. Ralph hopped over to the window. The engine revved again and the whole building shook. Ralph opened the window, punched out the screen, and tossed out the rifle. The engine quieted and the ratcheting sound of the gearbox echoed loudly. Ralph threw his body up onto the window sill. And that's as far as he got, ass up, shit out of luck. The room exploded all around him.

Cathy had just put out plates and coffee cups when a loud gunshot rang out. She paused. When a steer or heifer goes down, and is past the hope of medical care, that's how it is euthanized more often than not. But it seemed strange that it happened right at the time when Ralph was supposed to be coming down to the house. She looked out the window through the morning fog and didn't see anything unusual in the backyard or up at the barn, so she didn't think any more about it.

A minute later the coffee cups started rattling. She recognized the sound of the tractor but normally they didn't run it so loudly until they got it out of the barn. She looked out the window again and saw some commotion up at the office. She hurried to the backdoor and got outside just in time to see Ralph hanging out of the office window. And then, a second later, the tractor smashed through the building and ran him over. She let out a horrified scream and watched in disbelief as the driverless tractor plowed forward, smashing through tables and bushes, before finally running into a ditch and tipping over. Cathy turned back toward the house just as Ollie rushed out. She yelled, "Call 911! Get an ambulance!" And then she dashed up to Ralph.

His upper body lay face first on the ground but his hips and legs had been grotesquely twisted and mangled. She knelt down and saw his eyelids fluttering. She said, "Ralph, Ralph, can you hear me?"

His eyelids stopped fluttering. She lowered her head down to his and held his hand. He focused on her face and moved his mouth.

"It's ok, Ralph. It's OK. Help is on the way. Please, just be strong one more time."

He smiled. Cathy fought back the tears.

"Cathy, listen to me. I lied to you. I'm sorry but I had to protect Cisco and Ollie. Look in my hand, Cathy, and you'll know the truth. Look in my hand. And please take care of my boy. Please take care...."

"No Ralph! Please! Please! No!" She shook him, and called his name, but he was gone. She lowered her head and sobbed.

A voice that she knew well interrupted the bitter tears. It said, "I'm sorry, mother. I had to do it."

Cathy slowly raised her head and saw Cody standing in the mist. He had wild hair and a crazy man's beard. And he held a rifle in his left hand. He walked toward her. She stared without saying a word.

"He tried to kill me, mother."

Cathy looked down at Ralph. She saw a fabric bundle in his hand. She said, "Why would Ralph do that, Cody?"

Now hovering over her, he said, "For the treasure. He stole it from me. I swear that's what happened, mother. You have to believe me."

Ollie ran up to them and said, "The ambulance is on the way." But then he saw Ralph's body and fell to his knees.

Cathy took the bundle from Ralph's hand and opened it.

"You see! That's the proof right there! I gave him those coins to prove that I found the treasure, and then he threw me down the shaft! He tried to murder me, mother! I swear it's the truth!"

Cathy looked at the coins. She held up one of them and said, "This coin was minted two years after Jubal robbed the payroll wagon."

"Well...uh...then he switched it to frame me! It's obvious! You can see that, can't you?"

"No, Cody. You're lying like you always do, and I'm calling the police," said Cathy. She stood up.

Cody pointed the rifle at her. "I'm sorry, mother. I can't let you do that."

Ollie jumped to his feet and grabbed the rifle that lay amongst the debris. Cody swiveled and fired, but he missed.

"No Cody! Stop it!" yelled Cathy.

Ollie cocked his rifle and aimed it at Cody. Cody cocked his rifle and aimed it at Ollie. Now both of Cathy's boys had guns pointed at each other.

"Put it down, Ollie," said Cody. "You know you'd never pull the trigger."

"No, I never would, Cody, because I always loved you. And I thought you loved me. But then you tried to kill me and Cisco. And now you killed Ralph. I'll shoot you, Cody, and that's no lie."

The boys stared each other down.

"Put down the gun, Cody. It's over," said Cathy.

A subtle smile slowly formed on Cody's mouth. He took a step backwards. "What a bunch of idiots," he said. Then he turned and ran into the barn. A few seconds later a motorcycle fired up and Cody raced it out of the barn, popping a wheelie as he passed and whipping up a trail of dust on his way down to the highway.

Chapter 27

The postmark on the envelope said Banff, Alberta, Canada. For their honeymoon Ollie and Mariah had chosen a month long trans-Canadian train ride and these letters had been arriving regularly for the last couple of weeks.

"Cisco, you got a letter from your mom and dad," said Cathy, as she stepped through the front door with the mail. Cisco ran out of the studio. He grabbed the letter, got comfortable on the living room couch, and opened it up. Cathy sat down beside him.

The envelope contained a letter and a drawing. Cisco went straight to the drawing. And so did Cathy because she recognized the subject of it. At a very sad time in his life, Ollie had created hundreds of similar drawings, and Cathy thought that she had seen all of them. But she hadn't seen this one. She looked closer.

Like the others, it depicted a section of the shaft where Ollie had fallen. But, unlike the others, this one focused on a specific rock ledge at the bottom of the shaft where it opened up into a large chamber. And on that ledge sat a very old pair of saddlebags. They had cracks and gaping holes in them, and the contents had partially spilled out onto the ledge. At the bottom of the drawing Ollie had written a note, which Cathy read:

"Dear Cisco, When I get home, we have some special business to take care of. Love, Dad."

"What does it mean, grandma?"

Cathy pointed to the drawing, and the pile of coins that had toppled from the saddlebags. She said, "What do you think it means?"

"Oh boy!" said Cisco.

Cathy wrapped up her grandson in a great big hug.

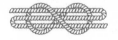

Acknowledgments

While researching acquired savantism, I became acquainted with some very special people who have either that condition or the more common autistic savant syndrome. Specifically, I want to acknowledge Leslie Lemke, Alonzo Clemmons, and Stephen Wiltshire MBE, whose amazing talents and inspiring lives make a book like this possible.

I also want to thank Dr. Darold Treffert whose lifetime of work in the fields of autism spectrum disorder and savant syndrome has educated and benefited countless people, including myself. I found his book *Islands of Genius* and his research in the area of acquired savant syndrome to be especially helpful.

Special thanks to Ujala Shahid for her stunning cover and interior illustrations. She did Ollie proud!

I also want to thank my wife, Martina, for her never-ending support and encouragement. Like a feisty angel, she takes care of me and keeps me in line.

And, finally, to my readers, I am grateful for your support and want to thank you for reading my books. If you have enjoyed *Ollie Come Free*, I would be very grateful for any review you might care to write. I enjoy hearing your feedback, and your reviews will help other readers to discover my work.

Sincerest Thanks,

Tim Patrick

The Author

Tim Patrick is a graduate of UCLA. He and his wife live in Southern California and are the parents of two grown children. In his spare time, Patrick enjoys aviation, bicycling, and experimenting in the kitchen.

Made in the USA
Middletown, DE
25 May 2021

39990909R00187